LAST OF THE GADERENE

The Doctor Who *50th Anniversary Collection*

Ten Little Aliens
Stephen Cole

Dreams of Empire
Justin Richards

Last of the Gaderene
Mark Gatiss

Festival of Death
Jonathan Morris

Fear of the Dark
Trevor Baxendale

Players
Terrance Dicks

Remembrance of the Daleks
Ben Aaronovitch

EarthWorld
Jacqueline Rayner

Only Human
Gareth Roberts

Beautiful Chaos
Gary Russell

The Silent Stars Go By
Dan Abnett

LAST OF THE
GADERENE

MARK GATISS

BOOKS

3 5 7 9 10 8 6 4 2

First published in 2000 by BBC Worldwide Ltd.
This edition published in 2013 by BBC Books, an imprint of Ebury Publishing.
A Random House Group Company

Doctor Who is a BBC Wales production for BBC One.
Executive producers: Steven Moffat and Caroline Skinner

The Random House Group Limited Reg. No. 954009
Addresses for companies within the Random House Group can be found at
www.randomhouse.co.uk

A CIP catalogue record for this book is available from the British Library.

ISBN 978 1 849 90597 8

The Random House Group Limited supports The Forest Stewardship
Council® (FSC®), the leading international forest-certification organisation.
Our books carrying the FSC label are printed on FSC®-certified paper. FSC is
the only forest-certification scheme supported by the leading environmental
organisations, including Greenpeace. Our paper procurement policy can be
found at www.randomhouse.co.uk/environment

Editorial director: Albert DePetrillo
Editorial manager: Nicholas Payne
Series consultant: Justin Richards
Project editor: Steve Tribe
Cover design: Two Associates © Woodlands Books Ltd, 2012
Production: Alex Goddard

Printed and bound in Great Britain by CPI Group (UK) Ltd, Croydon, CR0 4YY

To buy books by your favourite authors and register for offers,
visit www.randomhouse.co.uk

INTRODUCTION

This book was first published in 2000 (or the Year 2000 as it was known in my youth. Possibly even the *Space* Year 2000. Or did I imagine that?). I wrote a little introduction and this is how it went:

It's still possible to transport some of us of a particular age back to a magical childhood time when all nights seemed wintry and dark, the football results never ended and *Doctor Who* was the best show on television. All you have to do is utter the simple words, 'Remember the one with the maggots?' It's no good trying to explain what the show meant to us then; suffice to say it was the great constant in our little lives: the heroic Doctor, Jo Grant, the gently moralising stories, the fantastic monsters, action by HAVOC. And during the eternity between seasons we always had the Target books. They gave us exciting versions of stories we had seen, and glimpses into a strange and mysterious past where the Doctor had been someone else. Whenever I was off school, my medicine of preference was always *Planet of the Daleks* (and maybe oxtail soup), because it took me light years away from my four walls and into the Doctor's Universe. What a comfort and a genuine inspiration those books were. Incidentally, I feel I must point out that the cover of this book portrays the Third Doctor, whose physical appearance was altered by the Time Lords when they banished him to Earth in the twentieth century.

So, if I may, I'd like to dedicate this book to that happy time and to two men: Terrance Dicks and the late, great Jon Pertwee; for all those Saturday nights.

What I couldn't possibly have foreseen (without a Space/Time Visualiser at any rate) was that only a few years after the release of *Last of the Gaderene*, *Doctor Who* would return triumphantly to our screens, instantly rediscovering a 'family' audience long thought extinct. Not only *that*, but I would write for it and even appear in it! To say these things were dreams come true would be to put it mildly.

With the incredible success of the new show has come a renewed interest in its past, and the one thing those of us raised on Typhoo-tea wall charts and Weetabix dioramas were always denied: proper toys. Now, I am 45 years old. I don't *need* a model Zygon, a K1 Robot or every variation of the Daleks. What place can three different versions of Jon Pertwee possibly hold in my non-dimensionally transcendental home? But resistance, as they say, is useless.

All those beautiful Cybermen! A Hartnell TARDIS that makes the dematerialisation sound! Omega – complete with snazzy cloak (though I wish his helmet hinged up to reveal there's nothing left of him). And isn't it a shame that on the box containing the action-figure of the Last of the Osirans it doesn't say 'Plaything of Sutekh'? I have comprehensively given in to nostalgia and sometimes there's nothing wrong with that.

But what's truly wonderful is that all these things, books, audio plays, toys are part of an *ongoing* history of fantastic escapism. A brand new, vibrant TV show that viewers of all ages will be nostalgic about in years to come. In that spirit then, my renewed dedication must be to the man whose incredible energy, imagination and sheer enthusiasm brought the Doctor back to us. To Russell T Davies. For all those *new* Saturday nights.

Mark Gatiss
October 2012

'For Jesus said unto him, "Come out of the man, thou unclean spirit."
And he asked him, "What is thy name?"
And the man answered, saying, "My name is Legion: for we are many."
Mark 5:8

PROLOGUE

The woman's eyes were as brown as the Bakelite wireless on the high shelf behind her head.

The song coming from the wireless was muffled and crackly, as though the singer were far away. But the voice still managed to sound sweet, wistful and achingly melancholy all at the same time. There would be blue birds over the white cliffs of Dover, the singer promised, her sweeping tones washing over the crowded bar.

A stocky young man with a neatly clipped moustache leant on the bar, his lively eyes sparkling with good humour.

He watched the woman as she looked around the room, which was a blur of blue serge. She hitched up her skirt a little and tugged at her stocking, but she was careful that other men surrounding her, their faces flushed with high spirits and too much beer, didn't see. Such things were for his eyes only.

The young man pushed his officer's cap back on his forehead and forced his way through the crowd, four pints of bitter clutched precariously in his hands, his handsome face wreathed in smoke from his pipe. He moved the pipe from side to side between his clenched teeth and navigated a careful path through his fellow airmen to a red-leather upholstered seat.

The slim and rather beautiful woman watched his approach and a delighted smile lit up her round face. He felt a little thrill of joy dart inside him. Perhaps he'd ask her now. There was nothing to lose. And so much to gain. In his imagination he'd always seen them walking arm in arm through some sunny glade, not jammed behind a little table in a bar. But the war made everything much more urgent.

The young flyer pushed two of the pints across the table towards his friends and then settled down next to the woman. She thanked him and took a sip of the foaming beer.

'Are you sure that's what you wanted?' he asked, tugging the pipe from his mouth.

She nodded and pushed a stray strand of long chestnut hair from her eyes.

He rubbed his chin nervously and tried to think of the best way of saying it.

They'd been thrown together by the war – almost literally. An incendiary bomb had gone off just outside the shelter where he'd been hiding and the young woman had rushed inside just in time. The sweat was standing on her forehead and her eyes were bright and frightened. But, at the sight of him, she had broken into a broad grin.

He looked at the pint of beer on the table in front of him.

'Well, I suppose if you're going to be my wife, you'll have to get used to this grog.'

Her pretty eyes disappeared into half-moons as she smiled. She sipped at her pint and then almost choked on it. She span round in her seat.

'What did you say?'

He feigned innocence. 'When?'

'Just now.'

'Oh,' he took a great draught of his pint. 'You mean about marrying you?'

She looked suddenly vulnerable and terribly pretty. He leant over and kissed her.

'Oh, Alec…' she mumbled. After a while, she pulled away, grinning happily. 'OK, mister. I'll marry you.'

'Good show,' laughed the flyer.

'On one condition.'

He frowned. 'Oh?'

She cradled his face in her hands and smiled a little sadly.

'Get through all this alive, won't you?'

He nodded, beaming, and embraced her. He glanced around the room, taking in the ceiling blackened with smoke where men had burnt their names and squadron numbers into it with candles; the knots of young flyers in their blue uniforms, the fug of smoke and laughter. He thought of the nights he and the girl had spent together since that first meeting in the air-raid shelter. Her funny laugh. The time he had flown his aeroplane over the factory where she worked and looped the loop just to impress her.

He lifted her hand from her knee, squeezed it and then pressed it tenderly to his cheek.

Distantly, there was a low, rumbling drone.

His senses were immediately alert. Whirling round, he looked up at the ceiling, her hand still in his. A few of the airmen had heard it too.

He opened his mouth to speak; to tell the wonderful girl by his side to get down or to run for it. It was a buzz bomb. Had to be. But the sound was different somehow. A stuttering, shattering roar. Then the sound stopped and silence fell.

A moment later, the room exploded into white nothingness.

It was some days later that the young man found himself wandering over the devastated ground where the bar had stood. Soft cotton pads covered the severe burns he had sustained to his cheek, and one arm was painfully supported in a sling. He had been lucky.

The beautiful girl with eyes like Alice Fey; the girl he'd waltzed around the Pally one night; the girl he'd asked to marry him; she had not been lucky.

The young man in the blue officer's uniform took his cap from his head and tucked it under his uninjured arm. Ahead of him, the ground was little more than a blackened hole. Mud was churned up in a wide crater and fragments of debris – glass, chair legs, even a girl's handbag – were scattered around the rim.

The young man looked up as, with a throbbing roar, a squadron of fighter planes passed overhead.

He would get through this war. For her.

Something caught his eye, stark and incongruous against the black earth like a shark's tooth in caviar.

Reaching down, he plucked it from the ground. It was about three inches long, jade-coloured and crystalline. In his ruddy palm, it seemed to glow.

He frowned and tucked it into his jacket pocket, then turned on his heel and walked towards the aerodrome gates, the roar of the Spitfire engines still ringing in his ears.

Deep in the earth, under cover of the flattened mud, something stirred…

CHAPTER ONE

SUMMER LIGHTNING

A ladybird dropped out of the clear blue sky on to Jobey Packer's hand; bright against his skin like a bead of blood.

He paused in his work and, instead of swatting it away, watched it amble slowly over his knuckles. The ticklish sensation, he decided, was rather nice.

The ladybird's wing-case cracked open and, in an instant, it was gone.

Jobey smiled to himself and craned his head backwards to take in the enormity of the sky. Out here, away from the village, it dominated everything, like a vast canvas only precariously fixed to the narrow strip of the earth. Curlews arced and fluttered in it – dark flecks against the perfect blue. Jobey closed his eyes and listened to their sad cries muffled by the warmth of the summer afternoon.

The land rolled out under the sky like a great streak of muddy watercolour, dotted here and there with stubby trees or the shining mirrors of inland waterways.

Jobey craned his old head back further till his straw hat almost flopped to the ground. Its tightly bound weave was coming undone, exposing the peeling red skin on his tanned forehead. Perhaps one day he'd treat himself to a new hat. He let the sun beat at his face.

He'd never even been tempted to move away from Culverton, though he'd seen plenty of life elsewhere.

Even in the parched deserts of Alexandria, under the stars where the pharaohs once walked, Jobey had always dreamed of his little village. Safe, secure, always the same. As old as the hills – except, of course, that there were no hills in Culverton. None to speak of in all his beloved East Anglia. Just land and sky.

Land and sky.

Nowhere else ever seemed quite the same.

Jobey had found himself in London once, many years ago, crushed together with other countless thousands when the king and Mr Churchill had emerged on to the balcony of the palace to celebrate the end of hostilities. He had cheered and wept with the best of them, of course, but after a couple of days in the capital he was desperate to come home. London was such a mean, filthy, rabbit warren of a place. Everyone in such a rush. No time to say a 'good morning' or a 'how d'you do?' Not like Culverton.

When he was a little boy, Jobey would stand and windmill his arms round and round and round, just to make the most of the emptiness. Sometimes, when no one was looking, he still did.

He shaded his eyes now as he looked out across the marshy farmland. There was the green with the old pump, the post office with its subsiding wall, the hotchpotch of cottages and houses clustered around the russet-coloured church as though seeking sanctuary. The air hummed with insects and the mournful song of the birds, turning and turning. Jobey gave a contented sigh and turned back to his work.

He lifted the hammer and, with a few swift strokes, banged a couple of nails into the sign he'd spent most of the morning attaching to the gates in front of him. Jobey paused and shook his head. There he was, getting all misty-eyed about Culverton never changing, yet here was change staring him in the face. The end of an era. He took a step back to take in his handiwork. The sign, red on white, glared back at him like an accusation.

CULVERTON AERODROME CLOSED
BY ORDER M.O.D

Commander Harold Tyrell decided the time had come to say goodbye.

A great bear of a man, his rumpled face and infectious laugh had endeared him to the whole village throughout his time in charge of the aerodrome. He had seen it through some of its finest hours. Postwar at any rate.

There had been the splendid air show to celebrate the coronation. And then the dramatic rescue which he'd co-ordinated in person, sending cargo planes to the aid of a stricken tanker off the coast. When was that? '64? '65?

Tyrell sighed and ran his finger over the big oak desk in the control room. It left a broad, brown streak in the dust. He looked around the room he'd known so well. The panoramic window, stained and partially boarded up; the radar monitors, the model Wellington bomber. He picked this up and clutched it to his chest. He'd saved it until the very end because it meant the most to him.

Always a churchgoer, a line from his favourite hymn came back to him and ran round and round his head like looped tape:

'Change and decay in all around I see…'

He squinted as he peered through the great, curved window. The sunlight coming through it created a wide prism on the old carpet.

There was someone out there, walking swiftly across the broken tarmac of the airstrip.

Tyrell frowned. This was odd. And not a little annoying. He'd taken great pains to see that his final day in the job would leave him alone with his beloved old aerodrome. The one thing he didn't want before he closed the gates for the last time was to send some vandal off the premises with a flea in their ear.

With a grumpy sigh, he headed for the door, then stopped dead.

There were footsteps coming up the staircase outside. Whoever it was, they had the audacity to come straight to him. Unless it was an urgent message, of course. Perhaps his wife was ill. She'd taken the closure of the aerodrome almost as badly as he had.

Suddenly concerned, Tyrell stretched out his hand towards the doorknob.

The door opened before he could reach it.

Jobey was sad to see the old place go. Everyone was sad, naturally.

He stepped over his tool bag and peered through the diamond-shaped mesh of the fence.

The airstrip stretched ahead, broken and weed-strewn now, with grey parabolic prefabs on either side. Fringed by long grass, with the great control tower just to one side, it wobbled dizzyingly in the heat haze.

He could still imagine the place as it had once been, crowded with aircraft, their engines thrumming with power; knots of young flyers in buff leather sitting around in canvas chairs, waiting for the call to scramble…

Jobey shook his head. Those days were gone. And he wasn't paid to stand about idling.

Somewhere, not too far away, there was the sound of someone shouting.

Jobey tensed, but the sound cut off.

Despite the heat, he shivered and bent down to pick up his old navy-blue tool bag. He would stop off at the pub for a swift half, he decided, just to reassure himself that everything else was just as it should be. Adjusting his straw hat, Jobey straightened up and sniffed, then set off towards the village, hobnail boots ringing off the road. He could hear the quiet chirrup of crickets in the grass, the lazy drone of a fat bumble-bee as it bounced from flower to flower.

Away towards the horizon, there was a sudden flash of white. Jobey blinked and could see it quite clearly, imprinted on his retina. Summer lightning, he thought, and waited for the accompanying rumble of thunder. None came.

Jobey shrugged off his nostalgic mood and smiled broadly. It was a good day to be alive, even if he was alone on this old, parched lane.

Jobey was not quite alone, however. He met someone on the road. Someone who shouldn't have been there. Someone with dark eyes and a wide, wide smile. Jobey's shriek of terror shattered the calm of the summer afternoon but no one heard it over the melancholy cries of the curlews.

*

Jo Grant gave a little yelp as a dark shadow passed in front of her. She had expected to remain undisturbed, stretched out on a gaudily patterned sun lounger up on the flat roof of one of UNIT HQ's outbuildings and trying desperately to top up her tan. Her week's leave had been depressingly short of sunshine and she'd spent most of it reading three-day-old newspapers eulogising Britain's record heatwave.

Small and very pretty, Jo pushed large, round, green-tinted sunglasses on to her forehead, shaded her eyes and squinted. A man was looming over her, a solid black silhouette against the glaring disc of the sun. Self-consciously, Jo's hands fluttered to her chest to cover up the skimpy pink bikini she was wearing.

'Sorry, miss,' said a familiar voice. 'Didn't mean to startle you.' Jo heaved a relieved sigh. 'Oh, it's you, Sergeant Benton,' she said, flashing a winning smile. 'Thank goodness for that.'

'Who were you expecting?' said Benton, moving to her side, his big, good-humoured face creased into a frown.

'No one,' said Jo. 'No one special. It's just you never can tell what might be lurking around here.'

'Thanks very much,' laughed Benton with mock indignation. 'I'm not sure I like being thought of as a lurker.'

'You know what I mean.' Jo raised a finger and dragged her sunglasses back down over her eyes. 'It's either some slimy monster or…'

'Or?'

'Or the Brig on the prowl.'

Benton lowered a broad hand and promptly lifted the sunglasses clear again. 'Right second time. The Brig wants to see you.'

Jo made a face and, with a sigh, swung her legs off the sun lounger. 'He can't say I didn't try to find him. My name's in the log. But when I got here, there was no one about.'

She shrugged on a light summer dress as they made their way across the hot roof. 'And, anyway, I'm still officially on leave.'

She walked quickly on tiptoe, the scorching asphalt under her feet as hot as she'd expected her Spanish beach to be.

'The Brigadier's been away too, miss,' said Benton, helping Jo on to the metal ladder which ran up the side of the building.

'Where to?'

Benton shrugged. 'All I know for certain is that he's running a very tight ship today.'

Jo gave a low groan and began to climb down the ladder. The metal was warm under her hands, its hot, rusty stink reminding her of school playgrounds. Benton clambered down swiftly, his big army boots smacking the tarmac as he reached the ground.

'Where's the Doctor?' asked Jo.

Benton gave a small, humourless laugh. 'I'll leave the explanations to the Brigadier,' he said, giving her a cryptic wink and heading off in the opposite direction.

Jo frowned and, pushing at the double doors, made her way inside the building.

She blinked repeatedly, the contrast to the brightness outside making the interior seem unnaturally dark. The water fountain and bubble-hooded phone booth loomed ahead, wreathed in shadow. After a while, she grew accustomed to it and soon found her way to the Doctor's laboratory.

Jo pushed open the door and looked about her as it swung back into place. The room was hot, stifling and silent. The lab bench with its Bunsen burners and hooked sink taps was in its familiar place as was the hat stand where the Doctor hung his cloak. Three stools had been moved carefully into the corner, forming a neat triangle.

Jo turned at a thudding, buzzing sound close by. A bluebottle was banging itself repeatedly against the windows and she moved swiftly across the room to release it. Warm air filtered inside as she opened the window but the fly continued its pointless attack on the glass.

'Go on you stupid thing,' cried Jo exasperatedly.

As she moved across to open another window, she stopped. There was something wrong. The stools were arranged too neatly. The hat stand was bare. The lab bench, usually so cluttered by the Doctor's complicated electronic lash-ups, was wiped clean. And in the corner permanently occupied by the battered blue shape of the TARDIS, there was nothing.

The empty space yawned like the dusty rectangle left after a painting has been removed from a wall. Jo blinked slowly, then turned as the door opened again.

Brigadier Lethbridge-Stewart was standing there, hot and uncomfortable in his uniform. There was a sheen of sweat over his face. He looked Jo in the eye and then glanced down at the floor.

'That's right, Miss Grant,' he said flatly. 'He's gone.'

CHAPTER TWO
AWOL

A decaying jet stream had left a wide, wispy track across the cobalt blue sky. Alec Whistler, DSO, Wing Commander, late RAF opened one rheumy eye and gazed at it with some disdain. A small, neat-looking man in his sixties, he was comfortably ensconced in a deck chair in the garden of his cottage, dozing in the afternoon heat, a heavy book spread across his mustard-coloured waistcoat like the wings of a butterfly.

He snapped his eye shut and snuffled to himself, enjoying the warmth of the breeze which stirred at his curly grey hair and the pressed neatness of his summer blazer. His face was deeply tanned except for one whole cheek which was badly scarred and remained white as an aspirin.

Another jet chose that moment to boom across the sky like the echo of a distant thunder clap and Whistler sat up sharply, his beady green eyes fiery with indignation. 'Blast those things!' he bellowed to no one in particular. 'Can't a fella get a moment's peace?'

A softer, sweeter voice drifted down the garden in response.

'Now, now, sir. No need to get yourself into a lather. You were just as bad in your day.'

Whistler smiled to himself as the comfortable

plumpness of his housekeeper, Mrs Toovey, hove into view. She was carrying a tray of tea and biscuits. 'That was different,' he grumbled in response. 'We were fighting a war, remember.'

'I remember,' said Mrs Toovey gently.

She set the tray down on a table next to the Wing Commander and began to pour the tea. Whistler watched her with quiet satisfaction, enjoying the rich orange colour of the liquid and the diffused sunlight filtering through the delicate bone china of the cups.

Whistler slurped his tea and shot another venomous look up at the sky where the jet streams had formed a crisscross grid of cloud. Wild horses wouldn't get him up in one of those modern things. He'd seen them up close, of course. Fast enough, pretty enough. But not a patch on the crates he'd flown in the forties. By God, they knew how to design a plane in those days. He let his gaze wander across the garden.

It was large and beautifully tended, with a large barred gate at the far end which led directly on to one of Culverton's small roads. Close to the gate was a bulky tarpaulin which occupied much of the land beneath a cluster of lime trees. Whistler gave it a little smile and then turned as Mrs Toovey began speaking again.

'Today's the day, then, sir,' she said with a sigh.

'Mm?'

Mrs Toovey gave a sad smile which creased up the sides of her squirrel-like eyes.

'The aerodrome, sir. Officially closed as of today.'

Whistler set down his tea cup on the table and shrugged. 'Oh that. Today is it?'

Mrs Toovey gave him an admonishing look. 'As if

16

you didn't remember, Wing Commander. Sitting there, pretending you're not fussed about it when it's been getting your blood pressure up, regular as Big Ben, these past six months.'

Whistler harrumphed and fiddled with one of the buttons of his waistcoat. 'Can't say I care one way or another now. Country's gone to hell in a handcart and that's that.'

Mrs Toovey smiled to herself. 'Max Bishop says there's going to be some sort of announcement tomorrow morning.'

'Who?'

'Max Bishop. At the post office. He says there's some people arrived and they want everyone to come to the church hall tomorrow at ten.'

Whistler, who didn't think much of Max Bishop, looked round and frowned. 'What do you mean, some sort of announcement?'

'What I say,' muttered Mrs Toovey, pulling a crumpled tissue from the sleeve of her cardigan. She sneezed suddenly. 'Ooh,' she said, dabbing at her nose. 'Bloomin' hay fever. There's nothing worse.'

Whistler cleared his throat. 'I thought it was all decided. Defence cuts. Aerodrome mothballed. Isn't that what the men from the ministry said?'

Mrs Toovey shrugged. 'Max says it's not the Ministry of Defence that want to talk to us. It's someone else.'

Whistler stretched back in his deck chair and closed his eyes. 'Well, I've said my piece. No one wanted to hear. So this particular old soldier is going to quietly fade away.'

He crossed his hands over his chest; a splendid figure still with his precisely clipped grey moustache and striped tie.

There was a distinct flash of light between the trees. Both of them saw it and Whistler scanned the sky for any sign of cloud.

'Storm coming, you reckon?' he said.

Brigadier Alistair Gordon Lethbridge-Stewart was not having a good day. First, of course, there was this blasted weather. Heat, he maintained, was not good for the military mind. Made everyone far too sluggish. It was, after all, Britain – a cold, wet, sensible sort of place – which had once ruled half the globe. There was a patience and level-headedness that came from living on a damp little island which other countries simply couldn't match. Hot weather bred intolerance and downright bad temper. No wonder all those Latin countries were in a permanent state of revolution. If Cuba had rain and cricket to concentrate on, decided the Brigadier, Castro would never have had a look in.

Secondly, there was the inactivity. After a particularly busy spell, UNIT had suddenly gone awfully quiet, leading Jo Grant to take leave and the Brigadier feeling like a form master presiding over a summer-term class that had gone on too long. After one morning too many shut up in his stuffy office, he had wandered down to the laboratory to see the Doctor. But when he got there, as the nursery rhyme had it, the cupboard was bare...

The Brigadier rubbed his forehead with a handkerchief and downed a tall glass of lemonade in one go, ice tinkling as he lifted it to his mouth. He set the glass down on the lab bench and swivelled round on his stool to face Jo Grant.

'So that's it, essentially, Miss Grant. While you were away on leave, the Doctor simply vanished.'

Jo smiled wryly. 'Is that why it's so neat and tidy in here?'

'Quite. The Doctor never lets the cleaners anywhere near this place. They've been making up for lost time.'

Jo chose a stool for herself and sat down heavily. 'But he'd never just go without saying goodbye. I mean… he just wouldn't.'

The Brigadier wiped lemonade from the ends of his moustache. 'Well, he's free to come and go as he sees fit now, Miss Grant. To be perfectly honest, I'm surprised he's hung around as long as he has.'

Jo shook her head. 'No. There has to be an explanation. He's gone off somewhere in the TARDIS and got held up.'

The Brigadier nodded. 'Perhaps.'

Jo ran a hand through her unruly blond hair. 'Everyone else seems to be taking a holiday,' she said brightly. 'Why not the Doctor?'

The Brigadier frowned. 'He's not exactly the type to take notice of the factory fortnight, is he? I mean, what if something important came up?'

Jo let her gaze wander over to the empty corner where the TARDIS always stood. 'He'll be back. I know he will. In the meantime, sir, I think you should mellow out for a bit.'

'I should what?'

Jo grinned. 'Relax, Brigadier. The weather's gorgeous. The summer's here. Nothing's going to happen.'

CHAPTER THREE
THE VISITORS

The hand which hovered over the controls was plump, pale and waxy, like a doll's.

It moved in a swift and silent pattern over the winking panels, depressing delicate, membranous panels and switches. Then two hands were at work, tracing a spiralling red line that rose and fell across a row of small black screens inset in the controls like dark, watchful eyes.

The red line was stationary for a moment and then spread across the screens like a blossoming flower. A detailed map, coloured a luminous green, rose beneath the red tide. Culverton's church appeared as a full, three-dimensional image. The wave of red light washed over it but its appearance didn't alter.

At the side of the screens, nine rectangular holes yawned empty, like sockets in a metallic jawbone.

The hands moved towards them and rapidly slotted in eight objects. The ninth remained empty, shadow pooling inside it.

The red light on the screen grew noticeably more intense. Someone moved forward: a bulky shape, dressed in black. Its hands, pale as winter berries, came to rest on the controls, fingers dancing about on the cold metal as though in great agitation. Just visible in the flaring red and green light, something beneath its skin began to shift…

Whistler heard the engines first. Throbbing low and with an almost menacing growl.

Buzz bomb!

She was there again and he was trying to warn her, grabbing her hand and dragging her from the crowded mess bar. He opened his mouth to speak but everything seemed to have slowed down. His voice came out like a wound-down gramophone record.

Any second now and the noise of the bomb would cut out. Then it would fall. Fall as it had that night and take her away again…

The noise of the engine continued. Whistler opened his eyes and, with a start, realised he was in the living room of his cottage. He stayed in his armchair for a moment and then moved to the window, drew the curtain to one side and peered out into the purplish glow of the dusk.

A convoy of lorries was trundling past, the beams of their headlights bouncing off the old stonework of Culverton's houses. On and on they went, perhaps twenty of them, shattering the warm stillness of the summer night. He stayed by the window, watching the ominous black shapes, until he realised Mrs Toovey had come into the room.

Whistler turned back inside and clicked on a lamp, throwing a warm orange light around the parlour of his cottage. It was a beamed room, its thick plaster walls hung with horse brasses and large watercolours of old aeroplanes.

Mrs Toovey had taken a seat and was listening, her

head cocked to one side, to the rumbling wheels and the occasional hiss of brakes. The small bay windows rattled as the convoy passed by.

'Well,' said the old woman at last. 'What's all this about then?' Whistler shrugged. 'They seem to be heading for the aerodrome.'

Mrs Toovey frowned. 'These new people Mr Bishop was on about?'

Whistler turned his fob watch over and over in a ruddy hand. 'Seems likely.'

He cast another glance towards the window. 'Damned inconsiderate if you ask me.'

They listened to the convoy in silence. Finally, Whistler glanced down at his watch. 'I think I'll go for a pint,' he muttered, slipping the watch into a waistcoat pocket.

Mrs Toovey rose too. 'All right, Wing Commander,' she murmured. 'But…'

Whistler turned round, eyebrows raised.

'But what?'

Mrs Toovey was wringing her hands. She unlocked her fingers and let them fall to her sides. 'Be careful, sir.'

Whistler gave her a cheerful smile. 'My dear woman, what do you mean? This is Culverton, you know. And…'

'And nothing ever happens here,' she said, completing his familiar maxim. 'I know, but I mean… the lorries and everything. Mind yourself when you're crossing the road.'

She raised her hands and gently tightened the knot of Whistler's tie. He gave her hand a little pat. 'Of course I will, dear lady.'

Whistler walked into the hallway and selected a tweed hat from the coat rack, then turned back to Mrs Toovey.

'No need to worry, anyway,' he smiled and reached over to where a small, battered box lay on the telephone table. He flipped it open and picked something out. 'I've got my lucky charm.'

He held up a small, crystalline object about the size and shape of a rabbit's foot. It looked like jade and glinted dully in the light from the fire. Whistler dropped it into his waistcoat pocket and a moment later was standing outside the door of the cottage.

A chalk-white face jerked forward into the light from the screens. Its eyes were large and dark and glinted wetly as it peered at the green map. A small dwelling-place rose up from the digital read-out, the red light washing over it. Quite suddenly, a sharp, bright light began to wink steadily above it.

The figure began to smile…

Pausing for a moment outside the cottage, Whistler let the sweet fragrances of the summer night wash over him. The sky was a hazy navy-blue with a few stars visible and a miasma of insects swirled around the yellow light of the porch. The desiccated remains of their fallen colleagues lined the bottom of the lamp forming a carpet of wing-cases and compound eyes.

Whistler looked back at the house. Mrs Toovey was just settling herself back into a chair. It was a warm, Saturday evening. Perhaps she'd switch on the wireless or listen to a play or a concert. She might even risk the television. But tonight she seemed distracted. She was already knotting her hands together once again, pulling at her rings, her face wreathed in anxiety.

Whistler straightened up and made a conscious effort to throw off his melancholy mood. He took a deep breath of the flower-scented air and folded his hands behind his back. His posture was ramrod straight, his walk brisk. He began to whistle, softly and rather tunelessly and, at last, he began to feel a little better.

It made him smile to think it, but his whistling hadn't improved. The fact was it had always been his hope that the men under his command would dub him with some affectionate nickname and 'Whistling' Whistler had been the one he'd naturally favoured. Yet, despite the many hours he spent deliberately plugging away at popular wartime tunes, the men had resolutely failed to catch on. 'Stubby' Parkinson had a nickname, of course, and 'Beaver' Kirk, Whistler's old commander. But, as the war years had progressed, Whistler had found himself depressingly without a moniker of his own. He was beginning to think that even something like 'Stinker' would be appropriate when he'd accidentally discovered the truth. The memory made him chuckle, even after all these years.

Suddenly, with a roar of protesting engine, a lorry thundered past, its brakes hissing explosively, its wing mirror slicing through the darkness just inches from Whistler's face.

He pulled up sharp and jumped back from the road a little shocked, feeling cold sweat spring to his skin. Mrs Toovey would not have been pleased. He had been wandering through the dark, lost in remembrance and quite forgetting the great dangerous things that were throttling through the village.

Whistler stood on the kerb and watched three or four of the vehicles disappearing into the night, their cargo invisible beneath heavy black tarpaulins. What on earth was going on? If they were doing something to the old aerodrome, surely the villagers should have been consulted. Unless, he thought, tapping his lip with a finger, unless it was very hush-hush. Now there was a thought. He might ring some of his old contacts at the MOD in the morning. See if there was something brewing. You could never really rest easy. Not with the Russians and the Chinese sitting on all those missiles…

He waited till the road was clear and the warm, silent blanket of night was restored and then set off for the pub. Just as he began to move, however, he heard the sound of approaching feet. It was a very particular sound, and familiar to him.

Troops. Marching.

Without quite knowing why, Whistler ducked down into a narrow alley between two thatched cottages. He pressed himself close to the damp plaster walls and bent down, his old knees cracking noisily. The footsteps came closer.

Whistler peered out at the road, listening to the sound of his own breathing. He rubbed his eyes and sniffed, every sense alert. Then he saw them.

A group of perhaps a dozen black-uniformed men marched into view. Their handsome faces seemed to glow in the soft moonlight, as did the buckles on their black shirts.

Whistler felt himself go cold all over.

He felt in his pocket and rubbed his lucky charm until it felt warm beneath his fingertips. Then, as stealthily as he could, he ran towards the pub.

CHAPTER FOUR
CARGO

When Max Bishop was a very small boy his parents had taken him to the theatre. It wasn't a very impressive place, its red walls scuffed and peeling, the photographs of old music-hall turns sun-faded and falling out of their frames.

Max, though, in his grey school blazer and neatly polished shoes had been immediately entranced. He had taken his seat in the stalls, wedged between his ample mother and skinny father, a bag of sherbet on his lap and a bubbling surge of excitement in his tummy. A fanfare of music had sounded, the threadbare velvet curtains had swung back and the stage was suddenly full of wonders. Jugglers, people in glittering costumes, even a troop of little people with the faces of old men whom Max had found more than a little disturbing.

It must only have taken an hour or two but, by the time Snow White and her handsome prince were married, Max Bishop's life was transformed. He was going to go on the stage. His brother Ted, by contrast, had never really wanted much except to take over the post office business from their parents. He hadn't much time for socialising or courting, preferring to spend time with his books rather than attend the village dances where he might meet a likely girl. Max had always despaired of him.

27

Even in their dressing-up games, when Max had been the ruler of some foreign land, complete with home-made turban and harem of wives, Ted had been content to play a palace guard or a eunuch.

As time went by, the brothers had grown apart. Max was going to go to drama school, everyone in Culverton knew it. Ted, of course, would take on the business when their parents passed away.

But things hadn't quite worked out as expected. Ted had been the one who had married. A lovely woman, but carried off in childbirth like someone from a Victorian novel. It had fallen to Max to take on the post office because Ted, he told everyone, simply wasn't up to it, being so griefstricken and all. As the years passed, Max insisted upon staying on. His brother was a good man, a decent man, but business was never his forte. Max owed it to their parents' memory to keep the business afloat. So, he had martyred himself on the altar of duty, slipped into his niche on the opposite side of the counter and scaled down his dreams to an annual production of *Annie Get Your Gun*.

What a trial his life was! As if the daily grind of pension books and postal orders was not enough he had to deal with Ted's reckless son, always shirking his duties and getting into scrapes. Well, the busiest period of the year, barring Christmas, was almost on them and young Noah would have to do his bit now.

It was early in the morning and Max Bishop glanced at his wristwatch. He had convened a meeting in the church hall to take everyone through the final details of the summer fête which – yet again – he had burdened himself with organising. This year, however, he'd taken great pains to tell everyone that it really was someone else's turn and, no, nothing could persuade him to change his mind. The villagers, of course, said it couldn't be done without him and had sent the new vicar, Mr Darnell, to plead with him personally. After a great show of reluctance (which reminded him rather nicely of that wonderful scene where Richard III refuses the crown), Max had agreed.

Now, with a fluting sigh, he ran his hand through his thinning grey hair and pushed his spectacles up his nose. Around the table were five empty chairs. Only Miss Plowman, a tiny, bird-like woman with round grey eyes which seemed to sit on either side of her nose like pince-nez, had turned up on time.

'Really,' opined Max, rolling his eyes. 'They begged me to look after this blessed fête. The least they could do is turn up.' He turned to the little woman at his side. 'Who're we missing?' he asked sharply.

Miss Plowman turned a few pages on her spiral-bound notebook. 'Erm… Miss Arbus. Your nephew…'

Max grunted.

'Mr Packer…'

'Well, he's never on time, anyway…'

'Wing Commander Whistler…'

Max shrugged. 'Probably cleaning that aeroplane of his.'

'And Mrs Garrick.' She closed her pad. 'Funny. I saw Jean last night. She said she was coming in early to do the flowers on the altar.'

Max wearily rubbed his eyes behind the thick lenses of his glasses. 'You haven't seen her?'

Miss Plowman shook her delicate little head.

Max sighed and smoothed down the front of his seersucker shirt. A long morning of sack-race registrations, tombola prizes and hoopla stretched ahead. It would be a relief when those new people from the aerodrome turned up for their meeting. At least he wouldn't have the weight of the world on his shoulders.

He looked about the room and threw up his hands theatrically. 'Where is everybody?'

Across the village, by the post office, Noah Bishop sat with his knees tucked up under his chin. He was a rangy, rather striking teenager and was wearing a loose T-shirt and cut-off denim shorts. As the traffic thundered by, he picked idly at the raised rubbery emblem on his old baseball shoes.

It was getting hot now, the sun glinting harshly off the paintwork of the lorry convoy which continued unabated, destroying the calm of the village and filling the pollen-heavy air with the smell of diesel.

Noah sat on a flaking metal bench set slightly to one side of the village green.

Another lorry rounded the corner and he squinted against the sunlight to try and make out the shape covered by the black tarpaulin. As he watched, the lorry took the corner rather too quickly. Noah saw it thundering towards him.

There was a long, drawn-out moment, as though time were slowing down, and Noah felt his heart beat very fast. He jumped to his feet and scrambled out of the way just as the lorry mounted the kerb, brakes screeching. Its massive wheels instantly cut through the turf of the green, throwing up a muddy furrow like a brown wave.

Noah backed away and dropped to his knees, eyes fixed on the vehicle which had come to a halt only yards from the bench.

There was a sudden silence.

The lorry's engine steamed madly.

Noah jogged cautiously forward, straining to see through the tinted windscreen.

'Hello?'

He walked up to the front of the lorry, frowning. The driver didn't seem to be in any hurry to reverse or even get out of the cabin.

'Are you OK?' called Noah.

He walked to the other side of the lorry, resting his hand on the bonnet. He pulled it back in shock, surprised at how hot the casing was.

It was only as he reached the back of the truck that he realised the tarpaulin had come loose and some of the cargo had spilled to the ground.

He cocked his head to one side, not at all sure what he was seeing.

Three large, cylindrical caskets were splayed out on the parched grass. They were about seven feet long and rounded at one end like torpedoes. In the sunlight they seemed sleek, black and glossy like wet liquorice. Noah couldn't see any break in their smooth surfaces but they reminded him at once of coffins.

As he bent down on one knee and put out his hand to examine one of them, a large, pale, cold hand grabbed his wrist and pulled him to his feet. He stepped back in surprise.

A man – some sort of officer judging by the braiding on his black shirt – was standing over him, his eyes hidden behind dark sunglasses and a wide smile on his handsome face.

'We'll take it from here, son,' he said. His voice was low and gentle, like a breeze through a cornfield.

'I don't mind giving you a hand.'

'We'll take it from here,' repeated the man, releasing Noah's wrist.

Noah shrugged. 'Suit yourself.'

Half a dozen more men appeared from the top of the green, like shadows detaching themselves from the side of the old water pump. They were dressed in identical black uniforms and sunglasses and immediately began to manhandle the caskets back on to the lorry.

The senior officer marched swiftly up to it and pulled open the door. Noah shifted his weight to see inside.

To his surprise, the driver wasn't moving. He was merely staring ahead, blinking slowly and, of all things, smiling. A pair of sunglasses lay broken on the dashboard.

Shock, Noah reasoned.

He remembered the time he'd come off a scooter while on holiday in Greece. The friction burns on his elbows and legs were nothing compared to the strange, cold feeling that had swept over him and the nebulae of spots that had exploded before his eyes.

Rather than move the driver to one side, however, the officer spoke to him in the calm, level tone he'd used to Noah.

'Reverse. The cargo has been replaced. Reverse and continue to the aerodrome.'

The driver didn't react, save for a momentary widening of his smile. He turned the ignition key and shifted the gear lever. The engine thrummed into life.

The officer clambered down from the cab in one swift movement and slammed the door behind him.

'Is he all right?' queried Noah. He glanced behind him. The lorry was now reloaded, the tarpaulin stretched back into place, as taut as a bat's wing.

The officer placed a gloved hand on Noah's shoulder.

'There's no problem, son. You go home now.'

Annoyed, Noah shrugged off the officer's hand. 'Would you mind telling me who you are exactly?' he said loudly.

The officer said nothing, merely moving back to rejoin his men. Noah followed him, his straight, blond hair fluttering in the breeze.

'Is something going on up at the aerodrome? We've got a right to know.'

The men had formed a neat line and were moving rapidly up the village green like a phalanx of cockroaches. Noah tugged at the officer's shirt.

Without warning the man swung round, his fixed grin wavering slightly. He raised a hand as though about to strike Noah.

'You heard the boy, identify yourself,' barked an authoritative voice.

Noah and the officer both looked round to see Wing Commander Whistler standing by the road, striking an impressive pose as he leant on his shooting-stick.

'Well?' he insisted, walking right up to the uniformed men, his old face flushed with fury.

The officer slowly lowered his hand. His eyes flicked from Whistler to Noah and back again. 'My name is McGarrigle. Captain McGarrigle.'

Whistler looked him up and down contemptuously. 'Captain, eh? Army?'

McGarrigle shook his head. 'Civilian.'

He touched his fingers to the tip of his cap. 'There's nothing to see. Good morning to you.'

Once again he grinned, tiny beads of saliva sliding over his long, brownish teeth. He turned on his heel and marched his men away.

Whistler and Noah looked round as the lorry finally moved off. It backed away from the churned-up soil of the green, executed a neat three-point turn which got it back on to the road and trundled off towards the aerodrome.

'Well, what was all that about?' asked Noah.

Whistler said nothing, but stared at the boy for a long, thoughtful moment. Then he marched swiftly to the phone box on the edge of the green.

He hauled open the stiff door and pulled a battered blue address book from his coat pocket. Vaguely he registered the unpleasant smell of urine and the carpet of dust and mouldering bus tickets beneath his feet, but his mind was elsewhere. He found the number he'd been looking for and laid the address book on the scuffed black shelf next to the phone. He dialled a long number, the circular dial crawling back round, digit by digit, with agonising slowness.

Whistler cradled the receiver under his chin and peered through the dirty glass panes of the phone box, sure that the troops would appear again at any moment. Noah was watching them go, gnawing anxiously at his knuckles.

'You have reached the offices of Panorama Securities,' said a recorded woman's voice at the other end. 'Please hold.'

Whistler sighed impatiently and hastily slotted three ten-pence pieces into the box.

There was a click at the end of the line and this time a man spoke. 'Hello?'

'Yes, hello,' said Whistler, his throat dry. 'I need to speak to Brigadier Lethbridge-Stewart. It's urgent.'

CHAPTER FIVE
ESCAPE TO DANGER

A very, very long way from the village of Culverton, three moons were rising in a sky the colour of burnt orange. A dense jungle, alive with the hooting and whistling of strange creatures, was disappearing into shadowy night as a man made his way swiftly and urgently through the trees.

The Doctor was running for his life.

He pulled up sharply, resting the flat of his hand against a tall, willowy tree trunk; the bark was still warm from the heat of the planet's day. Behind him, there was a sudden rustling sound.

The Doctor snapped his head round and squinted through the fading light to try and make out his pursuers. Only the jungle looked back at him, however, now beginning to glow bone-white in the light of the moons.

The Doctor leant back against the tree and listened to the harsh sound of his own breathing and heart beating.

A very tall, slender man, with a mane of white hair and a prominent, rather beakish nose, he was used to cutting something of a dash in his current form. But his rich blue velvet smoking jacket was torn and the collar was hanging off his ruffled white shirt as he stood in the strange three-mooned shadow, catching his breath.

The rustling from the jungle came again and the

Doctor looked swiftly behind him. If he could only make it down to the lake…

Making a snap decision he ran on, peering ahead to try and make out the reflection of the water ahead. A boat was meant to be waiting for him. A boat across to the island where he had materialised the TARDIS at the start of this whole sorry, ill-advised adventure.

He had made friends and allies, of course, during the past – how long was it? – a week? Two? But the terrible regime which ruled the planet had not taken too kindly to his meddling and, not for the first time in his life, the Doctor found himself a marked man. Desperation had got him over the walls of the prison and into the dense jungle beyond, but the soldiers were hot on his track as the increasingly raucous rustling behind him showed.

The Doctor dragged off his ruined jacket and hurled it into the undergrowth. His shirt was wet with perspiration as he hurtled on, aware that the spongy surface beneath his feet was crumbling. The jungle was giving way to a steep escarpment. The lake couldn't be far away.

Staggering down the hill, his boots plunging deep into the muddy ground, the Doctor suddenly saw the lake stretching ahead, like a drop of quicksilver in the moonlight.

He allowed himself a smile of satisfaction and raced on, ignoring the jets of watery mud that splashed up at him from the shallows.

A rotting wooden pier about twenty feet long extended out into the lake and a small boat, like a coracle, was bobbing gently nearby, attached to the legs of the pier by a thick, tarry rope.

The Doctor plunged on through the water. It was very

cold and he could feel it pouring in through the tears in his shirt, ballooning the fabric as he waded towards the boat.

Just visible in the centre of the lake was the small, heavily wooded disc of the island. The Doctor gave a sigh of relief and hauled himself over the lip of the boat. He sank back against the wooden struts and closed his eyes.

'You took your time, my friend,' said a voice, cutting through the silence.

The Doctor's eyes snapped open. He was staring down the barrel of a very large, very vicious-looking gun.

'Now don't do anything rash, old chap,' he said patiently, holding up both hands. 'I'm a friend, remember?'

The man holding the gun was small and thin with a dome-shaped head and the pale yellow, almond-shaped eyes characteristic of his race. His name was Rujjis and he had been the Doctor's constant companion for the last few hectic days. The alien lowered the gun and smiled. 'We'd all but given up on you, Doctor.'

The Doctor dropped his hands and glanced over his shoulder. 'Well, it was certainly a near thing. And they're not far behind now. I suggest we start rowing.'

With a nod, his companion pulled himself over the edge of the little boat, slipping silently into the waters of the lake where he began to untie the rope from the jetty. The Doctor pulled a stubby paddle from the wet planks at his feet and made ready.

Rujjis's nimble hands fiddled with the soaked fibres of the rope. The Doctor looked round sharply as a loud crash came from the jungle behind them.

'Quickly, man!' rapped the Doctor.

Rujjis gave a final tug and the rope came free, uncoiling

from the wood like a water snake. 'There! Go, Doctor!'

A bullet sliced into the still water next to the boat. Rujjis waded across and extended his wiry arm. The Doctor took his hand.

'Goodbye, my friend.'

Rujjis smiled. 'Goodbye, Doctor. We owe you much.'

The Doctor shook his head dismissively. 'The power was within you all the time. All I did was give it a little encouragement.'

Rujjis smiled, his leathery face dimpling.

Another bullet smacked against the fragile hull of the boat. Rujjis glanced down worriedly and, with a final wave, pushed with all his might so that the Doctor's little craft sailed off towards the island.

At once, the Doctor began to pound at the water with the paddle, plunging it deep below the surface again and again. The boat began to move swiftly forward. Peering through the night, the Doctor could just make out the lamp on the top of the TARDIS glittering with reflected starlight.

On the far shore, a troop of soldiers had emerged from the jungle. One of them, the ratty, obnoxious figure the Doctor had come to know as General Gogon, stood with hands on hips, a crooked smile disfiguring a face that was, in any case, none too pleasant.

The Doctor shot a look over his shoulder. Gogon was gesturing to his troops to line up and fire. About half a dozen followed his instructions, stepping into the shallows of the lake and raising their long, deadly rifles.

Redoubling his efforts, the Doctor paddled on, the little round boat skimming through the calm water like a well-aimed stone.

A volley of shots rang out like a smattering of hesitant applause and the water just behind the boat broke up into a choppy wake. The Doctor smiled grimly. He was just out of reach.

Rujjis's people had planted the explosives at the general's palace. A nationwide rising against his cruelty was already under way. It was time for the Doctor to slip quietly away in the TARDIS, now only twenty feet or so away on the tiny island in the middle of the lake. Time to slip into the mists of legend. Perhaps he might pop back one day and see how his legend was getting on.

'Doctor!'

The cry rang out through the still night air. The Doctor didn't stop paddling, but looked back briefly towards the shore. What he saw made him stop at once and the boat coasted to a gentle halt, bumping against the sandy foreshore of the island.

Gogon was visible at the far side of the lake, still surrounded by his heavily armed troops. But now the repulsive commander held a gun to the head of Rujjis. The Doctor's friend seemed calm, his hands held high above his head.

'Doctor,' called Gogon again. 'You will come back. Or your friend will not live to see the dawn.'

The Doctor sat still in the boat as it bobbed gently on the water.

Rujjis looked at his captor. 'Don't worry about me, Doctor,' he cried. 'It is the general whose days are numbered.'

Gogon's face twisted into a snarl and, for a moment, the Doctor thought he was going to shoot Rujjis there and then. But the dictator kept his temper. He continued to train the gun on his captive and once again addressed the Doctor.

'I am Gogon, Lord High General of Xanthos. Do as I command.'

The Doctor sat up in the boat and shouted back, his voice ringing with authority. 'You, sir, are a butcher!'

Gogon chuckled to himself. 'Whatever you think of me, Doctor, you know that I am a man of my word. I will kill this insolent savage unless you row your little boat back to me.'

Rujjis risked another outburst. 'Please Doctor! Go! You have done enough. This is our struggle now!'

The Doctor looked at him and heaved a heavy sigh. Then, slowly and deliberately, he began to paddle his way back across the lake.

CHAPTER SIX
GOGON OF XANTHOS

A few minutes later the Doctor was standing up to his ankles in the cold water of the lake, the little boat knocking against his legs as it gently rose and fell.

Gogon, still holding the gun to Rujjis's temple, smiled his reptilian smile and nodded to himself.

'You're very wise, Doctor, but you should know by now. We... dictators never keep our word.'

His finger closed on the trigger. The Doctor's face fell. He had only seconds to act. Hurling himself out of the water he hit Gogon full in the chest with his shoulder, knocking the general backwards just as the gun went off. A bullet hissed through the air and into the dense jungle, smacking the big leaves of the nearest tree.

Rujjis flung himself to the ground, scarcely believing he was still alive. He rolled over and over, just able to see Gogon and the Doctor falling backwards into a nest of leathery foliage which snapped explosively as they grappled.

Gogon's men advanced forward but the general spat venomously at them. 'No! Back! Leave him. He's mine!'

He managed to throw the Doctor off and the opponents shunted backwards, like wrestlers sizing each other up. The Doctor rose to his full height and ran a hand through his mane of silvery hair, now flattened and soaked with perspiration.

'You're finished, Gogon,' he said calmly, his eyes darting from side to side to assess his chances of escape. 'The people have risen against you. And if you cut us down, there will be countless thousands to take our place.'

Gogon sneered, a trickle of blood threading from his mouth.

'I do not know who you are, Doctor. Or how you came to my world. But I swear I will be avenged for the chaos you have brought in your wake.'

He stretched out both his arms, shifting from one foot to the other. The Doctor did the same and moved left, inch by inch, his boots sliding through the muddy ground. Soon the two men had completed a circuit, surrounded by Gogon's troops who once again held Rujjis at gunpoint.

'You might as well give up,' said the Doctor with a sly grin. 'Perhaps the new regime will be kinder to you. There are always prospects for a fella with ambition, you know.'

With a roar of anger, Gogon launched himself towards the Doctor who immediately grabbed his shoulder, lifted him off his feet and threw him into the jungle. There was a splintering crash and the general cried out as he hit the earth with a force that sent a plume of mud shooting into his eyes.

Rage transformed his face into an ugly mask as he came at his opponent again. This time he caught him off-balance and it was the Doctor who ended up on the ground. He rolled over at once, ignoring the sharp pain in his side, and jumped to his feet.

Gogon ran forward again screaming and, with a high-pitched Venusian war cry, the Doctor landed a devastating chop to the back of his neck.

Gogon crashed to the ground but hurled himself bodily at the Doctor's ankles, dragging the Time Lord down to his level and pummelling his chest with his fists.

The Doctor struggled to fight back, but Gogon's claws closed inexorably around his neck.

Tighter...

Tighter...

The Doctor could feel the alien's long, black nails digging into the flesh of his throat. His eyes began to bulge and he had to fight for his next breath as Gogon pressed down on his chest with his knees.

At last he managed to pull his hands from under him and chopped the sides of both palms simultaneously into the general's sides.

Gogon gasped and slumped forward, easing his throttling grip just enough for the Doctor to thrust his knee upwards into the alien's stomach and then continue the trajectory so that Gogon flew over his head and splashed into the shallows of the lake.

The Doctor sprang up, shaking his woozy head to clear it. Gogon emerged from the water, dripping wet, dashed to one of his soldiers and grabbed the weapon he was holding.

The Doctor gave a small laugh. 'Run out of options, Gogon?'

'The last refuge of the scoundrel,' hissed Rujjis.

Gogon wiped the moisture from his face and pointed the long weapon directly at the Doctor. 'Better a live scoundrel than a dead fool.'

'No!' cried Rujjis.

Just then the night sky was brilliantly illuminated by a blinding white flash. The percussion of a massive explosion hit them and everyone ducked instinctively as it rolled down from the mountains like thunder.

The Doctor kicked out one long leg and knocked the gun from Gogon's hand. The general backed towards his troops.

'Kill him!' he screeched.

The Doctor looked up at the distant mountains, now a broad band of fiery orange that could only mean the destruction of Gogon's citadel.

'Your palace, I presume,' said the Doctor evenly.

He turned his attention to the troops and his voice took on a tone of unmistakable authority. 'Gogon's rule is now finished. I advise you all to think very carefully about what you do next.'

There was a long, expectant pause. Gogon looked at his men, his yellow eyes twitching nervously. The soldiers looked him up and down, their expressions uncertain.

Rujjis swallowed nervously.

Then, one by one, the soldiers turned to point their guns towards the general. The last in line released Rujjis, retrieved the fallen gun and put it into the rebel's hand. With a smile, Rujjis turned the weapon on Gogon.

'Gogon of Xanthos,' he stated in a voice shaking with emotion. 'You will stand trial for the crimes you have committed against our people. Take him away.'

Gogon shot a last, hate-filled glare at the Doctor as his arms were pinioned and he was marched away into the jungle.

Rujjis walked slowly up to the Doctor and smiled.

'Once again, Doctor, we owe you so much. How can we repay you?'

The Doctor rubbed his chin, then tapped the barrel of Rujjis's gun. 'Tell you what, as soon as you can, get rid of that. And try and do without it in future.'

He flashed Rujjis a broad smile which took years off his heavily lined face then shook the little alien's hand. 'Now, if you'll excuse me, I really must be going.'

This time, the journey across the lake was a placid experience.

The Doctor paddled quickly but calmly, enjoying the smooth splash of the oar through the silky water. He reached the island and walked swiftly through the trees to where the comforting rectangle of the TARDIS stood, almost black in the embrace of night. He felt in his trouser pocket for the key and let himself inside.

The double doors opened with a low murmur.

The Doctor found the insistent hum and glaring white of the console room inexpressibly comforting. He stumped to the console and pulled the lever to close the doors, then rested the flats of his hands against the machinery, like a drunken man relishing the cool peace of his own pillow.

With a few flicks of switches, the time rotor of the TARDIS began to rise and fall, filling the air with the raucous, grinding noise of her engines.

Jo Grant sat on a laboratory stool, staring down at the pale grey rectangle of concrete below the window. It glared unpleasantly in the sunshine and left bright after-images on her eyes as she blinked.

A parade was under way with about two dozen UNIT

troops standing smartly to attention under Sergeant Benton's instruction. To one side stood the wiry, slightly anxious-looking figure of Captain Mike Yates, baton under one arm, and behind him was the Brigadier, looking rather splendid, Jo thought, in full dress uniform. She smiled. It was just like him to organise something like this to keep everyone on their toes.

'Never forget, Miss Grant,' he had told her solemnly. 'UNIT is first and foremost a military concern.'

She sighed and glanced around the empty laboratory. The place was beginning to take on the sad, neglected feel of an empty nursery; somewhere usually full of life, now fallen eerily silent.

Jo closed her eyes, thinking of the adventures that had begun within those four walls. She was proud of the way the Doctor had come to accept her, first as an assistant, then a colleague and, finally, as a friend. It was strange to think that it might all have come to an end.

She glanced at the empty corner, its bare, plaster walls depressingly sterile in the hard sunlight.

Perhaps it was for the best. Things had to change. She would have wanted to move on soon, she was sure of it. It was better to have the decision taken for her than have to choose the moment herself.

A little knot of fear and emotion suddenly rose in her and she felt hot tears spring to her eyes. Life after UNIT. What would that be like?

It might have been the sounds of the summer afternoon but, for a moment, Jo could hear the grinding, scraping engines of the TARDIS once more, as though from a long way away. Then she whirled round on the stool.

A familiar blue shape was slowly materialising in its old corner. Double doors, frosted windows, flashing lamp, all suddenly taking on solid form like a ghost stepping through a wall. Jo's pretty face was suddenly wreathed in smiles.

With a satisfying thump, the TARDIS was once more fully formed. The door flew open and the Doctor stepped out. He looked tired and filthy, his normally elegant clothes virtually shredded.

Jo cannoned into him and hugged him tightly.

'Well,' he smiled, patting her fondly on the back. 'Quite a welcome!'

Jo disentangled herself. 'We thought you'd gone. For good!'

The Doctor frowned. 'Really, Jo. Now why would I want to do a thing like that?'

He crossed the room, looking about him, a frown of displeasure creasing his tanned face. 'I see the Brigadier didn't waste much time. He's had the char in.'

He ran a finger over the workbench and shook his head. 'See what I mean? Not a trace of dust!'

Jo grinned. The Doctor walked to the wall and examined his reflection in a mirror.

'Oh dear,' he said, running a hand through his white hair. 'Oh dear, oh dear.'

He turned as the laboratory door opened and the Brigadier marched into the room.

'Doctor!' Lethbridge-Stewart cried delightedly, his face betraying a rare display of real emotion.

He cleared his throat as though to reassert his official credentials. 'Glad to have you back.'

The Doctor smiled too. 'Thank you, Brigadier.'

The Brigadier laid his baton down on the workbench. 'As a matter of fact, you're just in time. Something's come up.'

CHAPTER SEVEN

LEGION INTERNATIONAL

Charles Cochrane MP cradled the receiver of the red phone under his pointed chin and examined his nails.

'No, sir,' he said softly. 'No problem at all.'

He frowned, greatly displeased at the quality of his morning manicure, and very carefully snipped away at the side of his thumbnail with a pair of shiny silver scissors.

'Very well, sir. Of course.'

He sat up straight and smiled smugly to himself as the man on the other end of the line showered him with praise. 'Thank you, Prime Minister. My pleasure.'

He put down the phone and spent another five minutes attending to his nails before spinning round in his swivel chair and examining his face in a big, gilt mirror which hung just above his desk in the old, dark-panelled room.

He had handled the situation well, it was true, and it would only be a matter of time before the PM moved him upwards in the next reshuffle.

He tightened the knot of his Old Etonian tie and smoothed down the waistcoat of his favourite three-piece suit, then cocked an eyebrow at his reflection. His impish features stared back.

Handsome devil, he thought.

'Clever devil,' he said aloud.

He swung back round and turned his attention to his morning mail.

Cochrane was, by general agreement, one of the government's brightest stars. A high-flyer who had risen from Chief Secretary to the Treasury to Secretary of Defence in little more than eighteen months. Well bred, well educated and with a beautiful wife, he was still only forty-one years old and the way he had forced unpopular defence cuts on to the Chief of Staff had hugely impressed the Prime Minister. The Home Office beckoned, he was sure of it.

He was still smiling to himself when he opened an envelope and three freshly printed photographs spilled out on to the desk.

He could smell the fresh developer on them.

Despite the fact that they appeared to have been taken through a hotel window, they were staggeringly clear. Cochrane appeared in all three. He wasn't alone. And he wasn't wearing his three-piece pinstripe suit.

Cochrane felt a wave of fear wash over him like cold water. When he finally pulled himself together, he opened the envelope wide and checked it for further contents. A tiny slip of paper fell out. On it was printed a phone number. Cochrane rubbed his eyes and then, with shaking hands, picked up the phone and dialled the number. There was a click at the other end but no one spoke. Not at first.

Cochrane swallowed. 'This is Charles Cochrane.'

He turned the photographs over one by one so they were face down on the desk.

'What… what do you want?'

*

Whistler tipped a pinch of snuff on to the back of his hand and raised it to his bulbous nose. He inhaled briskly and then sneezed, causing more than one of the villagers gathered in the church hall to shoot him reproving glances. He glared back at them and blew his nose loudly, oblivious to the speckles of brown dust which now peppered his face like liver spots.

Sitting back in a rather uncomfortable chair, he looked around with a bored sigh.

The long, rectangular room was hung with gaily embroidered Bible scenes; woollen shepherds visited a woollen manger, a risen Christ gazing down on an earthly kingdom made of silver paper.

Since Max Bishop's abortive meeting earlier in the day, trestle tables piled with slim, leatherbound hymn books had been pushed back against the walls to provide more space. Wide-hipped, middle-aged ladies clustered around in little groups, like dodgem cars in flowery frocks, chatting and laughing.

Whistler gave a little wave to Miss Plowman but she didn't see him as she was too busy talking to Mrs Toovey. She, at least, glanced over at him and smiled. Next to them was the lean, rather sallow-faced Max Bishop from the post office complete with his bow tie and baggy cardigan. He was sipping from a cup of weak tea and talking to his pale, wiry brother Ted who, as usual, looked in fear of his wrath. Ted was standing in front of a scene from the Crucifixion, looking very sorry for himself. Whistler smiled. He didn't know who looked the more worse for wear: Ted Bishop or the Son of Man.

Ted's son Noah was close by. Whistler had arranged to meet him, keen to bring him up to date with the results of his call to his old friend Brigadier Lethbridge-Stewart.

Whistler sneezed again but it could have been because of the musty dampness of the unheated church hall as much as the snuff.

Shuffling from group to group was the vicar, Mr Darnell, a tall, young man with a pleasant, rather bland face. He exuded a permanent smell of dust and spice. Only in the village a month or so, he had lost no time in bounding up to Whistler's front door, all open-toed sandals and neckerchief.

'Oh, hello, Vicar,' Whistler had said.

'Call me Steve!' trilled the newcomer.

'No,' muttered Whistler, slamming the door in his face.

Now Darnell was orbiting those silly women, dressed in open-neck shirt, jeans and gym shoes – if you please – and not acting very much like a vicar at all.

Whistler pulled a sour face.

'What price the dog collar, eh, Wing Commander?'

Whistler turned round. To his surprise, Noah Bishop was sitting next to him, smiling broadly. He was dressed in bell-bottom corduroys and tight T-shirt and his snub nose creased up as he smiled. Max Bishop was always complaining that the lad was a bit of a troublemaker but Whistler had been fond of Noah since he was a child.

'What's that?'

Noah shrugged. 'The vicar. I get the feeling you disapprove of him.'

Whistler grunted. 'Well, naturally. Dispensing with all the "thees" and "thous". It's what church is all about. Used to be anyway. Take the wedding service. Used to be "with my body I thee worship". What a wonderful phrase.'

He stared into space for a long moment. 'All gone now.'

He cleared his throat. 'But that's neither here nor there. Are you all right, lad?'

Noah nodded. 'Why shouldn't I be?'

Whistler shrugged. 'Well, after this morning's shenanigans.'

'I'm fine. Really. It takes more than a bully in sunglasses to put the wind up me.'

Whistler grinned. 'Good lad.' He looked at his watch. 'Well, if those were our mysterious visitors, then you and I have got a handle on them already, Noah, wouldn't you say?'

Noah nodded. 'Didn't take to them at all.'

'I got through to my old chum Lethbridge-Stewart. He says he knows just the fella to look into it. Sending him down forthwith.'

Noah nodded. 'Cool.'

Whistler glanced round. 'Well, these aerodrome johnnies are going to be late if they don't show soon.'

Noah nodded. 'Well, I make it just ten, they should be...'

He stopped speaking abruptly as a flash of light illuminated the room. A murmur of surprise ran through the assembled villagers but, before anyone could comment, the main doors to the hall swung open.

A breeze rushed through the long room, making the parish notices pinned to the wall flutter like butterflies testing their wings.

Three figures were framed in the doorway.

For a moment they stood in silence, as though pausing for dramatic effect, the morning sky forming a burnished blue canopy at their backs.

Two of them were athletic-looking men in neat black

uniforms. Noah and Whistler recognised one of them as Captain McGarrigle, still sporting the same sunglasses.

The two men flanked a tall, rather fat woman, in a neat black trouser suit and white blouse. She had large, dark eyes which stood out from her pale face with the clarity of ink spots on blotting paper. An oily comma of black hair was slapped flat across her forehead.

She looked about at the assembled villagers and swept her intense gaze across them. Then she broke into a huge grin, exposing teeth that were small, even and perfectly white, like those in the head of a ventriloquist's dummy.

'Good morning, my friends,' she said. Her voice was rich, deep and soothing.

For no reason he could fathom, Noah shivered.

'I apologise for the abruptness of this meeting,' continued the newcomer.

She crossed the room in a few swift strides, the two black-uniformed men keeping perfectly in step with her, and took her place at a lectern made of pale, blond wood. She smiled again and Whistler noticed how many of the villagers were responding to her evident cheerfulness.

'My name is Bliss,' said the newcomer, flattening down still further the black fringe which hung like a silky curtain across her forehead. 'And I bring great news for you all!'

CHAPTER EIGHT
THE NEW ORDER

'My dear Brigadier,' said the Doctor, stretching back in a chair and folding his hands behind his head. 'Running errands is not my forte. If you want someone to pop round to see your old friends, I suggest you try the Women's Institute.' He put his feet up on the Brigadier's desk, the corners of his mouth turning up into a small smile. 'I believe they make excellent jam.'

The Brigadier raised an eyebrow and shot a venomous look at the Doctor who had now closed his eyes, completing the picture of indifference.

He was glad the Doctor had returned, of course, and he was certainly looking back to his usual dapper self in emerald-green smoking jacket, narrow black trousers and bow tie. However, he was displaying his familiar contempt for the Brigadier's methods and seemed damnedly disinclined to get back to work. Or, at least what the Brigadier regarded as work.

'Perhaps if you could explain a little more, sir,' said Jo helpfully.

'Oh very well,' sighed Lethbridge-Stewart. He sat down and leant forward over the desk, crossing his hands in front of him. 'Alec Whistler is an old friend. He was a pilot during the war –'

'Which war?' said the Doctor, still with eyes closed.

'Well, the last one, of course,' cried the Brigadier in exasperation.

'Oh, yes. I lose track. You have so many.' The Doctor settled himself further into the chair.

The Brigadier cleared his throat. 'Whistler flew Spitfires out of a base in East Anglia. A village called Culverton. He liked the place so much he decided to stay on there. It's a lovely spot. Been down there myself more than once.'

The Doctor sighed theatrically.

The Brigadier pressed on. 'Well, anyway, as I thought I'd explained, the old aerodrome closed down recently. Defence cuts and all that…'

'And then these new people bought the place up?' asked Jo.

The Brigadier nodded. 'That's right, Miss Grant.'

The Doctor spoke without opening his eyes. 'And what has that got to do with us?'

The Brigadier looked down at his hands, a troubled expression flitting over his features.

'Well?' demanded the Doctor.

'It may be nothing. But Alec Whistler says these new people are acting rather strangely. Convoys of lorries going up to the old aerodrome. Acting rather… officiously.'

The Doctor's eyes opened and he nodded towards the armed guard at the door. 'There's a lot of it about.'

He sat up at last, a flicker of interest in his eyes. 'Go on, Brigadier.'

'Whistler asked me if I could do a bit of digging. I like the old boy, so I said I'd do what I could.'

'And you dug?' said Jo brightly.

'I did. Or at least I tried to. It should have been fairly routine. The MOD is always selling off redundant property. But I can't seem to get a straight answer out of anyone.'

The Doctor rubbed his chin thoughtfully. 'And it feels like more than just the usual bureaucracy?'

The Brigadier nodded. 'These new people seem to have friends in high places. The order comes from the top. Leave well alone.'

Jo chewed thoughtfully at her lower lip. 'And what are they called?'

The Brigadier glanced down at a sheaf of notes. 'Legion International.'

The Doctor looked up. 'What did you say?'

'Legion International,' repeated the Brigadier. 'A new outfit apparently. Lot of foreign investors. And that's about all I could find out.'

The Doctor seemed lost in thought. Jo looked at him. 'What is it, Doctor?'

He continued to think in silence for a moment and then shook his head. 'Nothing, nothing.' Jumping to his feet, he crossed straight to the door and pulled it open.

'Where are you going?' cried the Brigadier in surprise.

The Doctor looked puzzled. 'Culverton, of course. Isn't that where you wanted me to go?'

He strode out, his cloak flapping behind him.

The church hall was buzzing with chatter. Bliss held up her hands for silence. Whistler and Noah had folded their arms simultaneously, unconsciously mirroring each other's scepticism.

'My friends,' continued Bliss in her syrupy voice. 'I can

understand your concern. The news of the aerodrome's closure must have come as a shock. Who can forget the heroic exploits of its fighter squadrons during the last war?'

Whistler cleared his throat. 'Plenty by the sound of it. Otherwise, why close the place down?'

Bliss eyed Whistler carefully and flashed her huge smile. 'Time marches on, sir. The old order passes away.'

Whistler harrumphed. 'And what, pray, are we to expect in its place?'

Bliss nodded to the black-uniformed Captain McGarrigle at her side. The muscular man crossed swiftly to a slide projector which had been set up at the back of the hall and switched it on. The machine was of a dull, grey, planished metal and hummed with power.

McGarrigle slotted a slide into place and suddenly Bliss's face was bathed in coloured light. A huge image was projected across the room on to the white plaster of the far wall. Bliss stepped aside so the assembled villagers could take it in.

The image was an artist's impression of the aerodrome, but in a very different state to the neglected, weed-strewn place that everyone knew.

The parabolic prefabs had been replaced by tall steel and glass towers. Sleek passenger aircraft, even the odd jumbo jet, were dotted around the broad black band of a new runway, disgorging hundreds of happy, tanned passengers. Everywhere, airline crew in black uniforms and peaked caps were smiling and waving. A flag flew boldly from the top of the highest tower.

'What the hell do you call that?' cried Whistler from his seat.

Bliss's smile grew even broader. 'The future, my friend.'

She stepped back into the projector's beam and an aeroplane was instantly superimposed across her pale, fat features. 'I give you Legion International.'

There was an audible gasp from the assembled villagers, then a smattering of clapping.

Bliss accepted the applause like a soprano during a curtain-call, bowing slightly and plucking unconsciously at her blouse. She looked up, her huge black eyes glittering, and gave a little nod.

McGarrigle and the other uniformed man moved swiftly and silently to the doors of the hall and opened them wide.

At once, a dozen or so similarly dressed men marched inside, tall, handsome and immaculate in their uniforms. They split into two columns and moved to flank the figure of Bliss who stood at their head like the general of an army.

Jo had never seen a sky like it. Not on Earth anyway. The Doctor had driven his little yellow Edwardian car, Bessie, at a frantic pace out into the Essex countryside and, hugging the coast, up towards East Anglia.

The land had quickly flattened out and it was possible to see for miles and miles with only the occasional church spire to break up the horizon.

At first Jo had found the journey monotonous, but as the hot summer afternoon wore on she came to relish the wind rushing through her hair and the glorious colour of the sky which dominated the landscape: a kind of deep, burnished blue like a fresh coat of paint.

The Doctor pressed his foot down and Bessie put on

a turn of speed, taking on the narrow corner of a lane with amazing dexterity. Jo gripped the car door to steady herself and turned to the Doctor, her sunglasses glinting.

'We all missed you, Doctor,' she cried above the roar of the little car's engine.

The Doctor nodded absently. 'Did you?'

'Of course. The Brig was in quite a state. I don't think he'd quite know what to do with himself if you weren't there.'

The Doctor gazed ahead, his eyes disappearing into a mass of lines as he squinted into the sun. 'Well, he'll have to get used to it, Jo. I can't hang around here for ever, you know.'

Jo nodded a little sadly. 'I know.'

The Doctor changed gear. 'I mean, there's little point in having my exile lifted if I choose to stay put on twentieth-century Earth, now is there? I have my reputation to think of. People will go around saying I've become institutionalised.'

Jo's puzzled look was visible through her large sunglasses. 'Pardon?'

'Institutionalised. An old lag. Someone who comes to depend on their imprisonment.'

Jo shook her head. 'Oh, I'd never think that. But you must... you must...'

The Doctor looked quickly across at her before refocusing on the road ahead. 'Must what?'

Jo shrugged. 'Well, I mean, it must mean something to you. UNIT, the Brigadier... me, or else why are we going to East Anglia instead of Metebelis whatever?'

'Three, Jo,' said the Doctor levelly. 'Famous blue planet of the Acteon galaxy.'

'I know,' smiled Jo. 'Well?'

'Well?'

'You haven't answered my question.' Jo looked hard at the Doctor.

He was silent.

Charles Cochrane MP wasn't used to travelling by the tube. Even during the thankfully brief period he'd spent as a member of Her Majesty's Loyal Opposition, he'd managed to use his family connections to wangle a car with a driver. He was very careful never to use it when travelling around his grim little Northern constituency, of course, but then politics was chiefly about the art of concealment.

He walked swiftly down the escalator at Tottenham Court Road station, uncomfortable in the shabby clothes he'd adopted as a disguise. The jacket was too small and horribly constrictive in this hot weather and the trousers were far too big, forcing him to keep them pulled together at the waist. Despite the rush and his worry about the whole situation he was still feeling rather pleased at the neatness of his ruse.

The voice on the phone had told him to come to an address in the East End, without his usual round-the-clock security guard. It had been difficult to convince the officer but, in the end, Cochrane had succeeded.

'I'm going undercover,' he had said. 'It's a way to connect with the voters again and find out what people are really thinking.'

What concerned him most, naturally, was what the voters would really think if they saw those photographs splashed across the Sunday papers...

He changed trains at Liverpool Street, threading his

way through the commuting crowds, and made his way east, shrugging a bulky holdall over one shoulder. Tired of standing, he finally found a seat on the packed, oppressively hot vehicle but an old man, head lolling, kept falling asleep on his shoulder. Cochrane grimaced and wiped some of the man's drool from his cheap suit, then adjusted the sunglasses which disguised most of his face. He hugged the holdall to him.

It was dangerous, of course, to give in to a blackmailer, but the alternative was too frightful to contemplate. Anyway, there was something else inside the bag, in addition to ten thousand pounds in cash. His father's revolver. Just in case these crooks had anything nasty in mind.

Cochrane got off the tube at a dingy, decrepit station which he'd never even heard of. It still had wooden escalators, the corner of each stair packed with paper and old cigarette butts. As he sailed towards ground level, Cochrane made a mental note to do something about such firetraps if he became Home Secretary.

'When I become Home Secretary,' he muttered aloud.

He would hand over the money and they would give him the negatives. Then he could go back to doing his job. And he'd never stray again. Ever.

The address he'd been given turned out to be a warehouse of some kind. Gantries crisscrossed the buildings above him and there were huge iron hooks projecting from the brickwork.

He walked down a dark, narrow alley. A drain was overflowing, pooling filthy water on to the cobbles.

Cochrane found a narrow door painted in peeling green and pushed at it. The door opened soundlessly, as though freshly oiled. He stepped through.

The room beyond was clearly vast. Despite the darkness, Cochrane could make out rafters high up, fitfully illuminated by dirty skylights. The whole place stank of turpentine.

He lifted the bag up to chest height. 'I've brought the money,' he said in as clear and steady a voice as he could muster. There was no response.

Somewhere a tap was dripping.

Cochrane lowered the bag and placed it carefully on the floor in front of him. He unzipped it and felt inside until he found the butt of the gun.

'And I've ordered the Culverton aerodrome out of bounds. Just as you ordered.'

He lifted the gun clear of the wads of bank notes and slipped it into the waistband of his trousers.

'So…'

He held up one hand in what he hoped was a conciliatory fashion.

'Do we have a deal?'

Something moved far back in the shadows.

Cochrane steadied himself. His hand moved to touch the gun. The tap dripped steadily in the silence.

Then there was a deafening noise, somewhere between a scream and a howl of rage, and whatever was in the room with Cochrane came powering through the pitch darkness and overwhelmed him.

He scrabbled for the gun but it fell down the inside of his baggy trousers and clattered to the floor.

And when he tried to yell, something slithered inside his mouth.

CHAPTER NINE

THE CONTROL ROOM

She felt its agony as though it were her own.

Out there, out of sight, it lay. Blood thumping through its massive body, bringing life and energy to the great sinews and muscles. But the brain... the mind...

She felt it reaching out to her and a wave of terrible regret flooded through her body.

She had been lucky. The other had not, succumbing to the instabilities of their passage through the darkness. And now he was lost, an insensible, monstrous thing.

Almost insensible.

Somewhere in the dark pit of his brain, he knew. He knew what he had become and he screamed his pain and resentment into her mind.

She sank back into her chair and closed her huge, dark eyes. Blood dripped from her palms where she had sunk her fingernails into the flesh.

Wing Commander Whistler crouched down behind an oil drum and rubbed his tired eyes.

Just ahead of him, the gates of the aerodrome had been opened and pushed back as far as they would go. The familiar convoy of lorries was rattling through and, from his hiding place, Whistler could see they all had the same tightly covered black tarpaulins over their hidden cargo.

As the latest lorry roared past in a cloud of dust, he looked over to where Noah Bishop had concealed himself. The boy held up his hand, signalling for Whistler to wait, as two Legion International troopers pulled the aerodrome gates closed behind them.

When all was clear, Noah slipped out from behind a pile of packing crates and joined Whistler.

'Did you get a closer look?' asked the old man.

Noah shook his head. 'They're not going to make another mistake like that.'

Whistler pulled a small pair of binoculars from his jacket and squinted through them. 'Might get a better view – ah!'

'What is it?' Noah sprang up, peering into the distance.

Whistler handed him the binoculars. 'They're starting to unload. Can you see?'

Noah fiddled with the focus. 'Yes. They've pulled up… about… three hundred yards down the airstrip.'

Whistler shielded his eyes. 'Can you see what they're unloading?'

Noah nodded slowly. He handed the binoculars back to the old man. Through a shimmering heat haze, Whistler could make out the shapes of a dozen or so men hauling bulky equipment and crates on to the concrete.

He let his hands flop to his waist. 'Hmm. Not what you saw before?'

'No,' muttered Noah. 'Concrete-mixers or something.'

Whistler shook his head. 'Whereas…?'

'They were more like coffins.' Noah looked him in the eye and then his head snapped up suddenly. 'Look.'

Whistler followed the line of his outstretched finger. There was a freshly painted sign attached to the gates, announcing that the aerodrome was closed. It hung loose now, swinging from one corner.

'Oh yes,' muttered Whistler. 'Old Jobey was talking about that in the pub. He's been contracted to paint a few of them…'

He tailed off, frowning.

'What is it?' said Noah.

Whistler shrugged. 'It may be nothing. But I haven't seen Jobey in days. He's always in his usual place in the pub. I've never known him miss a night.'

Noah looked steadily at Whistler. 'But he wasn't there last night?'

Whistler shook his head. Jobey's sign creaked gently in the breeze. 'Question is, why would anyone bother to announce the closure of the aerodrome if they were about to flog it to a private airline?'

Noah wiped the palm of his hand over his face and sighed. 'I'd better be getting back. Uncle Max's got me working this afternoon.'

Whistler smiled. 'Me too. Mrs Toovey's been on at me to get my act together for the fête. She treats me like a little boy most of the time.'

He smiled, then glanced back towards the aerodrome. 'Perhaps we should come back tonight.'

Noah nodded. 'Yeah. Let's do that. I'm sure between us we can find out what's going on.'

'I might have some news from my friend,' said Whistler. 'He's promised to do some poking about at the MOD. Find out what they know about these Legion International beggars.'

'Cool.'

'Eh? Oh yes.' Whistler held out his hand and Noah

took it, his grip warm and firm. 'Until tonight, then.'

Noah grinned. 'Until tonight, Wing Commander.'

A tall, rather florid-faced man stood just inside the closed gates of the aerodrome, hot and uncomfortable in the uniform of a police constable.

John Trickett pulled a clean white handkerchief from his trouser pocket and rubbed it around the inside of the collar of his short-sleeved blue shirt. Then he dabbed his forehead and moustache and blew air noisily from his mouth. His thick woollen trousers were clinging to his legs, annoying him as much as the heavy helmet he cradled under one arm.

He thought back to his holiday in Rome and the cool, light wearable summer clobber he'd seen the Italian police wearing. Luxury. 'Sensible fellas,' he'd said to his wife. 'They may not know how to run a country but they don't force their coppers to wear winter woollies in the middle of July.'

A black-uniformed guard appeared, obviously senior in rank to the one who had admitted Trickett to the aerodrome. To Trickett's annoyance, and in spite of the newcomer's heavy black uniform, he didn't seem uncomfortable in the slightest. In fact, he was smiling broadly, his smooth face untroubled by perspiration.

'Yes?' The man's voice was even and relaxed. 'My name is Captain McGarrigle.'

Trickett cleared his throat. 'I'm here to see your Mrs Bliss.' He glanced down at his notebook. 'Is it Mrs or Miss? I don't think anyone's said.'

The captain didn't reply directly. 'Is she expecting you?'

Trickett nodded.

'I'll just confirm that if I may.' The broad smile didn't falter.

'By all means.'

McGarrigle turned away. Trickett expected him to walk back to one of the outbuildings but he just stood there with his back to the constable, for several seconds. Then he swung back, the sun glinting off his black glasses.

'I'll show you up,' said the captain, extending a hand towards the centre of the aerodrome.

Trickett looked to see where the man concealed the radio he must have used to receive his instructions, but didn't see anything. He gave a mental shrug. Probably miniaturised like everything else these days. Discrete technology, they were starting to call it.

He raised his fingers almost unconsciously to a glinting chain tucked into his shirt pocket. He knew that when the chips were down he could still put his faith in a tin whistle and a good pair of lungs.

Puffing slightly, he followed McGarrigle up a flight of metal steps to what used to be the old control tower. The steps clanged beneath their boots.

The captain pressed a button, which turned green beneath his thumb, and ushered Trickett inside.

The room beyond still resembled the interior of the control tower the constable sergeant remembered from his childhood. There had been grey metal consoles and primitive radar equipment then, but now the antiquated machinery had been gutted to leave a huge, circular, white-walled room with a continuous window stretching all the way around. It had been freshly reglazed and the room was flooded with light.

Outside, Trickett could see that work was well

under way on the new airport. There were lorries and uniformed men scattered all over the airstrip, assembling what looked like concrete-mixers. The slamming racket of a pneumatic drill occasionally broke the stillness.

There was little else in the room except for posters advertising the coming of Legion International and two tall rectangular boxes, with spinning spools of magnetic tape inside them, which Trickett assumed to be some kind of computer.

Behind a huge, oak desk shaped like a half-moon sat the tall, fat figure of Bliss, already smiling in greeting and holding out a pudgy hand for Trickett to shake. He took it and couldn't help but notice what looked like tiny, semicircular cuts in the palm.

'My dear Constable,' cried Bliss. 'How nice, how nice. Can I offer you some tea?'

Trickett took a seat across from her.

'No tea, thank you, ma'am. Although they do say it's the best thing on a hot day.'

Bliss frowned. 'Hot? Oh… yes. Yes, I suppose it is.'

Her smile reasserted itself. 'Now you said something on the telephone about complaints?'

Trickett nodded and pulled his notebook from his trouser pocket. It was damp with sweat. 'That's right, ma'am. Various parties aren't taking too kindly to these convoys driving all through the night.'

Bliss shook her head. 'Oh dear.'

Trickett smiled kindly. 'You see, ma'am, you mustn't think that we aren't happy for your company… for…' He glanced down at his notes again.

'Legion International,' said Bliss with a flourish.

Trickett nodded. 'We're very happy to have you move

72

in. It's grand to think the old aerodrome will be up and running again. It's just the speed of it all has got some of the more… shall we say, set in their ways, among us a little rattled.'

Bliss held out her flipper-like hands, palms upwards. 'I quite understand. Progress is a bitter pill for some. But I'm afraid the conditions on which we purchased this place from the Ministry of Defence were quite specific. We need to get Legion International up and running immediately. We must. It's our…' She looked to the ceiling, her dark eyes glinting, '…priority.'

Trickett gave a tight smile. 'It's a funny thing, ma'am. But Commander Tyrell never told us anything about your coming.'

Bliss's smile didn't falter. 'Commander…?'

'Tyrell, ma'am. Surely you dealt with him? He was in charge of the aerodrome right to the end.'

Bliss shook her head. 'I'm afraid we dealt directly with the MOD.'

Trickett glanced down at his notebook again, refraining from mentioning that no one had seen Harold Tyrell for quite a while.

'Is there someone at the ministry I could speak to?' asked the constable at last. 'I'm sure a proper statement would set everyone's mind at rest. There are enough rumours going round as it is.'

'Are there now?' Bliss's smile broadened even further. There were little spots of foamy saliva gathering at the corners of her lips.

Trickett gave a little chuckle. 'Well, yes. Mystery men turning up out of nowhere. One minute the aerodrome's closed down, the next we're the new Heathrow!'

Bliss laughed too, a small, harsh, dry chuckle. 'Quite.'

She got up and walked to the window, quite impressive in her dark suit despite her bulk. Her big dark eyes scanned the activity below with interest. 'As a matter of fact, Constable, there is someone you can speak to.'

Trickett produced a pencil and licked the end. 'Excellent, ma'am. If I could just take his name and telephone number...'

Bliss turned back. For a moment, as a long shaft of dusty sunlight poured through the window into his eyes, Trickett couldn't see her face. 'Oh there's no need. He's coming to Culverton. Coming very soon.'

CHAPTER TEN

'FOR GOD'S SAKE GET AWAY FROM HERE!'

And now night comes to this place of almost perpetual darkness.

The ground boils like molten tar; an impossibly bleak landscape, pitted by great bluffs of volcanic rock. Pools of seething, viscous liquid belch and ripple over the steaming soil. Night smothers all; a sky of thunder-black cloud, lowering over the desolation.

But something is alive out here. Something is crawling across the ground towards a huge steel structure; as incongruous as a cathedral in a desert, this great shimmering building. Its once-fine lines are scarred and bent, the metal pocked by the impacts of a million million meteorite strikes.

Inside there is still warmth. There is safety.

The thing moving painfully over the black dirt knows this. It claws its way forward. There must be a way in. Must be.

Yet it knows it has not been selected. It is not one of the chosen.

It remembers a better time, a sweeter time when the darkness was pleasant and comforting, not this nightmare of storms and destruction.

A convulsive shudder rumbles through the ground, spewing volcanic dust high into the air and shaking the structure of the building. The huge glass frontage rattles and threatens to splinter. Within, a cyan-blue light throbs gently like a beacon.

The thing moves forward on its claws.

Lightning splits the sky open like a fissure in rock. The thing *looks up, its round, black eyes swivelling in their sockets. Then it moves on, slowly, desperately, towards the steel palace…*

'Now don't you worry, my dear,' said Alec Whistler soothingly. 'We shan't be gone more than a couple of hours.'

Mrs Toovey's face was creased with worry. 'But I still don't see why you think you've got to go up there in the first place. If this UNIT man's coming down…'

Whistler nodded. 'Yes, yes. But if young Noah and me can find out as much as possible, we'll make this Doctor's job all the easier won't we? Now do stop clucking over me, Mrs T. I'm quite capable of looking after myself.'

The housekeeper gave a little shrug, tears springing to her eyes. 'And we're to expect the Doctor tonight?'

Whistler nodded. 'Lethbridge-Stewart says so. Make him comfortable and I'll be along as soon as I can.'

He turned to go, but Mrs Toovey laid a hand on his arm.

'What do you think's going on up there, sir?'

Whistler blinked slowly. 'Haven't a clue, dear lady. But there's something not quite right. You don't get through the Battle of Britain without scenting evil, and there's evil abroad up at that aerodrome, I'm certain of it.'

Mrs Toovey looked even more anxious. Whistler patted her hand. 'Not to worry,' he muttered.

It was only when the Wing Commander was long gone that Mrs Toovey saw something glinting on the table by the fire. It was the little tin case in which Whistler kept his good-luck charm. The old woman sighed, crossed herself, picked up the tin and made her way out into the garden. She knew a safe place to put it.

*

High, wispy red clouds like splayed fingers echoed the dying rays of the sun as the sky bruised into darkness. Whistler made his way swiftly along the old road to the aerodrome, his shoes scuffing on the dusty track. There was little other sound save for the familiar chittering chorus of insects.

Ahead, he could see the silhouette of the tall perimeter fence. Legion International had made no effort to set up security lights or alarms. All the better for he and Noah.

He slipped silently up to the fence and crouched down behind the oil drum he'd used earlier that day. Quickly, he scanned the area surrounding him, his breath coming out as a short, excited pant. No convoys tonight, he noted with disappointment. It would have been so simple to slip through the gate while one of the big vehicles was lumbering through. He pressed his face to the mesh of the fence and peered through. The aerodrome was shrouded in shadow yet he was sure he could detect movement. Figures seemed to be moving about, working noiselessly, silhouetted against the deeper black of the buildings.

Whistler's ears pricked up as he heard what he was sure was a police whistle, sounding feebly from somewhere inside.

'Evening.'

Whistler jumped as Noah's whispered harshly in his ear.

'Oh God!' hissed the old man. 'Don't do that! I'm not as young as I was.'

Even in the darkness he could see Noah grin. 'Sorry.'

Whistler nodded to himself. 'I'd hate to see this campaign founder because I keel over with a dicky ticker. Now, let's press on. Did you bring the cutters?'

Noah bent down to a large canvas rucksack which he'd brought with him. There was a loose rattling sound and he pressed a pair of bulky wire-cutters into the Wing Commander's outstretched hands. Swiftly and efficiently, Whistler snipped a large hole in the mesh and kicked it back until it was large enough to crawl through.

'You've done this before,' said Noah admiringly.

'Naturally.'

Noah replaced the cutters in the rucksack and hauled the bag on to his shoulders. 'Aren't we supposed to blacken our faces with burnt cork or something?'

Whistler tutted. 'If I didn't know you better I'd think you were taking the mickey, young man. Now, shut up and follow me.'

With surprising alacrity, the old man slipped through the hole, his clothes catching briefly on the ragged wire. Noah followed, crouching so low that his face almost brushed the dry grass.

When both were safely through, they kept low and sprinted to the nearest cover, a stack of cylinders partially covered by a thick grey tarpaulin. Closer now, they could see about two dozen Legion personnel unloading equipment from a line of lorries.

'More of those cylinders,' cried Noah excitedly.

Whistler strained to see through the darkness. 'Where are they taking them, I wonder? The control tower?'

Noah shook his head. 'Doesn't look like it. I think they're heading for the far side of the place.'

Whistler tutted to himself.

'What is it?' asked Noah, looking round.

'Extraordinary thing, don't you think?' said the old man, clucking his tongue.

'What?'

Whistler's gaze swivelled round to Noah. 'No lights.'

Noah shrugged. 'Well, they're obviously up to something. Maybe something illegal. They don't want to advertise it.'

Whistler waved a hand. 'No, no, no. I mean there's not a light anywhere. Not in the control tower. The old barracks. Not even a torch to help them unload. Not one.'

Noah nodded slowly. 'I see what you mean.' He sucked on his lip. 'That is strange.'

'So,' said Whistler, moving around the cylinder in front of him, 'our mission is to find out what they've got in those containers and why they think they can go around like they own the village.'

'Maybe they do,' murmured Noah.

'Hmmph. Not a pleasant thought, lad. A lot of my pals gave their lives to defeat this kind of behaviour. I'm not about to let another lot of blackshirts take up where the old ones left off.'

Without another word, Whistler moved off into the night. Noah followed and they raced through the darkness towards the airstrip, then peeled off to one side, sliding down against the wall of one of the parabola-shaped buildings which made up the old barracks. Whistler caught his breath and bobbed his head around the corner. His eyes moved swiftly from side to side as though photographing what he saw, then he ducked back.

'See anything?' asked Noah.

Whistler nodded. 'They're carrying those cylinders across the airstrip.'

Noah frowned. 'Where to?'

Whistler tucked his knees up and rested his elbows on them. 'There isn't anything beyond that section of fence, is there?'

Noah shook his head. 'Just marshland.'

Whistler thought for a moment. 'That could explain why they haven't driven down there. The lorries would be too heavy to drive over the ground.'

Noah took his turn to glance around the side of the building. To his astonishment, he saw that the Legion guards had formed a long line and were carrying the cylinders bodily on their shoulders like a huge, bizarre funeral procession.

'This gets weirder and weirder,' he muttered. 'What now?'

Whistler rubbed his hands together. 'Well, we could go back and wait for this UNIT fella to turn up.'

'Or?'

Whistler smiled. 'Or we could carry on and see what turns up.'

Noah clapped the old man on the shoulder. 'I'm game.'

Whistler was pleased. 'Good lad. Right. Here's what we'll do. As soon as that lot are out of sight, you pop out and check the coast's clear. Then we'll get into a lorry and see if we can't break open one of those containers – oh.'

'What is it?'

Whistler was tapping his waistcoat pocket. 'My lucky charm.'

Noah shrugged. 'Never mind, sir. I'm sure we'll be OK.'

'It's not that, son,' said Whistler, a little sadly. 'It's just I've never been on a… a mission without it. Not since I found it. It got me through the war, you know.'

'I don't doubt it,' said Noah, clambering to his feet. 'But

we'll have to trust to our own luck this time.'

He slipped around the corner of the barracks and nodded. 'OK. They've gone.'

Whistler nipped out quickly and joined him, both pressing their backs flat against the cold grey wall, and peered through the darkness where he could just make out the last of the line of guards moving away in silent procession. Nodding to Noah, he raced across the road to where the lorries were parked.

Noah crossed too and jumped up on to the back of the first lorry, immediately throwing back the tarpaulin that covered it. There was nothing beneath it. He cursed and let the canvas fall back, looking over towards the lorry with Whistler on board.

'Anything?'

'No,' hissed Whistler. 'Try the next.'

They continued in this way for several minutes, finding every lorry clear of cargo, until they reached the last two in the line.

'Ah!' cried Whistler happily, as Noah pulled back the tarpaulin and revealed that the lorry was packed full of sleek, black cylinders, stacked like wet cigars.

Noah felt all over one of them with the palms of his hands.

'I can't find an opening,' he murmured.

'There must be a way in,' said Whistler. 'Here, I'll shed some light.'

The old man reached into his pocket and pulled out a silver matchcase attached to the fob chain of his watch. He struck a match on its serrated base and the back of the lorry was briefly illuminated. Both men looked the casket over hurriedly. There wasn't a single flaw or crack on its smooth, ebony-black surface. Noah and Whistler exchanged glances just as the flaring light of the match snuffed out.

There was a sudden explosion of noise. Noah's heart began to thump. Behind them, he could hear booted feet on tarmac.

'We're rumbled!' he shouted. 'Run!'

He jumped down on to the tarmac and set off at a run, jerking his head back to see Whistler struggling down from the lorry. He hesitated, then tore back across the airstrip and grabbed the old man by the arm. 'Come on!'

Once on terra firma, Whistler was a different proposition altogether. Tucking his elbows into his sides he careered across the airstrip like a man possessed. Noah was just ahead, looking round wildly for an escape route. Booted feet thundered behind them and, even as he panicked, Noah thought it strange that the Legion men still hadn't turned a single searchlight on to them.

Behind him, he could hear Whistler beginning to tire, his breath rasping. He gripped the old man by the sleeve and urged him forward.

'Nearly there, sir. Hurry!'

Whistler shook his head, sweat streaming down his ruddy face. 'No. Can't –'

Noah pulled them both down to the ground. There, just visible in the gloom, was the hole they had cut in the mesh of the fence. Noah turned but found himself being pushed through.

'Go! Go on, lad!'

Noah's forehead hit the sharp mesh and he winced in pain as it cut into his skin. He shook his head involuntarily.

'It's OK, Mr Whistler. We'll just give ourselves up. Let

the police sort it out. We've done nothing wrong.'

Whistler thrust out both hands to propel Noah through the fence. 'There's more to this than breaking and entering, Noah. Those people mean business, now for God's sake get away from here!'

CHAPTER ELEVEN
THE BEAST

Noah tumbled through on to the other side of the fence just as the Legion men caught up with Whistler.

Through the gloom he could just make out the old man struggling to his feet and putting up his hands. A guard raised his gun and brought it down savagely on to the back of Whistler's head.

Noah felt anger rise like bile in his throat, and was on the point of trying to get back through the fence to help the old man when he pulled back. Better to get hold of Constable Trickett and sort out these bastards properly.

A guard was already halfway through the fence, shoulders flat to the ground. Noah looked around, decided where to go and then, in one swift movement, brought his foot round and kicked the guard under the chin. The man crumpled to the earth with a satisfying thud. Noah took to his heels.

Still there was no searchlight, no harsh klaxon breaking the silence of the warm night. Noah headed for the road back to the village and took the corner at such speed that he felt the ground give way beneath him. He hit the rough track chest first, knocking the wind out of himself.

He flipped over on to his back and lay there for a long moment, staring up at the sky, struggling to breathe. His ribs felt like they had an anvil resting on them.

As he recovered, he heard the Legion troops heading for the road and made a snap decision. They were bound to think he would head for Culverton. Instead, he would double back around the aerodrome, towards the marshland, and give them the slip.

He struggled to his feet, hobbling a little and wincing at the friction burns he had sustained on his long legs. He ducked out of sight as half a dozen guards ran past him towards the village and, crouching down by the grassy verge, he made his way back towards the aerodrome. He thought about Whistler inside there and what they might be doing to the old man.

Noah kept close to the fence and followed it all the way around for about a third of a mile until he could see the back entrance. The gates were open in order to allow egress from the base. A neat pile of the black cylinders stood just outside them.

Noah caught his breath and bent down, watching to detect any movement. Only two or three troopers stood guard, as immobile as statues.

He wracked his brain, unsure what to do for the best. Should he try and get past them and inside the aerodrome to rescue Whistler? Or scurry back to Culverton to raise the alarm?

The decision was made for him as he leant forward, slipped and put out his hands to break his fall. Both palms connected with the mesh of the fence, sending a shuddering rattle through the structure. Noah tensed.

As one, like identical weather vanes, the black-uniformed guards swung in his direction. None spoke. Noah could hear his breath streaming through his open mouth. Then they raised their guns and fired.

Bullets thudded – one, two, three – into the wet ground at Noah's feet. He flung himself down and rolled over as gobbets of soil spat out and covered his T-shirt. Without waiting for the guards to pursue him, he took off at a run heading blindly forward into the marshland.

The marshes extended for some acres behind the aerodrome, hillocks of tufty grass interspersed with great ponds of dank water. Noah splashed his way through, oblivious to the jets of mud that rocketed out and soaked his trousers. He had to get help. Had to get back to the village. Although he didn't stop running, he was vaguely aware that the guards hadn't bothered to follow him.

Noah pulled up sharp. Suddenly he didn't much care if the guards were on his trail. A deafening, bubbling sound was emanating from the ground ahead, as though great pockets of gas were belching to the surface.

He stepped back, feeling his heels sink slightly into the marsh. Despite the black night he could see that the wetland ahead was moving.

A huge shape was rising out of the darkness, dripping with water, its vast jaws clicking open, its fetid breath blasting all over him.

Noah opened his mouth to scream, but no scream came out.

Bliss gripped the arms of her chair until her knuckles blanched. The mind of the other reached out again. It was wild with energy, pursuing, attacking, wanting to kill. Yet the dark intelligence that survived at its core seemed to hold it back. In the void, it felt her mind and pleaded with her to end its agony.

Bliss shook her broad head. Shook it until flecks of spit flew from her mouth.

'I cannot,' she sobbed. 'I cannot help you. Let me be…'

The screeching in her mind abruptly ceased. Bliss put her head in her hands.

The Doctor's car approached Culverton a little after sunset. The dying rays of the sun set the flat landscape ablaze and he slowed down a little to enjoy the sight.

He remembered another evening like this, sitting alone by the Thames, trying to come to terms with his exile.

In his early days as UNIT's scientific adviser, a long time before Axons, Daemons and Daleks had come to bother him, he'd put on a good show of ignoring the Time Lords' sentence. But in truth, he'd found the routine unbearable. Stifling.

To think that he, of all people, should be marooned on one tiny world, in one time period – a heartbeat in the great scheme of things.

At first, he had thrown himself into his researches, working ridiculously long hours in the lab, trying desperately to work out a means of escape from the twentieth century.

I am no ordinary man.

The thought resounded again and again inside his head.

I am no ordinary man.

Yet how could he pretend to be otherwise when he was surrounded by the Brigadier's personnel, clocking in and out, going back to their families at night?

The winter evenings were the worst, the English

night pressing against the laboratory windows, black as molasses while the room's primitive yellow electrics blazed away.

For a while, he'd taken to wandering through the TARDIS, as though its endless labyrinth of corridors would somehow lead back to the wandering life he had known. But this had grown too painful, the paraphernalia of previous adventures bringing him sharply, and literally, back down to Earth.

After a time, though, something had changed inside the Doctor. He began to find the Brigadier's blinkered military mind less objectionable and rather more endearing. He secretly looked forward to each new problem, relishing the dangers it might bring. On an evening like this one, by the Thames, with the insignificant sun setting over this insignificant but wonderful little planet, the Doctor had felt suddenly... happy.

Then, out of nowhere, the Omega business had come up and, with its successful conclusion, release from his exile. The whole Universe was his to explore once again. He remembered the tiny twinge in his stomach as he stepped across the threshold of the TARDIS for the first time after his knowledge of the dematerialisation codes had been restored. What was it? Excitement? Adrenalin? Or was it just the slightest hint of fear?

It was an uncomfortable fact to face but the Doctor knew that his first thought as he'd leant, exhausted, on the console after his escape from Xanthos had been... home.

He glanced down at Jo, tucked up, fast asleep beneath her fur-collared coat, and brought Bessie in a large circle around the village green. He let Jo sleep on as he parked by an antiquated water pump, then swung his legs over the side of the car and stretched. It had been a long and rather tiring drive. Slipping into his emerald-green smoking jacket, the Doctor shot his ruffled cuffs and looked around.

Post office, pub, shop. He rubbed the back of his neck.

Green, pump, houses. Charming. Quite charming.

He leant over into Bessie and shook Jo gently by the shoulder. She groaned and rubbed her eyes sleepily.

'Come along, Jo,' said the Doctor brightly. 'We've arrived.'

Jo yawned. 'Culverton?'

'Culverton.' He glanced round again at the serene village, still bathed in the rosy glow of the sunset. 'Seems quiet enough.'

CHAPTER TWELVE
FRIENDS IN HIGH PLACES

The Chief of Staff, who rejoiced in the name of Jocelyn Strangeways, slammed down the telephone with uncontained fury.

A stout, ruddy-cheeked man, he was a soldier, like his father and grandfather before him and *his* father before that. He even sported the same enormous moustache that bristled so marvellously on the faces of his forebears.

Their portraits bore down on him from the walls of his book-lined study, splendid in their old uniforms, against a backdrop of the Sudan or India or the Transvaal.

Strangeways tried not to look at them. They seemed to have accusing expressions on their faces.

Damn it all, he was supposed to be in charge! What was the Prime Minister thinking about, cutting the country's defences back to the bone? A little friendly chitchat between the Yanks and the Chinese didn't suddenly make the world a safe place. It was imperative that Britain maintain a strong armed response.

Strangeways examined the tumbler of whisky in his hand then drained it in one go.

It was bad enough having to swallow his pride about these defence cuts, but to have to answer to that arrogant puppy Cochrane! Now the beggar wasn't even returning his phone calls.

There was a soft *click* somewhere close by.

Strangeways looked round but could see nothing unusual. Struggling to his feet, he reknotted the cord of his dressing gown and marched swiftly from the room, trying to shrug off the impression that his illustrious ancestors were laughing at him.

The knocker on the old front door of Whistler's cottage was matt black and shaped like a dolphin.

The Doctor lifted it with one hand and rapped twice, firmly. He looked around, breathed deeply and smiled to himself, relishing the scents of the warm summer night.

Jo stood close by. When there was no response after a full minute, she crept across the flowerbeds and peered through the window, shielding her eyes with the palm of her hand.

'Any sign of life?' asked the Doctor.

Jo shook her head.

The Doctor stepped back from the door and craned his neck to look at the upper storey.

He knocked again, then frowned. 'Funny.'

Jo joined him. 'The Brigadier did say he'd been in touch with the Wing Commander didn't he?'

The Doctor nodded. 'Yes. He's supposed to be expecting us.'

'Well, maybe he's just popped out –'

She broke off abruptly as the porch light came on and the door creaked cautiously open.

'Yes?' Mrs Toovey sounded anxious and not a little suspicious.

The Doctor stepped forward. 'Good evening, madam. I'm the Doctor, this is Jo Grant. We're here to see Wing

Commander Whistler.'

The old woman breathed a sigh of relief. 'Oh yes. I've been expecting you.'

She opened the door fully to let them inside. 'I didn't hear the door. I was in the garden.'

Jo nodded and smiled. 'That's all right. It's a lovely night.'

As she stepped over the threshold, the Doctor held back. He was looking towards the village green. Jo followed the direction of his gaze and made out the figure of a man walking slowly around the bench and staring down at the ground as though he'd lost something.

The Doctor indicated Mrs Toovey. 'You go on, Jo. I won't be a moment.'

He set off with long strides towards the green and soon saw the man more clearly. He was about thirty-five and dressed in an unironed linen suit and sandals. He had a pleasant but slightly vacuous look to him and a none-too-clean dog collar to complete the ensemble. The Doctor acknowledged the vicar with a cheery wave. 'Beautiful evening isn't it?'

The vicar nodded but he seemed troubled. 'Beautiful.' He held out his hand. 'Stephen Darnell,' he muttered.

'I'm the Doctor. Is there something the matter?' The Doctor looked down at the ground. The neatly cut grass had been churned up by heavy tyres, quite ruining the pretty verge.

The vicar pointed to the damage and then both he and the Doctor swung round at the sound of marching feet.

Jo poked her head around the door of Whistler's cottage and glanced at Mrs Toovey. 'What's that?'

A group of half a dozen black-uniformed men came

smartly round the corner, moving in a tight unit like a knot of glistening flies.

Jo looked at the Doctor who was frowning heavily. Completely ignoring both the Doctor and Darnell, the troops came to a halt on the village green, not far from the churned-up grass. Darnell regarded them intently and a pained look crept over his face.

The lead trooper withdrew a small black box from his jacket and laid it on the grass. The Doctor could see some kind of dial and a needle which swung sharply to the right. At once, another of the men began to dig at the green with a small spade.

Darnell gasped. 'Excuse me, but would you mind explaining what you're doing?'

The trooper, who wore the uniform of a captain, ignored him and picked up the box, replacing it in his jacket. The vicar persisted.

'This village has won prizes. I really don't think it's right for you to dig up the green. Those lorries of yours have done quite enough damage as it is.'

He cleared his throat and shuffled awkwardly. 'Do you hear me?'

The Captain scowled at Darnell and jerked his head in his direction. At once, two of the troops marched over to the bench and tried to drag the vicar away. He protested loudly and one of the man clamped a black-gloved hand over his mouth.

'You sir!' bellowed the Doctor. 'Do you mind explaining what you think you're doing?'

The trooper let his hand fall to his side. He looked to his Captain, who switched on a charming smile. 'It's for the gentleman's own good. He needs... looking after.'

The Doctor put his hands on his hips. 'I think he should be the judge of that, don't you?'

The Captain's grin broadened and, for the first time, the Doctor noticed the little clumps of saliva which clung like cuckoo-spit to his lips.

At a slight inclination of the Captain's head, his men released Darnell who slumped back on to the bench, his eyes flickering wildly from side to side.

The Doctor regarded the newcomers steadily. 'Legion International, I presume?'

The Captain nodded. 'I'm Captain McGarrigle,' he said, curtly. 'Aren't you from Culverton?'

'No,' said the Doctor. 'I'm not... local.'

The Captain looked about a little shiftily, taking in Bessie and then Jo and Mrs Toovey who were still standing in the porch.

'Well, it's good that you're here. We have plans for this village. Great plans.'

'Do you indeed?' The Doctor glanced down at the muddy tyre tracks on the green. 'May I ask what you were doing just now?'

The Captain's face assumed an innocent expression.

The Doctor pointed to the man's black uniform. 'That little box. Some kind of Geiger counter?'

The Captain laughed and a tiny fleck of saliva fell on to his freshly pressed jacket. 'Nothing like that. We had an accident. I was just checking that none of our... cargo was missing.'

The Doctor looked over at the remaining five troopers, standing in a line, still and impassive, like automata waiting to be wound up.

'And what is your cargo?'

The Captain's dark eyes glittered. 'Well, actually, we're more of a passenger service.'

The Doctor smiled. 'Is that so?'

There was a tiny flicker in the Captain's eyes. 'I simply mean that we're rebuilding the old aerodrome and converting it into a working airport. We use some things in our work which are rather dangerous. Chemicals and such. You understand.'

The Doctor bent down on one knee and fingered some of the soil. 'Well, I'm quite experienced in chemical analysis. If you like I could…'

The Captain's face was impassive. 'No. It's all right. My men will see to it.'

Without him giving an instruction, two of the troopers swung round to face the Doctor. He got slowly to his feet.

'Yes,' he said quietly. 'Yes, I see.'

The Captain touched the brim of his peaked cap. 'Good evening.'

The Doctor didn't move. 'Perhaps we could come up to the aerodrome tomorrow and have a look around? I'm sure it's fascinating.'

The Captain shook his head slowly. 'I'm afraid that's impossible.'

'Really? We have contacts at the Ministry of Defence, you know.' The Doctor smiled pleasantly as though talking to a child.

The Captain wiped his lips with the back of his hand. 'Then I suggest you refer the matter to them. No one is allowed in without an official pass.'

He turned on his heel and marched away, leaving the two troopers standing by the bench deterring any further investigation by the Doctor. The vicar got up and crossed to the Doctor's side. Jo came out from the porch.

Darnell introduced himself, proferring a shaking hand.

'Jo Grant,' said Jo quietly.

'And that,' said the Doctor with a sigh, 'was Legion International.'

The vicar nodded. 'You've heard of them?'

'That's why we're here. Wing Commander Whistler has expressed concerns about the newcomers.'

The vicar looked over at the retreating troopers. 'Concerns. Yes.'

'What now?' asked Jo.

The Doctor shot a stern look at the men by the bench and then put his arm around Jo's shoulder, guiding her back towards the cottage. 'Get on to Lethbridge-Stewart, would you, Jo?'

'OK.'

The Doctor shot one last look at the Captain's retreating form. 'I've a feeling he might be right about them having friends in high places.'

And now lightning rends the sky again. The broiling, unquiet black earth shudders as the thing presses itself against the glass of the steel palace. Its dark eyes shrink back into its fleshy skull as lightning sears its pupils. Moments later, with darkness restored, it looks again.

Through the blue haze it can see others like itself. They are lying in warm cocoons, their breathing regular and untroubled by the natural disasters outside. They are of all shapes and sizes; some little more than children, others fully grown, a waxy bloom like frost spreading over their sleeping faces.

Others, in the uniform of the Apothecaries, move in silence from one cocoon to the next, checking life-signs.

The thing outside raises a desperate claw and lets it slide down the glass. It leaves a sticky trail, like spittle, dribbling down to the baking soil.

One of the Apothecaries looks over. Its round, black eyes dilate. It moves towards the window…

There were more portraits lining the staircase of Jocelyn Strangeways's enormous house. From most of them, the familiar, slightly bilious countenance looked out, growing progressively darker as age and time stained the canvasses.

Strangeways shuffled up the stairs to his bed, the hem of his silk dressing gown whispering over each step. He clicked out the landing light and used the blue moonlight that spilled through the windows to guide himself to his room.

There was another *click*.

Strangeways whirled round, ears pricked, ready to face any intruder. He was spoiling for a fight after his outrageous treatment at the hands of Charles Cochrane. God help the cheeky bugger who dared to break into his house!

He jumped as a dreadful screeching sound suddenly emanated from beyond the window. Flattening himself against the wall, eyes darting from side to side, he tried to identify it.

It was horribly like a baby crying.

Strangeways thought of his ancestors, pulled himself together and made his way boldly across the landing towards the window.

Gingerly, he pressed his face towards the glass and

looked out into the dark night.

Slam.

Strangeways staggered back from the window as something hurled itself against the glass. His mind reeled and then he saw a sleek black cat glaring at him, its eyes blazing like green fire. He let out a huge sigh of relief and wandered back towards his bedroom door. The cat was joined by another. Both their hackles instantly rose and they began again the awful chorus he had heard moments before.

Strangeways pulled off a slipper and lobbed it at the window.

Both cats immediately scattered, disappearing into the darkness as though swallowed whole.

The Chief of Staff limped into his room, one foot slippered, one bare and threw off his dressing gown. It was a warm night and he lay on top of the sheets for a few moments, letting the events of the day filter through his brain.

It was during trying times like this that a fella could do with a wife. Someone to bounce ideas off, at least. Someone to reinforce his opinions about the Minister of Defence. Someone to give him a cuddle…

Strangeways turned on his side.

The space in the bed yawned emptily. His wife was long gone. Twice remarried now. He put out his hand to touch the cool pillow where once she had rested her lovely head.

His fingers met something warm and sticky.

Strangeways sat bolt upright, crying out in disgust. In the moonlight, he was suddenly aware of something; a bone-white, glistening thing like a crab scuttling over the sheets towards him.

Scuttling.

He thrust out his hands to fight it off but it moved with horrible speed. In a second, its warm, wet body was clamped to the skin of his face.

Somewhere, two black cats began to wail.

CHAPTER THIRTEEN
MISSING

Ted Bishop was a worried man. Those who knew him would say this was his natural condition and those who knew his brother would say he had plenty to be worried about.

Ted had got home around six to begin his nightly routine; shuffling into the kitchen in his old tartan slippers, putting the kettle on the hob, and setting out three mugs – well, two mugs and Max's rather fine china cup – on a tray. Four spoonfuls of rich-smelling black tea (one for each person and one for the pot) would be shovelled into the old brown 'Sadler six-cup' and then, when the kettle began to whistle, he'd rinse the boiling water round the pot to warm it.

While the tea brewed, he'd sit for a minute with the back door ajar and smoke a cigarette, taking great pains not to let the telltale tobacco fumes sneak into the house where Max's sensitive nose might detect them.

As usual, he'd poured out Max and Noah's tea and then carried the tray upstairs. His brother was always to be found in his room going over the day's takings at this hour of the evening, and Noah was usually making one of his models instead of doing his homework.

Ted had placed Max's cup on the edge of the desk and his brother had reached out a hand to take it without saying a word.

Ted then took his own mug and Noah's through to the boy's room. He liked to have a chat with his son before bed.

With both hands full, Ted had gently pushed the door of Noah's bedroom open with the toe of his slipper.

'Another day, another dollar!' he had cried, brightly, just as he did every evening.

Noah's room was empty.

Ted had stared at it blankly for a long moment, his gaze flickering over the neat bedspread and plumped-up pillows. He sighed and put Noah's mug down on a nearby bookcase. His son had promised to stay at home to help his uncle with some post-office paperwork. Max had got it into his head that Noah would one day take over the business, and he needed to start learning as soon as possible. Noah was far more interested in his model of a Sunderland flying boat but had agreed to help for his father's sake.

Ted supposed he'd better let Max know that Noah wasn't in but, to give himself a bit of courage, he took his time and sipped at his hot tea in silence before crossing back to his brother's room.

Max hadn't taken it well, of course, cursing Ted's son for being a no-good layabout and general ne'er-do-well before ordering Ted out to find him.

'I suppose I'd better get everything ready for tomorrow,' he'd said, running a well-manicured hand over his face. 'It's a good job someone's on the ball around here.'

Max had given Ted just enough time to put on his shoes before forcibly propelling him outside and slamming the door. Ted had sighed again and then, as he looked around at the village, he had smiled.

The night had a wonderful feeling about it, and he could smell the delicious scent of heavy summer flowers hanging in the air. It had been easy, for a moment, to imagine that he had slipped back into the past. The roofs of the houses which surrounded the post office were silhouetted against the purply sky. There was even an old-fashioned little yellow car parked by the green.

Probably there for the summer fête. There had always been evenings like this. And always would be.

But his good humour had evaporated and by now he was worried about his son. He fancied he knew all the places the lad was likely to go. Noah, however, was in none of them. Why would he stay out? Surely he knew how upset Ted would be and how his uncle Max would take it out on his dad.

Ted left the village and took the road that led towards the aerodrome. Perhaps he'd gone off up there. The new arrivals had certainly caused a lot of fuss. Yes, that was where he would be, seeing if he could resist getting himself in trouble. Unless, of course, it was a girl…

Ted smiled. The lad was growing up. So perhaps it wasn't so surprising that he'd failed to come home. Hadn't he seen a girl making eyes at Noah over the post-office counter? And the summer was at its height. Time for a young man's fancy to turn to thoughts of pretty girls. Cheered by this thought, Ted walked through the night towards the aerodrome with a lighter heart, and nothing disturbed him until he came across his son, spread-eagled in a ditch, eyes closed, a thick dribble of blood pouring from the open wound on his head.

*

The Doctor and Jo were seated across from Mrs Toovey on a small and comfortable sofa that seemed about to engulf them in its chintzy pattern. The Doctor smiled sweetly at the old woman and drained the last of his tea.

They had been made very welcome and Jo was already looking forward to the huge, comfortable-looking bed she'd been allotted in the attic room.

The Doctor nibbled on a biscuit and leant towards Mrs Toovey. 'Did the Wing Commander give you any idea how long he'd be?'

The old woman shook her head and stifled a sob. 'No, sir. I warned him. I said to wait until you got here but he's all for taking the initiative.'

Jo patted Mrs Toovey's hand gently. 'Good for him.'

Mrs Toovey gave a small smile. 'I reckon he misses the war, you see. He'd never admit it but it... made him feel alive. All this mystery with the aerodrome got his taste for adventure going.'

The Doctor rubbed the back of his neck thoughtfully. 'And you say he was planning to go up there?'

'Yes, Doctor. Him and Ted Bishop's lad.'

The Doctor nodded. 'What do you reckon to these... newcomers?'

Mrs Toovey rubbed her wedding ring, twisting it absently round and round her finger. 'Well, I'm sure it's a good thing. Everyone seems to think so. But all these fellas in black. Like soldiers...'

She tailed off.

Jo shot a glance at the Doctor. 'So what exactly did Mr Whistler suspect was going on up there?'

'Oh, he didn't confide in me, love,' murmured Mrs Toovey. 'Need to know, Mrs T,' she said, in imitation of

Whistler's military bark.

The Doctor rubbed his chin. 'Have you noticed anything else… unusual?'

Mrs Toovey cast her gaze towards the ceiling as if in search of divine inspiration. 'Not that I can think of… except, yes, the Wing Commander did mention that old Jobey Packer seemed to have disappeared. He asked about a bit. No one's seen him.'

'And that's not like him?' queried Jo.

'Oh no. If you knew Jobey, you wouldn't need to ask, love. He's a home bird and then some.' She looked down. 'Come to think of it, last time I saw him, he said he'd got some odd-job work…'

'Up at the aerodrome?' asked the Doctor.

Mrs Toovey nodded. 'Oh and there's the lightning, of course.'

Jo looked up. 'The lightning?'

Mrs Toovey nodded. 'Last few days. Everyone's seen it. Like the beginning of a thunderstorm, but it never comes.'

The Doctor frowned and then stood up decisively.

'Where are you off to?' asked Jo in surprise.

'The aerodrome,' said the Doctor matter-of-factly. 'I want you to stay here in case the Wing Commander returns.'

'Don't we have to wait for our passes?'

The Doctor looked indignant. 'Certainly not!'

Max stood in his accustomed place behind the post-office counter, fiddling with his rather flamboyant paisley bow tie. Hand on hip, he was tearing sheets of stamps free from a ledger, punctuating each rip with a bored sigh.

The place would be open again early the following morning, of course, despite his time being fully occupied making the final preparations for the summer fête. There was still no sign of old Jobey Packer – which Max put down to drink – nor of Mrs Garrick, which was less easy to explain.

Still, Miss Plowman had been a tower of strength and the parade of floats that would drive through the village would be the finest in living memory. Max had even had a message from the Bliss woman at the aerodrome, promising a spectacular display of some kind. That would put the icing very nicely on the cake.

The door was suddenly pushed open, setting the little brass bell clanging sharply.

Max swung round, mouth open, ready to start complaining. Ted was framed in the doorway, his son held in his outstretched arms.

'Oh my God!' cried Max, his hands flying to his mouth.

Ted's face was a mask of pained concern. 'Quick! Help me.'

He staggered inside the post office and gently let Noah down into his brother's arms. Max shunted the boy to a chair and pushed back his blood-matted blond hair.

'What happened? Has he been in a fight?' Max peered at the ugly wound on Noah's head. 'I told you, Ted Bishop. How many times did I tell you? That boy's a danger to himself.'

Ted came in from the back room, clutching a glass of water and bottle of brandy. 'It's nothing like that,' he said, struggling to get his breath back. 'At least I don't think so.'

He splashed cold water on to Noah's face and gently

106

slapped at his cheeks. There was no response. The boy's face was clammy and bloodless.

Max folded his arms. 'It's serious, Ted. I'll call an ambulance.'

Ted nodded absently, taking the seat next to his son and cradling Noah's head in his arms. He managed to raise a glass of brandy to the boy's lips and, for the first time since he had found him, there was some response. Noah licked his lips and groaned gently.

Ted looked up at his brother who was tugging anxiously at the tips of his bow tie. 'I found him in a ditch up by the aerodrome.'

Max tutted, reaching across the counter for the telephone. 'Well, that's it, then. Probably got himself clipped by one of those bloomin' great lorries. I said something nasty would happen, didn't I? Didn't I say, Ted?'

Ted nodded, frowning. There were great beads of sweat standing out on Noah's forehead. Max dialled a number and walked through into the back room, trailing the phone lead behind him.

Noah's eyes flicked open and he stared wildly ahead, as though waking from a nightmare. He started to breathe stertorously in and out, his hands gripping his father's arms as though for dear life.

Ted began to shush him gently, stroking the boy's hair out of his eyes. 'It's OK. It's OK, Noah. It's just your dad. I'm here.'

Noah shook his head, his eyes still fixed ahead, as though on a distant horizon.

'No,' he gasped. 'No!'

His eyelids fluttered and his head sank back on to Ted's

chest. In a moment, he was unconscious again.

Max returned from the back of the shop, biting his lip. 'Well?' said Ted.

Max shook his head slowly. 'You won't believe this. I dialled 999.'

'And?'

Max frowned. 'There was a voice at the other end.'

Ted nodded impatiently. 'Switchboard?'

Max shook his head. 'No. It was a funny kind of voice. They said... they said the number was unobtainable.'

The room was silent except for the occasional click and whirr of the computer banks standing by the far wall. Elaborate shades had been put up to cover most of the huge, panoramic window which dominated the office. Strips of black night were vaguely discernible through the heavy material.

Behind the wooden crescent of the desk sat the imposing figure of Bliss, still and alert, like a fat cat ready to pounce. She cradled the telephone in her hand, the receiver pressed close to her ear, listening to a faraway voice. She nodded and absently pushed the oily black fringe of hair out of her eyes. Her nose twitched from side to side in a constant tic.

'Yes.' Her voice was calm and confident. 'Yes. I understand.'

The voice at the other end of the phone spoke rapidly and with authority.

Bliss's fat fingers were splayed out in a fan on the desk, over a heavy sheet of blotting paper. Now they curled up into a tight, angry ball.

'Yes,' she said again, a hint of frustration creeping

into her carefully modulated tones. 'The operation is proceeding perfectly smoothly,' she insisted. 'To speed things up would only increase suspicion.'

The voice on the end of the phone seemed mollified by this. Bliss's balled fist relaxed and she began to drum her fingers softly on the cool surface of the desk. She nodded again and smiled, making a tiny, ticking sound as her lips parted.

'The swine are being gathered?' she asked.

The answer from the other end of the telephone seemed to please her. At length she hung up.

Bliss sat in silence for a few moments longer, enjoying the canopy of darkness which surrounded her. Then she leant forward, as though to flick an intercom. Instead, she spoke to the still and dusty air.

'Bring him in,' she said softly.

CHAPTER FOURTEEN
NIGHT TAKES BISHOP

Graham Allinson was an awkward boy.

He had been born prematurely and, for the first few years of his life, had worn callipers on his skinny legs. Even at night, he'd had to keep them on, those great metal encumbrances, cutting into his skin, preventing him from playing outside with the other children.

Now the braces were gone, but he had grown uncommonly tall for his age, like a nine-year-old's image in a distorting mirror. Together with his thick, pebbly glasses and shy manner he was always going to have trouble fitting in. But, just now, with the school holidays only a few days old, Graham Allinson's life was becoming unbearable.

The reason was the arrival of Culverton's new boy: Anthony Ayre, a big, bluff lad with messy hair and mean, stupid eyes. As soon as he'd turned up for his first day at Culverton Junior Mixed and Infants, Graham knew he was in trouble.

It had taken Anthony little more than a day to challenge Dawson, the school's reigning bully, to a fight, beat him and install himself as the new ruler. A clique of fawning hangers-on had risen around him with disgusting speed and, naturally, Graham had been instantly singled out for their attention.

For five miserable weeks, the bullying had got worse and worse until the blessed relief of the holidays. But if Graham thought he was to be spared, he was sadly mistaken.

He rode through the village that night on his old Raleigh bicycle, embarrassed by the clips his mother made him wear over the flares of his pale denim jeans. He'd spent the afternoon in the wood, splashing about in the little stream, looking for frogspawn and mayflies. Now he was heading home and hoping that his mother would have beans on toast ready for his tea. The last thing he expected to see under the yellow glare of a streetlamp was Anthony Ayre, but, as he pedalled furiously past the church and round the corner, he saw the bully sitting on the lichen-covered wall, chewing gum, a smug, arrogant look in his eyes.

Graham tried not to slow down, tried to keep going past the wall but Anthony jumped up and stuck a branch into the spokes of the bicycle. With a sickening lurch, Graham felt himself thrown forward and over the handlebars. He crashed on to the road with a groan and heard the Raleigh scrape its gold paintwork over the road.

Anthony walked towards him, laughing. All Graham could see was the front wheel spinning, spinning, spinning.

'Where're you off to, Bongo?' sneered the bully, using Graham's hated nickname.

Graham didn't reply. He tried to raise himself up on his spindly arms, wincing from the cuts on his palms and elbows. Anthony came closer and grabbed Graham's T-shirt. He pulled the boy close to his flushed face. His

breath smelled sweet and sickly, like baby's vomit. 'I said
–' he began.

Then both boys looked up as the night sky turned
from midnight blue to flashing white.

The strange summer lightning had come again.

The street was dark save for the occasional bedroom
light as Charles Cochrane let himself into the mews flat
he kept for himself off the King's Road.

He moved swiftly through the kitchen, dropping the
briefcase and red ministerial box as though they were
discarded sweet papers. They banged off the polished
wooden floors but Cochrane didn't seem to notice.

He opened the door into the front room and took
his place at a long, highly decorative table. Eight high-
backed chairs surrounded it. Two were already occupied
but Cochrane registered no surprise. He merely pulled
out the nearest chair and sat down, folding his hands on
the table before him.

Next to Cochrane sat a well-built woman with grey
hair and small, clever eyes. Two chairs along sat Jocelyn
Strangeways in full dress uniform. All three stared
straight ahead, their faces blank except for the wide grins
plastered across their faces.

None of them reacted when the front door opened
again and a stranger entered the room.

He took his place at the head of the table and glanced
from one to the other of them. His smile of satisfaction
did not quite match theirs, but then, he still had
responsibilities, after all.

Insects chirruped in the long dry grass which encroached

on the aerodrome's perimeter.

The Doctor crouched down and turned towards the shadowy complex of the aerodrome. Lifting his face from the parched soil, he peered through the diamond-shaped mesh of the perimeter fence for any sign of activity. He frowned. There was nothing. No movement. No lights.

Reaching a sudden decision, he leapt to his feet, rammed the toe of his boot into the mesh and began to haul himself up. With two or three swift moves he was up, then swung himself over on to the other side where he landed gracefully, spreading his feet wide to distribute his weight. He looked swiftly around. Still no sign of life.

Ahead, visible against the night sky, was the aerodrome's control tower. The Doctor thought he could discern movement of some kind through the panoramic window but, again, there were no lights on. Pressing himself against the lower wall of the building, his cloak-lining flat behind him like scarlet plumage, the Doctor paused and considered his next move.

There were a number of parked lorries close by which attracted his interest but the control tower seemed the logical place to start, despite the absence of any personnel.

Detaching himself from the wall, the Doctor walked swiftly and silently across the tarmac towards the tower. He put out both hands and grabbed the steel banisters of the staircase, hauling himself upwards until he was right outside the door.

He examined the lock quickly and then stopped as he heard voices.

A narrow, grilled catwalk extended around the circular tower just outside the thick glass window, and the Doctor jumped over a metal gate and on to it in one silent movement. Crouching down, he pressed his face close to the glass and tried to make out what was going on inside the darkened office.

Wing Commander Whistler sat upright in a chair, listening to the sound of his own breathing. He had come to in a grim-looking cell, his head pounding sickeningly, confidently expecting to be shot at any moment. But the hours had passed and none of the black-uniformed guards had appeared.

Fear had turned to anger and anger to boredom. Just when he had thought he'd prefer anything to simply sitting there staring at a blank concrete wall, the door had opened and two troopers had bundled him outside into the warm night.

They had made no allowances for his age or the darkness, and dragged him on whenever he stumbled. Now he was sitting in some kind of office, presumably about to meet whoever was behind all this.

He sighed, blinking slowly and expecting the door to open any moment. When a voice oozed through the dark, he almost jumped out of his skin.

'Show me.'

Whistler collected himself and peered ahead. He could just make out a figure behind a desk. He cleared his throat and set his jaw aggressively.

'I wouldn't mind being told just what the hell you people think you're playing at.'

There was no response. Whistler could just hear a soft, wet sound as though someone were smiling. 'Show me,' said the voice again.

115

Whistler scratched his chin. 'I can see right through your elementary psychology, you know. Really, I thought we might have got past sticking prisoners in darkened rooms.'

There was a thoughtful pause then an anglepoise lamp was clicked on, throwing a harsh white disc of light directly into Whistler's face. The old man laughed. 'Now that's even worse.'

Bliss swung the lamp round towards herself and the mechanism squealed in protest. The light shone on her pale, fat face and made her huge eyes glisten like raw meat. She winced slightly and swung the lamp away. Whistler noticed that there were dark smudges, like soot, below each of her eyes.

'Oh,' said Whistler with a small smile. 'I thought as much.'

'Your name is Alec Whistler,' said Bliss evenly.

'Bravo,' grunted Whistler.

'You were a soldier, I gather.'

Whistler bristled. 'Royal Air Force, if you please. Do you want my rank and serial number? Your interrogation methods would seem to demand all the clichés.'

Bliss cocked her head to one side, plunging most of her face into shadow. 'I'm not here to interrogate you, Wing Commander. You will provide me with the information I require, or I shall kill you. Right now.'

Despite himself, Whistler felt a cold pall of fear creep over him.

Max Bishop wasn't used to running. He could feel a sticky patch of sweat spreading across the back of his shirt as he hurried across the village towards the police house and he regretted putting on his favourite lemon-coloured pullover.

Flustered, he ran his hand through his thinning hair and trotted across the road to the small, grey, nondescript building where Constable Trickett was always to be found.

A place the size of Culverton had no need for a fully fledged police station. Instead, the whole operation was run from Trickett's house, a blue lamp – blazing now despite the collection of mummified moths within it – and a parish poster outside the only indicators of its true function. It was on nights such as this, thought Max, that the villagers could have done with a more impressive police presence.

The lawn in front of Trickett's house was neatly manicured, but had browned somewhat in the summer heat. A winding, crazy-paved path led up to the door and Max was careful to follow it. It didn't do to disobey 'keep off the grass' signs right under the nose of the constabulary, even in an emergency and under cover of darkness.

With two or three neat steps, he was outside the door and rang the buzzer urgently. There was no response. Usually, the constable's wife would answer, or even Trickett himself who was most often to be found behind the frosted-glass screen at the front desk.

Max waited a moment longer and then buzzed again, shrinking from the loud noise and regretting the upset to the natural order of things which it represented. There was still no response. Not even the barking of Trickett's Yorkshire terrier, a bad-tempered, yappy little thing which Max had always loathed. He looked around, tugging anxiously at the tips of his bow tie, and wiped the sweat from his brow. He was on the point of pressing the buzzer once more when he noticed that the front door was open a crack.

Max frowned.

For reasons of basic security, the door was never left ajar. Trickett or his wife would respond to the buzzer. They couldn't just pop out for a pint of milk and leave the door on the latch. Responsibility came with the job. Tentatively, and biting his lower lip, Max pushed open the door and went inside.

The darkness seemed absolute. Max put out a hand to steady himself, laying his palm flat against the cool green plaster of the wall. As the room began to take shape gradually, he peered ahead towards the desk, able to make out the chairs against the walls and the coat hook fastened to the door. There was a shadow behind the screen, a clear silhouette, its outline blurred by the frosted glass.

His hands slithering over the walls, Max tried to find the light switch. When his fingers finally fastened on the cold plastic he flicked the mechanism swiftly down.

Nothing happened.

He tried again, clicking the switch up and down rapidly, and sighed. Bulb must have gone, he thought to himself.

Max marched towards the desk, sure that Trickett would slide back the panel at his approach, but he reached the screen and there was no movement from behind it.

He shook his head and cleared his throat. This was getting ridiculous. After all, young Noah was hurt. Something out of the ordinary had happened to him and it was Trickett's job to be there for the villagers when help was needed.

A little angry now, Max slammed his hand down on to the desk bell three times. The silhouette behind the glass didn't stir. The sound of the bell dissipated in the hot, still air. Max let out a long, exasperated sigh.

'Mr Trickett?'

His voice sounded thin and a little hysterical. He cleared his throat and called Trickett's name again, this time using the authoritative tones he had perfected for his role as Buffalo Bill the previous Christmas.

When this failed to work, Max banged his fist on the desk and pressed his face close to the frosted-glass screen. He could see the constable on the other side.

'Constable Trickett? Could you come round, please. It's an emergency.'

Despite the fact that the policeman's face was only inches from his, Trickett seemed not to notice Max's plea.

Baffled, Max made his way sharply to the end of the desk where a door led into the back room. This too was open. He pushed his way inside, his gaunt face flushed with rage.

Despite the darkness, there was enough street light spilling in through the windows for Max to see that Trickett was sitting in a swivel chair, his back towards him. To Max's astonishment, he still didn't turn round.

Max's hand fluttered to his throat. 'Mr Trickett! I am not used to being ignored like this! Particularly when the matter is an urgent one.' He tried the light switch in this room, but, again, it didn't respond.

Max paused, breathing heavily, and a chill ran through him. He'd seen things like this in the films all the time.

Trickett was dead. He was sure of it. If he moved forward now and spun the chair around, the policeman would slump to the floor, face upwards, a small, neat bullet hole in the centre of his forehead. He swallowed nervously and shuffled one foot after the other, his shaking hand stretched out.

'Mr Trickett? *John?*'

He fixed his eyes on the heavy, dark blue cloth of the constable's uniform and placed his hand on Trickett's shoulder. With a deep, gulping breath, he swung him round. A small scream was rising in him at the expected horror.

Constable Trickett, however, was very much alive. In fact, he seemed rather pleased with himself. He was grinning all over his face.

CHAPTER FIFTEEN

THE WIND TUNNEL

Whistler recoiled as the back of Bliss's hand connected with his cheek.

He felt her sharp nails cut into his flesh and raised his own hand in instinctive defence. Bliss grabbed his wrist and twisted it painfully. The old man cried out, his eyes narrowing in agony.

There were already countless cuts and swellings disfiguring his weathered face and one tooth had been completely knocked out by his interrogator's fist.

'By God,' hissed Whistler between gritted teeth. 'If you were a chap I'd swing for you.'

Bliss stepped back, an almost noiseless exhalation bubbling from her lips, the nearest she came to a laugh. 'I've no doubt that, were you not tied to the chair, you'd have "swung for me" before now.'

Whistler looked up and peered through his puffy eyes at the darkness. He could taste little rivulets of blood running into his mouth from the cuts on his cheek. His mind was reeling with fragments of thought. The lorries barrelling through Culverton. Legion International's showy display in the church hall. The sleek black coffins he and Noah had found up at the aerodrome. And Bliss, the tall, flabby woman in well-cut black clothes, her pale, grinning face like that of a Victorian doll. Her eyes, huge and black as tar-pits. Whistler shifted in his chair, weak with fear and pain.

'Have you finished?' he croaked.

'Hardly.' Bliss cocked her head to one side. 'You're strong, for such an old creature,' she said flatly. 'But you can't last for ever. Why don't you tell me what I want to know?'

Whistler let his head sink on to his chest. 'I don't know what you're talking about.'

Bliss marched up to him and pulled back his hair savagely. Whistler yelled in agony. 'Show me!' she bellowed. 'Show me the ninth key!'

Whistler sat up. This was new. 'The ninth key?'

Bliss plucked at her blouse as though angry with herself.

'The ninth key to what?' persisted Whistler.

Bliss didn't speak. Instead, she moved to the side of the room where a small table had been set out next to the humming computer banks. Laid out on a white cloth were about half a dozen metal objects. Whistler struggled to make them out clearly in the gloom. They appeared to be chromium in texture but fashioned in such strange shapes that he had no idea what purpose they served.

Bliss stepped up to the table and passed her hand over the objects, settling on the third in line. She lifted it close to her milk-white face and Whistler made out a network of glittering blades, like the razor teeth of a lamprey, set into its circular head.

Bliss pressed a switch and the chrome instrument emitted a high-pitched whirr.

Whistler began to breathe very hard indeed.

*

Outside, on the catwalk, the Doctor strained to hear what was going on in the office. Frustratingly, a light seemed to have been switched on, but it did no more than illuminate what looked like the side of a man's face. The voices within were rendered indecipherable by the thick plate glass.

He pressed his face to the window and tried once again to peer inside. Could that be the Wing Commander? And was he being held against his will?

A bulky shape moved into the path of the lamp and the view was once again obscured.

Sinking to his knees, the Doctor turned away from the window and tapped his finger thoughtfully against his teeth.

Below him came the sound of booted feet crunching on gravel. The Doctor tensed and tucked himself under the lip of the window, looking down to see who was coming.

A Legion trooper, resplendent in his black uniform, was patrolling below. He was looking about alertly, his machine gun slung over his shoulder.

The Doctor slowed his breathing and tried to keep still. The trooper was directly below him and, despite the darkness, had only to look up to see him.

Shifting his weight only a fraction, the Doctor knew at once that he had made a mistake. The metal gantry creaked and the trooper tensed, pulling his machine gun down to waist level and pointing it into the shadows.

He looked left, then right, the muscles on his neck standing out like whipcord. Then he looked up, his face fixed in a crazed and disturbing smile.

The Doctor seized the moment and flung himself from

the catwalk. Cloak blossoming behind him, he fell like a great bat, cannoning his legs into the trooper's chest, sending him crashing into the gravel.

Not anxious to be caught when he had found out precisely nothing, the Doctor instantly took to his heels, racing from the gravel on to the broken tarmac of the old airstrip.

The trooper rolled over and jumped athletically to his feet, machine gun poised. He was about to open fire but then seemed to think better of it, shouldered his weapon and ran after the Doctor.

Putting at least two hundred yards between himself and his pursuer, the Doctor's immediate thought was to get back to Bessie and drive back to Culverton as quickly as possible. He had learnt nothing from his sortie except that Legion International were armed and dangerous. Jo was alone with Mrs Toovey and would be wondering where he'd got to.

However, he found himself diverting from the direct route back to the perimeter fence as soon as he saw the old hangar, looming through the darkness like the hump of a great whale. His insatiable curiosity got the better of him and he slowed to a fast walk, casting a glance behind him to check whether he was still being followed. The clatter of the trooper's feet on concrete told him he was, so he ran swiftly up to the hangar, turned the corner and flattened himself against the wall.

The trooper raced past, seemingly tireless, dark eyes fixed ahead.

The Doctor waited until he had gone and then walked back to the front of the old structure. Two massive doors designed for war planes to pass in and out stretched up into the darkness. For the sake of convenience, a smaller, man-sized door had been cut into one of them. The Doctor pushed it and, to his delight, it opened.

He peered through into pitch darkness, then glanced back towards the fence. He should get back to Jo, of course, but he had come to the aerodrome to find some answers. Perhaps this old hangar would provide them.

He stepped through the door and closed it softly behind his back.

Feeling in the pockets of his smoking jacket, he found a thin pencil torch and clicked it on. A narrow shaft of light sprang from it, immediately illuminating a landscape of filthy rags and metal fragments. Oil stained the floor everywhere, the relics of hasty repair jobs on fighter aircraft thirty years previously.

The Doctor swept the beam of the torch around the hangar. Benches and chairs had been stacked none too carefully against the wall, looking as though they might crash down at any moment. Then he saw why they had been moved out of the way. There were signs of recent activity. Part of the floor had been scrubbed clean and there were now over a dozen black, leather-upholstered surgical tables arranged in a row, stretching away into the gloom.

The Doctor examined the closest, fingering the heavy-duty straps that were firmly attached to its sides.

He sucked his lower lip thoughtfully then moved deeper into the hangar.

After a while, he came upon another door. This was new and had seemingly been carved from the wall. There were scorch marks around the steel frame and the Doctor examined them closely.

'High-intensity beam,' he muttered to himself. 'Laser?'

The light of the torch showed up what looked like a complex entry-coder but this didn't seem to be finished. Wires hung from it in a clump, like seaweed.

Shrugging, the Doctor pushed at the door. It swung inwards noiselessly.

The room beyond was vast and brand-new. The Doctor could smell the fresh plastic, even though he could see very little. For a moment he considered risking switching on the lights but decided against it.

'That's if there are any lights,' he said quietly.

Ahead of him, he could make out a semicircle of machinery, divided into sections like metal teeth. There was a swivel chair in front of each section and the Doctor sat down on the nearest one.

He clamped the pencil torch in his mouth and span round twice, then tensed as he heard a noise from the hangar beyond.

Just as he grabbed the torch from his mouth, the metal door sprang open and the trooper threw himself inside.

The Doctor didn't have time to react and took a direct punch to the side of his face. He crashed to the floor and tried to point the torch at his attacker but it was knocked from his hand, landing on top of the machines and spinning round and round, creating a dizzying halo of light.

The trooper came at him again, slamming a booted foot into his ribs. With a winded groan, the Doctor fell back against the ring of consoles and tried to grab hold of his assailant's leg.

The trooper was ready for him, though, and as the Doctor managed to haul the man's leg into the air, kicked savagely. The Doctor was sent flying. His chest barrelled into the nearest console and suddenly the whole room flickered into life.

The consoles whined and whole banks of lights blinked on. The Doctor saw that the back wall was made of thick plate glass and beyond stretched some kind of tunnel. Lights flickered along its entire length, like a runway.

The trooper stood with legs wide apart and unholstered his machine gun. He levelled the weapon at his opponent and prepared to fire.

The Doctor gazed into his big, dark eyes. An idea flashed into his head and he dived for the torch. He swung the beam directly into the man's eyes and the trooper hissed like a snake, shielding his eyes with a gloved hand.

'I thought so!' laughed the Doctor triumphantly.

Taking advantage of the trooper's disorientation, he delivered a chopping blow to the Legion man's chest, sending him smashing back into the consoles. A whole bank of switches clicked into life. Soundlessly, smoke began to stream into the tunnel beyond the glass. The Doctor cast a rapid glance towards it and made out the massive shape of a jet engine at the far end. It was a wind tunnel.

Still unaccountably smiling, the trooper struggled to his feet. The Doctor kicked out with a cry and caught him in the ribs. The man fell back again but this time managed to wrestle his machine gun from under him. Mindlessly, he opened fire.

The Doctor dived to the floor, covering his head with his hands as bullets sang off every available surface. Rolling over and over, he flung himself into the corner just as a whole volley of shots hit the plate glass, shattering it into fragments. Immediately, the room was filled with the roar of the jet engine in the tunnel beyond, as though a typhoon had been bottled and trapped there.

Wind tore at the Doctor's hair and cloak.

The trooper staggered towards him, the flesh around his grin buffeted by the incredible strength of the wind tunnel. He raised his gun again.

The Doctor grabbed a swivel chair just by him and sent it crashing into the trooper's knees. As the man crumpled, the Doctor jumped over him, landing on top of the consoles like a tightrope walker. But the trooper was ready for him, springing back to his feet like an unstoppable machine and pumping at the trigger of his machine gun.

Nothing happened. Something was jammed.

He glanced down and the Doctor span balletically round, his foot connecting with the weapon and sending it crashing against the wall.

Roaring like a beast, the trooper hurled himself at him and together they fell through the shattered glass and into the wind tunnel.

The force of the engine was incredible and the Doctor struggled to stay on his feet as the wind whipped and tore at his clothes.

The trooper advanced on him, teeth bared in his grinning face, hair streaming in the hurricane. The Doctor ran at him and gripped him in a bear hug. If he could only get the man on to the floor. He'd probably never be able to get up again... Squinting as the wind slapped at his face, the Doctor tried to force the trooper down, kicking at his calves in an effort to unbalance him. The Legion man fought back, strong arms moving to clamp around the Doctor's neck.

As they wrestled, the Doctor happened to glance upwards. To his astonishment there seemed to be another tunnel, like a great chimney, stretching high up towards an impossibly distant ceiling.

On the wall, just visible in the dim light, were two large buttons. One glowed red, the other a muted green.

The trooper pushed his opponent away from him with a grunt and the Doctor fell back against the wall. With a roar, the man raced at the Time Lord but the Doctor stepped out, struggling against the incredible wind, grabbed his wrist, twisted it and threw the trooper over his shoulder.

He slammed against the raised buttons and the green light suddenly flared brightly.

At once, the force of the wind altered. The distant jet engine cut out and another, high above their heads, powered up. This time, however, it was sucking the air upwards.

The Doctor felt the massive tug at his cloak and scrabbled at the floor like a cat trying to find purchase on wet tiles.

The trooper shot into the air, arms and legs flailing, but managed to grab hold of the Doctor's ankle.

Fingernails digging into the floor, the Doctor managed to grip on to a plastic tile. He could feel the glue coming away even as he did so, but it might hold long enough for him to reach the red button…

The trooper and the Doctor were strung out like acrobats, the latter clinging desperately to the floor, the former clutching on to the Doctor's leg as the huge engine overhead sucked air into its heart.

The Doctor twisted his neck round. 'Hold on!' he cried above the din.

The trooper had no intention of letting go, his grinning face seemingly untroubled.

One whole corner of the floor tile came loose.

The Doctor cried out, feeling his body jerking upwards like a cinder in a chimney flue.

He gripped the tile in both hands and tried to swing both himself and the trooper closer to the wall. They hung in the air like two links in a paper chain.

The Doctor swung again and this time he heard the trooper's foot smack against the metal wall.

'Try and hit the red button!' he shouted.

The trooper didn't react.

'Can you understand me?' yelled the Doctor above the colossal roar of the jet engine. 'Hit the red button! Kick it, man!'

He swung them again. The trooper's whole body slammed against the wall. His grip on the Doctor's leg loosened and he slipped back, his hands sliding until they came to rest on the heel of the Doctor's shoe.

'Don't let go!' bellowed the Doctor. 'You can reach the button. Try again!'

Sliding his hands deep under the floor tile, he swung his body again. There was a loud crack and three-quarters of the tile came loose.

The trooper's hands scrabbled at the Doctor's foot but it was no good. The whole shoe came away and, still clutching it, the man was sucked remorselessly upwards. He didn't scream and the strange smile never left his face even as he was pulverised by the deadly blades of the jet engine.

The Doctor swung himself wildly at the wall, just as the floor tile gave way. He felt the wind rushing past his face as he flew upwards but lashed out frantically with the foot that was protected by his remaining shoe as the red button flashed by. His toe banged into it with devastating force and, at once, the distant engine overhead shut down.

The Doctor fell a good ten feet to the hard floor and groaned as his chest connected with the tiles.

Panting with exertion, he struggled weakly to his feet and limped out of the wind tunnel.

Behind him, blood began to rain down on to the gleaming white tiles.

CHAPTER SIXTEEN

JO ALONE

Plumping up a cushion, Jo rearranged herself on the sofa and smiled.

Mrs Toovey shook her head and wiped a tear from her eye. 'Oh it's been such a tonic having you here, my dear,' she said, laughing. 'I've not enjoyed myself so much in ages.' She gazed into her teacup. 'Now… where was I?'

'The Wing Commander,' said Jo.

Mrs Toovey passed a hand over her face and let out a short squeal.

'Yes. You see, he always fancied they'd give him one of those… you know… "dogs of war" nicknames. He thought he ruled his men with a rod of iron and all that.'

'And he didn't?'

'Oh they respected him, right enough. Loved him, I daresay, but he's far too much of a pussy cat to be called, you know, "Bulldog" or something.'

Jo flicked her fringe from her eyes. 'So what did they call him?'

Mrs Toovey's laugh pealed like bells. 'Well, he was such a love to them all. All those brave boys… they named him after that painting.'

Jo frowned and shook her head.

'You know,' cried Mrs Toovey. 'The old Victorian woman in the black dress…'

A delighted smile crept over Jo's face. 'Whistler's Mother?'

Mrs Toovey nodded rapidly, her eyes disappearing in a forest of amused creases. 'Mother!' she chortled. 'Lord bless him!'

Jo laughed too, pleased she'd been able to cheer the old lady up. But there was still no sign of Wing Commander 'Mother' Whistler. Nor the Doctor, for that matter.

'So he decided to stay on here? After the war?'

'That's right. He loves it here. The countryside. The people...'

Mrs Toovey looked into the middle distance, suddenly lost in thought. She sighed deeply.

Jo leant over and gave her hand a reassuring squeeze. 'So he hasn't taken too kindly to these new people?'

Mrs Toovey shook her head. 'Oh you mustn't get the wrong idea, Miss Grant.'

Jo held up her hands. 'Jo. Please.'

Mrs Toovey smiled. 'Jo, then. No, the Wing Commander's not some old fossil, raging at the world. There's something... bad about those folk up at the aerodrome. He said it himself. Something... evil.'

Jo suppressed a shudder. 'I suppose it must've been very different in the war. When you knew who the enemy were.'

Mrs Toovey got up and smoothed down her skirt. 'Oh yes. He'd have just gone up in his Spitfire and given the Jerries the old one two! Now, I'd better see to the washing-up.'

Jo got quickly to her feet. 'No, no. You've done quite enough, Mrs Toovey. Let me.'

The old woman gave a grateful smile and sank back

into her chair. 'Well, if you're sure, my dear…?'

Jo nodded and began to clear away the teacups. Mrs Toovey crossed her hands over her chest and let her leathery chins sink into one another. 'When the Wing Commander gets back, you might ask him if he'll take you up in the old kite.'

Jo frowned. 'I'm sorry?'

'The Spitfire,' said Mrs Toovey evenly. 'It's out the back.'

Jo's face was a mask of surprise. 'You're joking?'

'No, no. He restored the old thing himself. It's in full working order. The Wing Commander gets her out, regular, every summer for the village fête. She's ready for tomorrow. That's if we have a summer fête with all this going on.'

Jo lifted the tea tray with both hands. 'Well, I can hardly wait to meet him. I feel like I know him already.' She laughed and shook her head. '*Mother!*'

As she moved to the door, there was a soft thump from upstairs. Jo stiffened and looked back over her shoulder at Mrs Toovey.

'What was that?'

Mrs Toovey glanced up at the ceiling and began to fiddle anxiously with her wedding ring.

There was a small, crisp sound, like someone clicking their fingers, and all the lights went out. Mrs Toovey drew in a sharp breath.

'There's somebody in the house.'

Ted Bishop placed a cool hand on to his son's forehead and bit his lip anxiously.

Max had been gone the best part of an hour, so Ted had moved Noah into the back room and stretched him out on the sofa. He seemed no better, his face lathered in sweat, his eyes rolling white.

Glancing at his watch, Ted gently lifted Noah's head from his lap and let it rest on a cushion before getting to his feet. He made his way across the room and picked up the phone.

In the absence of the police, there was always one person he knew he could rely on.

She was an old friend of his late wife and had been a great comfort to him in his grief. She was a cheery, sensible person who disliked Max and his theatrical ways. That made her all right in Ted's book.

He picked up the receiver and was about to dial when Noah groaned. One arm flopped over the side of the sofa and he trailed his fingers on the thin carpet. As Ted watched, the boy's eyes flicked open once more, wide and frightened, the whites glittering in the light of the fire.

Jo held her breath and looked up as another thump echoed through the little cottage. She reached out and gripped Mrs Toovey's arm, more to steady her own nerves than the old lady's.

Mrs Toovey opened her mouth to speak but Jo put a finger to her lips and shook her head. She looked around, listening as the clock on the stone mantelpiece softly marked time, then detached herself from Mrs Toovey and headed for the door to the hall.

'Where are you going?' hissed Mrs Toovey in alarm. Jo pointed to the ceiling.

The housekeeper shook her head violently and Jo gave her a reassuring smile. Creeping up close to her, she whispered in her ear.

'It's OK. I'll go out and open the front door. If there's anything fishy, just run. I'll be right behind you.'

Mrs Toovey frowned concernedly, clearly not happy with Jo's plan.

Jo shrugged. 'We have to do something,' she whispered gently. 'We can't just stay here like a couple of frightened rabbits.'

The old woman gave a small smile and patted Jo on the wrist.

Jo tiptoed across the room and softly opened the door. The corridor beyond suddenly seemed very dark indeed. Phantom shadows flitted over the walls as moonlight spilled in through the fanlight over the front door.

Jo swallowed nervously and then dashed swiftly across the uncarpeted floor. Her hands hovered briefly over the door before she found the lock and carefully unhooked the latch. She swung the door open and winced as it creaked noisily.

Warm night air washed over her and she took a moment to catch her breath. Turning, she looked back over her shoulder at the staircase which ascended into pitch darkness a few yards inside the hallway.

The housekeeper was leaning out through the open door to the living room, anxiously rubbing her wrinkled throat. Jo gave her a thumbs-up sign and then dashed to the stairs. She and Mrs Toovey passed each other. The old woman patted her shoulder and then Jo suddenly found herself climbing upwards.

She paused and took another deep breath. Ahead she could make out perhaps the first three stairs, their turkey-rug pattern bleached white by the moonlight. After that though, she could see nothing, just the yawning blackness of the top of the house where something might be waiting.

When she was very young, Jo had occupied a sizeable room on the second floor of her parents' house. Inside had been the usual girl's jumble; posters hanging haphazardly from the walls, piles of schoolbooks and unlearnt violin scores in every spare space. The room abutted her parents' and a large landing occupied the space just in front of both, at the top of the bannistered stairs. During the day, this was Jo's favourite playground, sometimes the sumptuous ballroom for her dolls' elaborate parties, sometimes a rolling pasture where she exercised her imaginary horses.

At night, however, it seemed very different. Her mother would always leave the bedroom door open and, waking up in the middle of the night, Jo would peer out into that lonely darkness and imagine all kinds of horrors. She could usually make out the skeletal banisters silhouetted against the window, the moonlight spilling on to the carpet.

Regularly, she would work herself up into such a pitch of terror that every nerve in her body cried out for her to flee across that landing to the safety of her parents' bed. But the fear of crossing the dark space was almost too much to bear. Who knew what might reach out and grab her? A rotted hand thrust out of the night? A gaping mouth, packed full of sharp, sharp teeth…?

Jo tried to push the memory to the back of her mind as she found herself once again in her childhood nightmare, approaching the dark landing in Whistler's cottage.

Tentatively, she put out her hand and found the wooden post that marked the top of the stairs.

Thump.

Jo's mouth turned dry. Her heart began to bang against her ribs and she could hear the blood pounding in her ears.

Thump.

The sound was very close by, seemingly coming from one of the three or four rooms that made up the upper storey of the house. She had only to cross the landing to find out.

Cross the landing.

Jo let out a shuddering breath and hugged herself. She wished very much that the Doctor was there. He would have strode confidently across, thrown open the door and demanded to know who – or what – was lurking there.

Jo almost smiled at the thought, but the darkness was too terrifying.

Thump.

It was coming from the room immediately to her right. She turned her whole body towards it and began to grope her way forward, hands waving about in front of her. With a burst of speed she raced across the landing.

She was doing well, she told herself. She'd got this far. Nothing to be scared of on the landing any more. Now she just had to deal with the door and whatever was behind it…

Jo steadied herself, thrust out her hand, twisted the knob and threw the door open.

The room beyond was very small. She could sense that, even in the darkness. It took her a few moments to register that it was some kind of boxroom, and that the window to the right was open. It was swinging gently in the night breeze, the metal fastener periodically banging into the old woodwork.

Thump.

Jo gave a sigh of relief and took a step towards the window to close it.

She stopped dead. There was a rush of air and something shot out of the shadows and ran at her. Holding out her hands defensively, she immediately backed towards the door, trying to scream.

The shadow was big and bulky. As it backed Jo out on to the landing she felt it brush against her and suddenly found her voice. She screamed and stumbled towards the stairs.

'Mrs Toovey! Run! Get help!'

She felt a cold hand slap over her mouth and tried to scream again. Her hot breath streamed around her assailant's fingers and she hurled herself to the carpet in an effort to extricate herself.

The figure came at her again, arms spread wide. Jo rolled over on the carpet and grabbed for the banisters. She pulled herself forward and took the stairs two at a time. The figure was right behind her.

Suddenly Jo pitched forward and felt herself falling. She threw out her arms and felt the stair carpet burn her as she crashed down towards the hall. Reaching the bottom, she flopped on to the bare boards, the wind knocked from her and a sharp pain shooting through her side.

Ribs aching, she lifted her head from the floor and tried desperately to breathe.

She could hear her assailant moving swiftly down the stairs towards her. There was no one to save her. She'd screamed at Mrs Toovey to flee and now she couldn't even cry for help. If only she could get her breath back…

The figure was standing over her now, bathed in moonlight. She could make out details of a black uniform and a chiselled, pale-skinned face. He reached out a hand towards her.

A harsh bell shattered the muggy silence. Jo blinked rapidly. Her assailant's hand hesitated. The bell rang again and again. It was the telephone.

Jo took advantage of the distraction and rolled on to her stomach, breath flooding back into her lungs. As she did so, a thin beam of light split the darkness illuminating the figure, which was now clearly revealed as Captain McGarrigle.

He reacted to the light as if physically struck, hissing like a vampire caught in sunshine and shielding his wide, dark eyes. He stepped back and knocked the telephone from its little table. It crashed to the floor and the receiver was dislodged. A tiny, tinny voice called 'Hello?'

The torchlight bobbed closer and the Captain ran for the door, barging into the person who was holding the torch. The light swung crazily about over the ceiling and Jo heard booted feet clattering over the floor and out into the night.

She sat up and shielded her eyes as the light from the torch bore down on her. Another hand, warm this time, reached out and gripped her shoulder. Jo gave a little yelp.

'It's all right, Jo,' said the Doctor soothingly. 'It's only me.'

Jo let out a huge sigh of relief. 'Oh, Doctor. Thank goodness.'

'What have you been up to?' he asked.

The small voice from the telephone sounded again. The Doctor set the torch down and squatted on his haunches. He reached out for the telephone and picked up the receiver, cradling it under his chin and giving Jo a cheerful smile.

'Hello? Who? No, no. She's not here, I'm afraid.' He covered the mouthpiece for a moment. 'Mrs Toovey's not here, is she, Jo?'

Jo shook her head.

'No,' continued the Doctor. 'She's... er... she's just stepped out. Can I help?'

His face looked grave in the beam of light that shone upwards from the torch. 'I see. Very well. Where are you? The post office. All right.'

He put down the phone with a soft click.

'Come on. Stir your stumps, Jo. We've got work to do.'

Jo struggled to her feet. She glanced down and noticed that the Doctor was missing a shoe.

'What happened to you?' she giggled.

The Doctor didn't look happy. 'It's a long story.'

He glanced up the stairs. 'I wonder if the Wing Commander has any spare boots?'

CHAPTER SEVENTEEN
SLEEPING WITH THE ENEMY

And now the thing outside the steel palace raises its balled claw and hammers against the glass. There isn't much time left. It must survive. It must...

The Apothecary glides forward, its legs skittering over the marble-tiled floor. It regards the thing outside with cool, detached eyes and then inclines its great head to one side. Two others like it emerge from the bluey shadows, carrying long, tubular weapons in their spiky claws. They peel off from the Apothecary's side and, moments later, an airlock opens on to the outside world with a startling hiss.

The thing falls back from the window, suddenly afraid. The two creatures that have emerged shrink back from the elements as though shocked at what they see. It is as if they haven't been outside in a long, long time. All around them is decay and desolation. After a time, the closer of the two glances down at the thing at its feet.

The thing tries to look appealing. It tries to look whole and healthy and useful. It raises a claw in greeting, in brotherhood. The closer of the two creatures responds and for an instant, hope lifts the thing's heart.

Then the other lifts its weapon and a bolt of red fire disintegrates the thing to the screaming wind.

Without a sound, the two creatures from the palace turn and re-enter the airlock. One of them turns as the door slides shut, taking a last, long look at the world he has left behind...

*

The Doctor placed the flat of his hand on Noah's brow. Ted Bishop and Jo stood to one side of the sofa, their faces fixed in concerned frowns. They had caught up with Mrs Toovey on the village green and she sat close by, frightened, anxiously fiddling with her rings.

The Doctor nodded to himself. 'Severe shock. Keep him warm. Plenty of fluids. He should be all right.'

Noah's father was hugging his arms around himself, as though for comfort. 'I found him up by the aerodrome. Just off the road. In a ditch. Max reckons he must've been hit by one of them lorries.'

Jo looked across at the recumbent boy. 'Is that true, Doctor?'

The Doctor got to his feet and shook his head. 'There's no sign of physical damage apart from the gash on his forehead. No, this boy's been frightened out of his wits.' He rubbed his chin thoughtfully. 'Where's your brother now, Mr Bishop?'

Ted jerked a thumb over his shoulder. 'He's gone to fetch the constable. Shouldn't be long now.'

The Doctor nodded. 'No sign of the Wing Commander and now a young man in shock.'

'And both connected to the aerodrome, somehow,' muttered Jo.

The Doctor walked to the window and pulled back the curtains in one swift stroke. The first streaks of dawn were beginning to lighten the sky. 'Well, it's been a long night. I suggest you all get some rest.'

Mrs Toovey nodded, quickly slipping back into the protective mode she knew so well. 'I'll see to your rooms then.'

The Doctor smiled pleasantly. 'Thank you, Mrs Toovey.

I'm sure Miss Grant will find hers satisfactory.'

Jo stopped at the door. 'You're not coming?'

The Doctor looked down at Noah. 'No. I'll stay here with young Noah. Then Mr Bishop can get some sleep too.'

Ted ran a hand over his drawn, exhausted face. 'I'd be very grateful, Doctor.'

'That's settled then,' said the Doctor, settling himself into an armchair.

Jo glanced at Mrs Toovey. 'Are you sure it's OK for us to go back there? After what happened?'

'I don't think they'll try anything else tonight, Jo. Now you get your head down.'

He patted her hand. A few moments later, the Doctor was alone.

He walked up and down for a while, wriggling his toes inside the cavalry boots he'd managed to dig out of the Wing Commander's wardrobe. They were slightly too tight but would do very well until proper replacements could be found. Throwing himself into an armchair, the Doctor pondered his experiences at the aerodrome. The wind tunnel intrigued him. The first horizontal one was no surprise. After all, a new airline would have a vested interest in experimentation. But what on Earth could be the function of the vertical chimney?

Unless...

He rubbed the back of his neck thoughtfully. Unless its function wasn't on *Earth* at all...

Noah shifted in his sleep, sweat still pouring from his clammy face.

The Doctor got up and stooped to examine the cut on his head, now encrusted with dark blood. The boy reacted to his touch and groaned as though in pain.

'It's all right, old chap,' said the Doctor soothingly. 'It's all right.'

'No,' croaked Noah, his lips dry and flaky. 'No. I saw it. Saw it.' He reached up and grabbed the Doctor's wrist.

'What did you see, Noah?' The Doctor crouched low to hear the boy's whispered words.

'I saw it,' repeated Noah.

'It's all right, Noah. You can tell me. What did you see out there? At the aerodrome?'

The boy suddenly sat bolt upright, his pale, bright eyes staring wildly ahead.

'Monster!' he shrieked. 'Monster!'

Whistler woke with a throbbing headache, the worst he had ever experienced. He tried to move on his bunk and immediately sank back, feeling waves of nausea pound through him.

He lifted a shaking hand to his face and gently examined his lacerated skin. He could feel bruising all over and his lips and cheeks were painfully swollen.

When he tried to sit up again the room remained steady. Glancing around, he saw that he had been returned to his cell. Bliss had not disposed of him as she had threatened, which meant he must still be of value to her.

The ninth key.

What had she meant? The old man silently congratulated himself on holding out against her terrible tortures. His squadron would have been proud of him.

He struggled to his feet, pressing the flat of his hand against the cold wall, groaning in pain as he took several deep breaths. His ribs ached terribly and he felt his tongue probe almost unconsciously the wet, bloody hole where his tooth had been.

Whistler straightened up and smoothed down his sweat-soaked hair. There was no mirror in the room, no furniture at all save for the bed and a small table clamped to the wall. A metal water jug and a bowl of what looked like porridge sat on the table. Whistler ate the porridge greedily with his bare hands, grateful for any sustenance, and drank almost all the water in one draught. He burped and then poured the remaining water over his head, hissing in pain as it stung his wounds.

After a moment, he glanced at the door of the cell. It was a plain, gunmetal colour with no grille or window. He couldn't tell if a guard was posted outside, but he knew Bliss would take no chances. Looking quickly around, Whistler began to formulate his plan.

He picked up the metal jug and clambered back on to the bed, curling his arm beneath his head and pushing the jug out of sight beneath the pillow. Then, summoning up as much phlegm as he could from his aching lungs, he began to utter the throatiest moan he could manage.

'Help,' he gurgled, his voice rattling. 'Help me... please!' There was no response from beyond the door.

Whistler rolled his eyes and upped the volume of his groaning.

'I'm... help me... I think I'm choking!' he shrieked, improvising wildly.

This time, the door was flung open. Whistler kept his back turned, restricting his movements to a writhing spasm which he hoped would convince the guard.

The black-uniformed man came swiftly inside and

advanced on the bed without saying a word. He extended a hand to pull Whistler over. The Wing Commander waited for his moment and, as he felt the man's fingertips brush his shoulder, he swung round and smashed the water jug straight into his jailer's face. The guard dropped like a felled tree, buckling at the knees and falling backwards on to the hard concrete floor.

Whistler stepped over him and raced for the door. He looked out into the featureless corridor, checked both ways, stepped out and then softly closed the door behind him.

As on most recent nights, young Graham Allinson had found it impossible to sleep.

He lay now, eyes aching and raw, staring at the ceiling, arm tucked behind his head, wondering what he was going to do. Sunlight was beginning to filter through a chink in the curtains like light from a film projector and he tried to take some comfort in this. But the only image that came to mind was Anthony Ayre knocking him from his bike and, even after the distraction of the strange lightning, losing no time in beating him up.

The bully was careful, though, to ensure that all of Graham's injuries looked like they could have been caused by falling from the old Raleigh.

The boy turned over to face the door of his room and groaned at the pain in his ribs. Hot tears began to well up in his exhausted eyes.

Why did he have to be so funny looking? Why did his ears stick out? Why was he so skinny? And how come Anthony Ayre was built like a boxer when all he ever ate was chocolate and crisps?

Graham was turning these burning issues over and over in his mind when a sharp sound from outside made his ears prick up.

Wincing, he shuffled across the bed to the window and drew back the curtains a fraction.

Someone was making their way down the garden towards the freshly creosoted shed. Graham pulled himself close to the glass to try and make out who the figure – dressed all in black – was. The door of the shed opened and the figure slipped inside.

Graham frowned and glanced quickly at his alarm clock. Whoever it was couldn't be up to any good this early.

He went back to bed, sank back on to the pillows and listened to the thudding of his own heart.

What he should do, of course, was to wake his mum and dad. They'd protest at the early hour, naturally, but then his dad would swing into action. He was always so good in times of crisis. That's what dads were for, Graham's grandma had once told him.

Yes, Mr Allinson would be down the garden in no time, still in his pyjama bottoms, wielding a golf club, with Mrs Allinson and Graham cowering behind him.

But not this time.

Graham jumped out of bed and put on his tartan dressing gown and slippers. He went swiftly downstairs and into the back kitchen, pausing only to slip on his anorak and give his dog a pat on the head. The dog looked up sleepily from its basket but didn't follow as Graham unlocked the door and slipped outside.

The morning was wonderfully fresh. Dew sparkled on the grass and the blossom-heavy trees but Graham didn't notice as, with pounding heart, he picked up his cricket bat and crept towards the shed.

Nervously, he fiddled with the rubber tube that covered the bat's handle, rolling it back and forth. As he approached the door, he lifted the bat to shoulder height, trying to remain calm and letting the smell of linseed oil drift into his nostrils. He reached out one shaking hand and lifted the latch on the shed door. It creaked open, exposing a black rectangle of darkness. He peered inside.

Someone stepped into his line of sight and Graham yelled in terror. He swung the cricket bat high above his head and then stopped dead as he realised the figure was his father.

Mr Allinson, however, seemed oddly changed. He was dressed in a smart black uniform, boots and epaulettes shining, his eyes hidden behind chunky sunglasses. He was smiling and holding out some kind of box with both hands.

'Dad?' said Graham in a small voice.

His father didn't speak, merely extending his arms so that the box was within his son's reach.

'What's going on, Dad?'

Graham looked down. The box was white and seemed to be made of some kind of translucent plastic. It was glowing. The boy was sure he could see something moving inside it.

He tried to back away, to call for his mother, to get up the nerve to smash the cricket bat down on to the box, but his father peeled it open, as smoothly as a lunch box, and the thing within leapt out and latched on to Graham's face.

A few minutes later, Graham Allinson wasn't worried about being bullied any more.

Constable Trickett, in his new pyjamas, swung back the bedclothes and walked slowly into the bathroom to brush his teeth.

He glanced up into the mirrored door of the medicine cabinet and his own smiling face looked back at him. His teeth were oddly stained and, as he lifted the brush towards his face, something seemed to stir in the darkness just inside his mouth.

Trickett cocked his head to one side as though listening to an instruction, then carefully laid down the brush, a bead of white toothpaste untouched on its bristles. He opened the door of the cabinet so that the mirror showed a view of the bedroom beyond. His wife Helen appeared to still be asleep but Trickett could see that she was staring into space, her eyes haunted.

She seemed to be aware that her husband was watching her and cast a quick, furtive glance towards the bathroom.

Trickett closed the cabinet, his grinning image looming up like a face drawn on a balloon.

'Morning, love,' he called. 'Sleep well?'

Helen Trickett didn't answer.

CHAPTER EIGHTEEN
RETURNS

Sergeant Benton was driving the Brigadier and Captain Yates along a narrow road lined with box-hedge. The big car hummed steadily. The Brigadier pressed the receiver of his car-phone closer to his ear and nodded.

'All right. Very well,' he rapped, passing the receiver to Yates.

'Trouble, sir?' asked Yates, replacing the telephone in its compartment below the seat.

'Not sure, Yates,' said the Brigadier with a frown. 'That was the defence secretary. It seems that our passes into Legion International come with one or two qualifications.'

'Qualifications?'

Lethbridge-Stewart nodded. 'We have precisely one hour to complete our inspection and then we have to be off the premises.'

'But why, sir?'

The Brigadier sank back against the red upholstery. 'To – and I quote – "enable the facility to go about its important work undisturbed".'

Yates shook his head. 'Somebody up there likes them.'

'Indeed,' said the Brigadier grimly. 'Let's hope the Doctor's got something to go on. See if you can raise Miss Grant, would you?'

He peered through the window. A road sign flashed past.

'Culverton, two miles,' he announced.

The parp of a car horn sounded and the Brigadier craned his neck to see. A big, black limousine was directly behind them, seemingly anxious to pass on the narrow country road. The horn blared again. The Brigadier leant forward and tapped Benton on the shoulder.

'Better let him pass, Benton.'

'Righto, sir.'

Benton twisted the wheel and the car moved to the left giving the limousine space to pass.

It roared by in a dark flash, without so much as a pip-pip of thanks. Benton watched it until it disappeared into the distance.

The Doctor was halfway through a plate of scrambled eggs which he'd rustled up when Ted Bishop came downstairs, looking refreshed and better than he had in a long while, except for his hair which was sticking up at the back in a cowlick.

He greeted the Doctor with a half-smile.

'Noah's sleeping fine now. I'm grateful, Doctor.'

The Doctor waved away his thanks. 'Don't mention it. Now, your brother hasn't returned, Mr Bishop. You say he went to find the local constable?'

Ted nodded. 'What do you think could have happened to him, Doctor?'

The Doctor shrugged. 'I've no idea. Let's hope he's all right. The most important thing is we have evidence that things aren't quite right in Culverton. That should help the Brigadier get official wheels moving. If he ever gets here.'

He glanced at his watch.

'In the meantime, I'd better get over there and see how Miss Grant –'

The Doctor broke off suddenly as they both heard the front door open and then quietly shut.

Ted Bishop looked up. There was muffled rush of water as someone turned on a tap.

'Max?' called Ted. 'Max, is that you?'

The Doctor indicated that they should go through into the kitchen. He pushed back the door and looked through. Max Bishop was standing at the sink, filling the kettle and laying out the tea things.

'Morning!' he said brightly. 'I didn't know we had company, Ted.' He shovelled tea from the caddy into the big brown pot.

Ted frowned. 'Where've you been?'

Max just smiled and hummed a little tune to himself.

The Doctor exchanged glances with Ted. 'I'm the Doctor, Mr Bishop,' he said, as though talking to a child.

'Doctor, eh? Somebody poorly?'

The Doctor rubbed his chin. 'Would you mind telling us where you've been?'

'I went to see a policeman,' said Max, his eyes shining with wonder.

The Doctor moved over to his side and held out his hand for the teapot. 'Let me help you with that.'

Max grinned. 'Oh, thank you.'

'Did you see the policeman?' asked the Doctor casually, setting out the cups.

'Oh yes,' said Max.

Ted sighed impatiently. 'You went to get Constable Trickett, Max. Noah's been hurt, don't you remember?'

Max continued to smile. 'There's nothing to worry about. Constable Trickett told me. There's someone coming to look after everything.'

The Doctor frowned. 'Who? Who's coming?'

Max looked up. The sunlight slanting through the kitchen window threw a bar of shadow across his face. It suddenly made his eyes seem very large and dark.

'Another policeman. An important one. He's coming from Scotland Yard.'

Jo had bathed and changed into a clean T-shirt and bell-bottom cords. A sweater was knotted around her waist and she tightened it as she popped her head round the door of the front room in Whistler's cottage.

'Ah, Jo,' said Mrs Toovey brightly, wiping her mouth with a napkin. 'How are you this morning, love?'

'Much better for a good night's sleep,' said Jo sincerely, stooping to pick up a piece of toast. 'Do you mind? I'm starving.'

Mrs Toovey got up and headed for the little kitchen. 'I was just waiting for you to get up. Would bacon and eggs be all right?'

'Smashing,' mumbled Jo, her mouth full of toast. 'What do you reckon that bloke was looking for last night?'

Mrs Toovey rubbed her ring finger. 'I wish I knew. You were ever so brave, you know. I was frightened out of my wits.'

Jo smiled. 'Well, I've been trained to just about hang on to mine.'

She looked into the middle distance thoughtfully. 'It was really dark up there but I'm sure he wasn't just waiting around to scare us. It was more like... he was looking for something.'

'You mean he was just a burglar?'

Jo shook her head. 'I think the Legion International people have set their sights higher than your candlewick bedspreads, Mrs T.'

The old woman gave a small, sad smile then straightened up, hands on hips. 'Well, if the Wing Commander's taught me anything it's the importance of positive action. He's been missing long enough. If we can't get our constabulary interested, we'll get on to the county coppers. See what they think. They'll sort these aerodrome buggers out, once and for all.'

She clapped her hands together. 'Now, love. How do you like your eggs?'

Jo gave a groan of happy expectation but was interrupted by a knock at the back door.

She shot a quick look at Mrs Toovey and got to her feet, but the housekeeper held up her hand. 'No. I'll go. It's about time I stood up for myself.'

Jo followed her through into the kitchen; a beamed room cluttered with pots, its ceiling blackened by the fumes of three centuries' dinners.

The back door was gated into two halves like a stable door. It rattled again as someone knocked twice on the outside.

Gingerly, Mrs Toovey unbolted it and swung open the top section. She gave an audible sigh of relief as a sunburnt old man in a battered straw hat was revealed.

'Morning, Annie,' he cried.

Mrs Toovey laid a hand flat against her chest. 'Oh, Jobey, thank heavens it's only you.'

She stepped back so that Jo could see the newcomer.

'This is Jobey, my dear. He does a few odd jobs for me from time to time.'

'Hello,' said Jo.

Jobey Packer raised his straw hat in greeting and leant over the bottom half of the door, crossing his brawny arms.

'The Wing Commander said you wasn't at the pub the other night, Jobey. He was quite concerned,' said Mrs Toovey, taking down the big, iron frying pan from the wall. 'Where've you been?'

'Oh,' said Jobey, his mouth widening into a huge smile. 'Here and there.'

The tiny point of light was almost white in its brilliance.

It moved across the concrete like a searchlight until it found its intended victim. The spider sat immobile, its hairy abdomen throbbing gently, its legs clustered together, unaware of what Anthony Ayre had in store for it.

The boy was sitting on the concrete drive which led to his father's garage, dressed in football shorts and a moth-eaten towelling shirt his mother made him wear when he was 'playing out'.

In one hand he held the thick lens from Graham Allinson's spectacles which he had stolen and broken the day before. He was putting the lens to good use, he thought, with a chuckle as he angled it towards the blazing disc of the sun and watched the focused beam crawl towards the spider.

He had caught the creature and slapped a piece of sticky tape over it to keep it rooted to the spot. It wriggled confusedly, trying to extricate itself from its prison. The beam of light came closer, closer.

This was the latest in a series of tortures which Anthony had devised. One of his favourites had always been to squirt water from an old washing-up-liquid bottle over the hundreds of red mites that seemed to crawl out of the concrete every summer and drown them.

The other kids in the street would be doing girly things like writing their names on the parched concrete with the stream of water. Anthony found his game much more satisfying. He imagined himself a great king, bringing destruction to an invading army; opening the floodgates and exterminating the heathen hordes of red mites.

Grinning, he shifted his weight on his ample buttocks and watched as the sunlight began to burn the spider's carapace.

Whitish smoke began to curl upwards. Anthony cackled with delight. The spider struggled. A tiny black hole had been scorched into its side.

Anthony suddenly looked up as he heard shoes scraping on the concrete driveway.

A lanky boy in shirts and T-shirt stood blinking in the sunlight.

Anthony grinned. Today just got better and better.

'Hello, Bongo,' he said in his surly way. 'Come back for some more?'

Graham Allinson didn't say a word. He stared at Anthony, then down at the trapped spider.

'What are you smiling at?' demanded Anthony.

He got to his feet, hands curling into fists, forgetting all about the spider.

Grinning madly, Graham turned on his heel and disappeared through the narrow alley that separated

DOCTOR WHO

Anthony's garage from his neighbour's.

The bully was after him at once, feet scrunching over the gravel. He emerged into the back garden and looked around wildly.

Graham was crouching on his haunches, his back to Anthony, peering down at something.

Anthony ran across and belted him in the small of the back. The skinny boy didn't flinch.

Enraged, the bully raised his fist to hit again, then paused.

'What have you got there?' he muttered.

Graham did not reply. He merely rocked on his haunches, gazing down at the object at his feet.

Anthony grabbed him by the shoulder and wrenched him back. He was startled to see some kind of container lying on the ground, and what looked very much like the spider he had been burning inside it. But this 'spider' was big. Horribly big. And it had dark, dark eyes. And they were staring up at him.

When it was all over, Graham picked up the empty container and he and Anthony set off to see if they could make some new friends.

160

CHAPTER NINETEEN
SLEEPERS

Jo found the Doctor just as he was emerging from the post office. The village was beginning to bustle with activity despite the early hour, and the green was already covered in refectory tables and boxes.

The Doctor shielded his eyes against the sun and frowned.

'What's going on?'

'It's the summer fête,' said Jo. 'Hey, guess what?'

'What?'

'That old bloke that Mr Whistler was worried about. He's turned up.'

The Doctor rubbed his neck. 'Has he indeed? Well, so has Max Bishop.'

Jo's eyebrows shot up in surprise.

'Tell me,' said the Doctor evenly. 'This fella... Packer wasn't it? Was he behaving... oddly?'

Jo shrugged and shook her head. 'No. He was all smiles.'

'Hmm,' said the Doctor thoughtfully. 'Same with Mr Bishop. Happy as a sandboy. Almost... too happy. He didn't seem to have any sense of what was going on. Or why he went off to find the constable last night.'

Jo watched as a large truck reversed into the village. Half a dozen brawny men with their shirts off got out

161

and began to unload stacked-up piles of gaily coloured sideshow booths and stalls.

'Perhaps we should call on the constable ourselves.'

The Doctor looked at his watch. 'Perhaps. Where is that idiot, Lethbridge-Stewart? We could get straight to the heart of this if we could only get inside the aerodrome.'

'Didn't you find out anything last night?'

The Doctor looked a little wounded. 'Little more than more unanswered questions. That and a grazed knee and a barked shin. Don't ever tell the Brigadier,' he added in a conspiratorial whisper, 'but sometimes it's better to take the official way in.'

Jo grinned. 'My lips are sealed.'

A knob of rapidly melting butter slid along the length of one of Helen Trickett's best knives. She watched it in silence as it crept across the polished Sheffield steel, pooling over the plate on which the knife lay, finally drip-drip-dripping to the tiled floor.

She stood behind the kitchen table, her eyes twitching, a pile of unbuttered bread before her.

She had things to do. A hundred sandwiches to prepare. Miss Plowman at the WI was absolutely counting on her. There was the tombola store to be organised and all the presents for the lucky dip to be wrapped in newspaper. Her daughter Nichola was twirling the baton at the head of the Culverton jazz band and her blue and silver costume still wasn't ready. Helen Trickett had so many things to do, but she stood and watched the butter slide off the knife and fall to the kitchen floor.

John Trickett came in. He was the picture of contentment in pale green shirt, beige summer trousers and open-toed sandals with socks.

'Lovely day, Helen,' he cried, smiling. His wife didn't reply. She dragged her gaze back to the piles of unbuttered bread.

'Haven't you got those sandwiches done yet?' he chided gently. 'Come on, love! Chop, chop!'

He flashed her his benevolent smile. Helen noticed that there were flecks of spit at the corners of his mouth. She picked up the knife and plunged it back into the runny butter.

John grabbed a pair of sunglasses from the worktop and bent to peck her on the cheek.

'Well, I've got to pick up our guest of honour. I'll see you later, then. Bye.'

He winked and went out through the back door.

Helen raised her hand to her cheek where John had kissed her. Her fingers trembled as she touched her skin.

There was a noise behind her and she swung to her left, dropping the knife to the floor. It clattered and span round and round like the needle on a compass.

Nichola was standing in the doorway, half in and half out of her majorette's uniform. She was holding her tall hat in both hands and her lip was trembling. With a sudden, ragged sob, she ran to Helen and threw her arms around her mother.

'Oh, Mummy,' she cried, her little chest heaving with sobs. 'That… that's not daddy… is it?'

Helen felt herself crying too and she stroked Nichola's hair rapidly back and forth, rocking the child gently.

Whistler had no idea that his old friend Lethbridge-Stewart was so close by. The old man was inside the hangar the Doctor had visited the previous night, his back to the thin wall, his knees tucked up under his chin. Outside, about a dozen Legion troopers were at work around the lorries.

He looked around. The hangar was familiar to him from the war and hadn't really changed that much. The skylight roof was filthy, allowing only a little of the summer sunshine through, and the concrete floor was stained with old engine oil. Benches and chairs remained much as they had in his day. There was even the remains of an old calendar on the far wall. Betty Grable peered through the accumulated grime of thirty-odd years. Smashing legs, thought Whistler absently.

He cast a puzzled look at the row of black tables, but decided his priority was to get out of the aerodrome.

Rising to a crouching position, he managed to shoot a quick glance through one of the small, broken windows that were at eye level. He quickly pushed a section of glass out of the way. The troopers seemed completely occupied, unloading yet more of the black containers from the backs of the lorries. Overseeing them was the tall, blond man whom Whistler and Noah had encountered. How was the boy? Did he get away?

Or did Bliss have him imprisoned too…?

Whistler dropped to the floor as one of the troopers walked right past the window. He bit his lip, thinking hard. He could stay where he was, of course, but the alarm was bound to be raised soon. He had to take his chance to get out of the aerodrome because he was unlikely to survive another session with Bliss. His face darkened as he thought about what she had done to him. The clicking, metal needles swirling towards his face, glittering in the light from the lamp…

He cleared his throat and wiped a sheen of sweat from his forehead. It was now or never.

Whistler stayed on his haunches and shuffled along the wall towards the massive hangar doors. He grabbed the edge and peered through, blinking rapidly at the brightness of the day.

Overhead, a jet was ploughing through the blue, leaving a puffy white vapour trail. Whistler focused on it for a moment and tried to gather his thoughts.

Around the corner, the troopers were at work. There was silence save for the occasional clank of metal or effortful grunt as the containers were lifted on to brawny shoulders. The Captain issued no orders, no rebukes, nor any encouragement. It was if the troopers knew exactly what was required of them and had no time for anything else.

Whistler took a deep breath and stepped out on to the tarmac, pushing the door closed behind his back. At once he dropped to his hands and knees and made his way swiftly past the hangar doors towards the other side of the building. He could see the perimeter fence only yards away.

And now activity is building inside the steel palace. The Apothecaries have shifted the young creatures back, lines and lines of them, into the dark blue recesses of the building. Others have taken their place in the centre of the room. Twelve tall figures on a nine-sided dais.

They are multi-limbed and chitinous. A thin film covers their round, dark eyes. They are unaware of the bustling activity around them.

Inside, they are shielded from the chaos, from the wind and rain which beats ceaselessly at the great window. Lightning flashes constantly. But the warm cyan-blue of the room does not change. Those within have been carefully selected. And their time is approaching.

For the moment, though, the twelve elders and three hundred thousand others of their kind sleep on…

Brigadier Lethbridge-Stewart heaved a sigh of disappointment.

'Not much to go on, Doctor.'

The Doctor and Jo sat next to him in the back seat of the UNIT car. They were finally heading for the aerodrome.

The Doctor nodded. 'I admit it's less substantial than we could have hoped for but really it only serves to deepen the mystery. These two missing people turning up still leaves the Wing Commander and the boy.'

The Brigadier frowned. 'I thought you said –'

'He's not missing, sir,' cut in Jo. 'But he's obviously had a very bad experience.'

'That's right,' said the Doctor, crossing his hands over his knee. 'Up at the aerodrome. He was muttering something about… monsters.'

The Brigadier cleared his throat. 'Well, that's as may be. The fact is, we've got to try and get something on these Legion International people in the short time we have. The Ministry of Defence is refusing to play ball.'

The Doctor looked interested. 'Is that a fact?'

Jo turned to him. 'Doctor?'

The Doctor rubbed his chin. 'What could Legion International be doing that's so important to the Ministry of Defence? They're just a private airline, after all.'

'And the MOD sold the aerodrome to them,' said Jo.

'Precisely. Unless of course…'

The Brigadier's eyebrows rose questioningly.

'Unless of course they're rather more than just a private airline.'

Benton threw a glance over his shoulder. 'We're here, sir.' The UNIT car drew up to the main gates of the aerodrome.

Jobey Packer's sign had disappeared and in its place was a shiny new placard bearing the legend:

LEGION INTERNATIONAL
GETTING US WHERE WE WANT TO GO

CHAPTER TWENTY
OUT OF THE SHADOWS

The Reverend Darnell sighed with relief as he saw Max Bishop approaching across the green.

'Oh Mr Bishop! Thank heavens,' he cried, clasping his hands before him. 'When we didn't hear we thought… well, you know we couldn't get along without you.'

Max grinned at him.

'Now, I've had your itinerary copied,' continued Darnell, handing Max a sheaf of photocopied papers. 'The hoopla stall is going next to knobbly knees, as you instructed. And we've left a big space for the aerodrome people. Though we don't know what their stall is going to comprise yet, do we?'

Max shook his head. 'I think it'll be good,' he grinned inanely.

Darnell looked him up and down. 'Yes, quite.'

One of the great, lumbering Legion lorries pulled up at the side of the green with a hiss of brakes.

'Ah,' said Darnell as ten black-uniformed, black-sunglassed men clambered from the back of the lorry. 'Here they are.'

The Doctor looked around Bliss's office with something like disdain.

'Hmm,' he sniffed. 'Minimal, isn't it?'

'It suits my purposes,' said Bliss evenly. 'My name is Bliss,' she purred, her nose twitching from side to side as though irritated by a particularly nasty odour. 'I gather you are from...' She glanced down at the passes, '... UNIT.'

'That's right, ma'am,' said the Brigadier crisply. 'Brigadier Lethbridge-Stewart. This is Miss Grant and the Doctor.'

Bliss looked at the Doctor with interest. 'I am not familiar with the organisation.'

The Doctor turned from his examination of the whirling computer spools.

'Oh you know. It's one of those dreadful quangos they have so many of these days. United Nations sponsored thing. We poke our noses in, have a look around.'

Bliss's smile widened. 'And today you've decided to poke around here?'

'Precisely.' The Doctor flashed her a winning smile.

'Why?' said Bliss.

The Brigadier shot a look at the Doctor as though the simple question had flummoxed him. 'Well... we... er...' he stammered.

'You're a new facility,' said Jo with confidence. 'On former Ministry of Defence property. It's standard procedure for UNIT to check how things are going.'

The Doctor nodded appreciatively at Jo.

Bliss looked Jo up and down, her black eyes liquid and inquisitive. 'I thought we'd been through all that when we... purchased the property.'

The Doctor thrust his hands into the pockets of his smoking jacket. 'You know the British, madam. Everything in triplicate.'

Bliss nodded. 'I see.'

The Doctor cocked his head to one side. 'Bliss. That's a lovely name. Where are you from, if you don't mind me asking?'

'We…' Bliss blinked twice, slowly. 'I… I'm originally from South Africa.'

The Doctor's eyebrows shot up. 'Really? Beautiful country isn't it? Where exactly are you from? The Transvaal?'

Bliss nodded impatiently. 'Yes.'

'I've always meant to go back to Johannesburg. You must be very proud of your capital.'

Bliss's dark eyes narrowed. 'Indeed we are, Doctor. Now, if you don't mind, I'm rather busy.'

She turned to the Brigadier. 'I'll arrange for you to see everything. A full tour. You'll have to forgive the mess. We're eager to get going.'

'Yes,' persisted the Doctor. 'You've been very busy haven't you? A lot of traffic. Especially at night.'

Bliss smoothed down her blouse. 'As I say, we're keen to get Legion International up and running.'

The Doctor gazed levelly at her. 'And what about Culverton?'

'I don't follow you.'

'Are you sure you have the village's best interests at heart?' said the Doctor coolly.

Bliss spread her hands. 'Naturally.'

'And does your philanthropy extend to threatening people… or frightening young men half to death?'

Bliss didn't react. The Doctor looked deep into her eyes. There was scarcely any white in them, just the huge, dark pupils.

'Order must be maintained,' said Bliss, smiling and showing her tiny white teeth.

The Doctor gave a low chuckle. 'Sounds wonderful. A rosy future for Culverton. A state of *bliss*, you might say.'

The Brigadier cleared his throat and tapped his watch. The Doctor nodded. Bliss swung round.

'You're right. We must be getting on. You people don't have much time left.' She smiled her wide smile. 'Do you?'

Whistler straightened up and made boldly for the perimeter fence. Far better to act as though he belonged here than skulk around waiting to be captured. He tried to stay light on his feet, conscious of the crisp ring his shoes made on the tarmac.

There was no sign that he had been spotted. All he had to do now was find the hole that he and Noah had made in the fence.

A hundred yards away the Legion troopers suddenly stopped work, as though frozen in time. As one, their heads swung upwards and to one side, as if listening to something. There was no sound save for the songs of the summer birds but somewhere, on a higher register than Whistler could ever hope to detect, an alarm was sounding.

Captain McGarrigle straightened up, his head snapping to one side. He saw Whistler at once and began running towards the old man.

Whistler heard his booted feet on the tarmac and shot a look back. Gathering all his depleted strength he tore towards the fence, gripping the wire with both hands and hauling himself upwards.

Cursing his old age, he managed to drag himself higher. An image flashed through his mind of an escaping prisoner of war. Imprisonment was a fate he had managed to avoid in real life and had only ever seen in those John Mills films. Now he was experiencing it first-hand, struggling over a fence with McGarrigle in pursuit. At least they didn't seem to have machine guns trained on him. Maybe they didn't need to…

The Captain's hand grasped Whistler's thick ankle and tugged hard.

Whistler immediately kicked at him, landing a heavy blow to his shoulder. An instant later, McGarrigle bore down again, this time grasping the old man's calf with both hands.

Despite his best efforts, Whistler felt himself sinking slowly towards the ground. He forced his hands into the mesh of the fence until he could feel it cut into his skin and kicked viciously at the Captain's exposed face. Whistler's shoes connected with the blond man's grinning mouth and McGarrigle gasped as the polished toe cracked into his stained teeth.

Whistler kicked again, this time landing a savage blow right in the Captain's windpipe. McGarrigle choked and staggered, then, with a roar of rage, jumped up and dragged the old man bodily to the ground.

Whistler fell heavily and lay there on the tarmac wheezing as the Captain, clasping his throat, loomed over him.

Blood was weeping from open cuts on Whistler's palms. His eyes flicked up as a dozen Legion troops formed a circle around him.

Captain McGarrigle, however, seemed to be in trouble.

He was breathing stertorously, his throat and chest juddering like those of an asthmatic. Saliva pumped from the corners of his wide mouth, trickling down his chin and spattering his neat black uniform.

A strange, deep, belching noise came from inside him.

He swung round to face Whistler, his dark eyes blazing like lava beneath the sea. Still clutching his throat, he advanced on the old man until he was astride him. Then, as Whistler watched, something inside the Captain began to move…

It was only a small flicker at first, reminding Whistler of the way ticks shuffled beneath the skin of his hand when he was a boy. Soon, though, there was more definition; a chunky, segmented shape, just beneath McGarrigle's rapidly tightening skin. Something was moving upwards through his throat.

Whistler let out a shriek of disgust. The Captain staggered forward, foamy spittle dropping in clumps on to Whistler's face. Then it came; brittle, transparent, spindly legs appearing around the sides of McGarrigle's mouth. Clutching the flesh of his cheeks, it began to haul its way out, sliding over his gaping tongue, probing out into the air, a vile, hairless, carapaced thing somewhere between crab and worm.

McGarrigle clutched the sides of his head as the creature extruded itself like paste from a tube.

Whistler slid on his back towards the perimeter fence, gagging in horror. The thing swayed as it emerged and, for the first time, the old man saw that above its gaping maw were a pair of dark, dark, pitiless eyes.

Helen Trickett was upstairs when she heard the car

arrive. Nichola was sitting on the bed, fiddling anxiously with the dress of her favourite doll while her mother rapidly packed their suitcases. There would be no village fête today. They had to get away. Something was wrong with John, something Helen couldn't rationally explain. All she knew was that he hadn't been the same since he came back from that visit to the aerodrome.

She clicked the lock on the cases and then froze as she heard one, no, two car doors slamming. Nichola looked up, her little eyes full of terror. Helen swept her up in her arms and raced to the window.

Pushing back the curtains she could just see a large, black, well-polished car in the street below.

She would have to sneak out the back, through the kitchen. There was no point in trying to reason with John. He was different. Changed. A crazy thought drifted into her mind.

He's not the man I married…

That's what they always said, wasn't it? In this case, it was true. Helen knew. She knew from John's voice, his manner, his touch. There was something terribly wrong. This man looked like her husband and sounded like him now, although at first he'd been horribly silent, just sitting there, smiling; his grin mad and wide like a cut in the taut skin of a melon.

She'd go to her parents. They wouldn't ask questions. They'd listen to her. Know what to do next.

With Nichola in one arm and the suitcase in the other, Helen ran down the stairs and into the kitchen.

She almost yelled when she saw John standing there, that terrible smile plastered over his face.

'Hello, love,' he said softly. 'Not going anywhere are

you?' Helen swallowed and felt tears spring to her eyes. She held Nichola very tight.

John took off his sunglasses and his eyes were very dark indeed.

'You must meet our guest of honour, Helen. He's come all the way up from Scotland Yard to open the fête. He'll be in charge of things from now on.'

There was a sound behind Helen. She turned on her heel.

A middle-sized man with swarthy, saturnine features and a neat, pointed beard walked through from the hallway, looking immaculate in his braided inspector's uniform.

'Mrs Trickett,' he said with what seemed genuine warmth. 'I've heard so much about you.'

Helen looked at her husband and then back to the newcomer. 'Who… who are you?'

The newcomer's smile faded and his eyes, as fiery and brown as a dusty Andalusian desert, blazed with power.

'I am the Master,' he thundered. 'And you will obey me!'

176

CHAPTER TWENTY-ONE
DISPLAY OF POWER

Bliss raised a fat hand, taking in the whole of the aerodrome with one sweeping gesture. She seemed unperturbed by the summer heat whereas Jo and the Brigadier were perspiring profusely.

'As you can see,' she purred, 'it's full steam ahead here. We aim to have a new airstrip laid within a fortnight and we have ambitions to rival the big airports for trade within the first few years. Once people see how competitive our rates are.'

The Doctor was leafing through the glossy brochure Bliss had given him.

'"Getting us where we want to go",' he quoted, looking up. 'Unusual way of putting it.'

Bliss let a little sigh escape from her. 'I don't follow.'

The Doctor smiled back. 'Nothing. Tell me, are you conducting any research here? Experimental aircraft, that sort of thing?'

Bliss shrugged. 'That would certainly be on our agenda for the future, Doctor. But for now we have to concentrate on the task in hand.'

'So,' said the Doctor. 'No wind tunnels or anything like that?'

Bliss looked him directly in the eye. The Doctor met her stare and cocked a quizzical eyebrow.

'No,' murmured Bliss at last. 'Nothing like that.'

The Brigadier looked rapidly around, as though hoping to find something incriminating. 'Well, thank you for your help, ma'am. I'm sure our report will be most encouraging.'

Bliss pressed her hands to her chest. 'Not at all.'

She inclined her head to one side. 'Now, I really must be getting on. We're organising a display for the village fête, you know. It wouldn't do to be late.'

The Doctor nodded. 'Of course. Good afternoon.'

Bliss smiled at them all and headed off back towards her office.

The Doctor thrust his hands into his pockets.

The Brigadier sighed. 'Nothing. Absolutely nothing.'

'Clean as a whistle,' concurred Jo.

'You think so?' said the Doctor. 'I had a little adventure here last night. In a wind tunnel. One of those Legion fellas didn't come out of it too well. And she knew. She knew that I knew.'

Jo glanced around. Benton had brought the car in through the gates. There was a strange patch of some kind of foam on the concrete by the fence. It reminded Jo of cuckoo-spit. She dismissed it and turned away.

'But we still haven't got any proof,' she sighed. 'I suppose it suddenly doesn't seem to amount to much. Apart from the Wing Commander going missing, it's all a bit flimsy.'

The Doctor shrugged. 'Well, we know one thing for sure.'

'What's that?' asked Jo.

'Bliss isn't who she says she is.' He moved off towards the car.

The Brigadier trotted behind him. 'What do you mean?'

'The capital of the Transvaal,' said the Doctor over his shoulder, 'is Pretoria.'

With the sun at its zenith, Culverton's village green shimmered in a heat haze. Mr and Mrs Neesham's little green sweet shop, tucked between two cottages like the filling in a sandwich, was doing a roaring trade. Children streamed in and out, clutching sherbet fountains or paper packets of midget gems.

One boy, bigger than the rest and faintly absurd in his grey school shorts, was twisting another youngster's arm behind his back in an attempt to steal his Action Transfer of Napoleon's retreat from Moscow. The other boy was putting up a good fight and had even sacrificed his bag of flying saucers which had fallen and split on the hot pavement. Sherbet blew from their hollow innards.

Other boys ran around squealing excitedly, getting grass stains on their knees and letting ice lollies drip unnoticed over their clenched fists. Little girls did handstands on the parched green, giggling and tumbling as their friends egged them on.

Close by, Graham Allinson and Anthony Ayre stood side by side. The other children were surprised that they seemed to be friends, but had to admit they looked pretty good in their matching black sunglasses…

The sound of kazoos and marching feet filled the air, accompanied by the strange, distant echoes of a public address system as the winners of the sack race were announced.

The Reverend Darnell watched the proceedings with

a slightly uneasy look on his bland features. Among the familiar stalls – pin the tail on the donkey, the tombola, win-a-goldfish – stood a huge and elaborate structure, tall and jet black like a mausoleum. Black curtains covered the entrance and the only clue to its function was the jolly, colourful placard standing on the grass just outside it. It showed happy, smiling children on the shoulders of Legion International personnel.

Darnell thought of his recent encounter with the troopers and shuddered.

Miss Plowman, who was standing next to him, set down a lemonade jug and frowned. 'Something the matter, Vicar?'

He managed a smile and shook his head.

Ted Bishop leaned over his son and closed the window. Despite the heat, he didn't want the booming sounds from the fête to disturb Noah who was now sleeping peacefully.

Sighing, Ted rubbed his face and sipped at his tea. He'd had no luck with Max, who seemed determined not to explain himself.

He'd gone over to take charge of the fête now, smiling happily as though nothing at all had happened.

Ted's ears pricked up as he heard activity downstairs. Swiftly, he crossed the room, closing Noah's bedroom door behind him with a soft click. He was down the stairs in a few seconds and found the Doctor, Jo and the Brigadier coming inside.

'Hello,' said Jo, apologetically. 'Sorry to barge in.'

'All I'm saying Doctor,' cried the Brigadier, 'is that given the amount of top-level obfuscation regarding this matter, it'll take a lot more than we've got to persuade the powers that be to act.'

The Doctor threw himself down into an armchair.

'Good afternoon, Mr Bishop,' he offered, before battle was rejoined.

'May I remind you, Brigadier, that it was you who requested my involvement in this matter in the first place.'

The Brigadier put a hand to his perspiring brow. 'Of course. But if you yourself were to speak to the Defence Minister... ' The Doctor's cry of exasperation could have been heard outside, despite the marching of the Culverton majorettes.

'Despite your best efforts, Lethbridge-Stewart, I have not yet succumbed to the level of petty bureaucracy in which you seem to revel. If there's any toadying to be done, I suggest you do it yourself!'

Jo slapped her hand down on to the table, rattling the uncleared breakfast cutlery and stopping the Doctor and the Brigadier in their tracks.

'For goodness sake!' she cried. 'What's got into you two?' The Doctor looked a little shocked.

Jo glared at him. 'The Wing Commander is still missing, Noah's upstairs in... a... a state of shock and Legion International are marching around this village like the SS. Surely we should be doing whatever it takes to get to the bottom of this, not arguing like kids!'

The Brigadier looked at her.

'Er... sir,' she concluded lamely.

The Doctor cleared his throat. 'Yes. Well, you're right, my dear. Of course you are.'

He looked up at the Brigadier and gave a tight smile.

181

'You said something about a telephone call, Brigadier?'

Lethbridge-Stewart nodded. 'Yes, Doctor. Charles Cochrane. Secretary of Defence.'

'Right.' The Doctor slipped his hands into his trouser pockets. 'Whenever you're ready.'

The Brigadier seemed pleased. 'I'll get on to it right away.'

There was a heavy, banging sound from upstairs and Noah Bishop suddenly appeared, stumbling down the stairs. He fell heavily into his father's arms.

'Dad,' he croaked, licking his dry lips. 'Out there! It… it's out there. On the marsh. I know where it is!'

The Doctor nodded excitedly to himself. 'Capital! I think I may have something to say to the Minister after all.'

Out on the village green, the sun blazed down.

A black-uniformed Legion trooper stood to attention outside the heavy black curtains of the fête exhibition. He stood stock-still and upright as an oak tree, his black sunglasses glinting.

A little boy in sandals and shorts was plucking at the curtain, eager to see what might be inside. The trooper turned his head and faced the boy. His expressionless face didn't alter but it was as though a statue had suddenly moved on its plinth. The boy felt his hair stand on end and, with a drawn-out wail, ran off to find his mother.

The inside of the exhibition tent was a perfect reproduction of an aeroplane interior, decorated in the exquisite black and yellow colours of Legion International. Rows of comfortable-looking chairs were arranged throughout the cabin and small windows looked out on to a simulated blue sky.

Bliss sat in one of the chairs, her fingers steepled together. Next to her, smoking a fat cigar, was the Master, his inspector's cap on the arm of the chair.

'It's an excellent service,' he said with a small smile. 'I'm sure everyone will be all too eager to fly with you.'

Bliss nodded, pleased.

'There's only one thing you've forgotten,' said the Master.

Bliss's dark eyes blinked slowly.

'My complimentary white wine,' he said with a chuckle.

Bliss chose to ignore him.

'The simulation is many years ahead of the technology on Earth. We aim to have most of the village passing through the aeroplane by the end of the day.'

She pressed a button on a small keypad at her side and the view outside changed into a spectacular night-time sky with twinkling lights below it.

'Rome.' She pressed again. The view changed to a pinky opalescence. Snow-capped mountains rose through fog. 'Dawn over the Rockies.'

The Master nodded. 'A charming toy.'

Bliss's fat, chalky white face beamed. 'More than that. There are some hidden extras on this particular flight.'

She snapped the machine off and the windows were plunged into darkness. 'But to business. The ninth key has still to be recovered.'

The Master tutted. 'Is that why you sent for me? You told me it had been traced.'

Bliss clenched her fat fists. 'There have been some -

complications. The key registered on my monitors and then… disappeared.'

She plucked at her blouse. 'It appeared to be in the general area of the dwelling of a man called Whistler. By chance, he came snooping around the aerodrome but my… interrogation was unsuccessful.'

'Oh dear,' said the Master, greatly amused. 'Where is he now?'

'My men have him. Unfortunately, there was an incident. He was… converted.'

The Master clucked his tongue. 'Thus rendering him useless for any further interrogation.'

Bliss let a hiss of anger slip between her teeth. 'Yes.'

'Well, once we have the village under our control, there'll be no need for further secrecy,' said the Master with a shrug. 'We can tear the place apart if necessary.'

Bliss's dark eyes blinked slowly. 'There have been developments. Some people came on an official inspection.'

The Master frowned. 'Official? I thought I'd blocked all avenues of inquiry.'

It was Bliss's turn to sound smug. 'So did I. Apparently you either failed or these particular visitors are able to pull strings.'

'I didn't fail,' said the Master with menace. 'Who were they?'

'A soldier of some sort,' muttered Bliss. 'A girl and a man they called…'

'The Doctor,' smiled the Master. 'Naturally. He's a wily old bird and no mistake. Well, well, well. It will be nice to renew our acquaintanceship.'

'Meanwhile,' said Bliss evenly, 'you will do your best to

find the location of the key.'

The Master's eyes glowed like coals. 'I am not accustomed to taking orders.'

Bliss's milky face suddenly clouded and, for an instant, something shifted beneath her skin, like an embryo stirring in the womb. 'The Gaderene are taking this planet,' she hissed. 'Take care that you are not swept aside!'

A wasp was buzzing around the eves of Whistler's cottage in a state of some confusion. The familiar, papery nest it had left seemed to have vanished, along with all its comrades. It flew angrily at the stonework until Mrs Toovey's rolled-up copy of *Horse and Hound* flattened it out of existence.

She tutted to herself and threw the magazine into the incinerator to which the pest-control man had recently consigned the wasp nest and brushed herself down, all ready to go to the fête.

She paused on the threshold of the cottage, resplendent in her summer frock and wide-brimmed hat.

It didn't seem right to be going when the Wing Commander was still missing. But what good would she be moping around the house all day? He'd have wanted her to go.

She mentally admonished herself for already acting as though he were dead. She might find out something that would be useful to the Doctor and Jo, after all.

Nodding to herself, she cradled a basket filled with jars of jam under her arm and was just closing the door when a familiar figure stepped on to the path next to her.

Mrs Toovey dropped the basket. 'Oh! Sir!' she cried,

her hand flying to her mouth. 'Wing Commander, thank God. Where've you been?'

Whistler walked a little closer but didn't speak.

'What's happened to you, you poor love? Look at the state of your face.'

She reached out a hand to touch the bruises and cuts that covered the old man's skin. Whistler grabbed her wrist.

'What are you –? You're hurting me!'

He pulled Mrs Toovey close to him and she could feel his breath washing over her. He smiled.

On the pavement, jam oozed on to the hot flagstones. Wasps settled among the shards of shattered glass.

CHAPTER TWENTY-TWO
GUEST OF HONOUR

Noah was back on the couch and dozing when Jo sat down beside him. He opened his eyes.

'Hello,' she said brightly.

Noah smiled and brushed his hair from his eyes.

'How're you feeling?' she asked.

Noah sat up and pushed a fat cushion behind his back.

'Pretty weak. Who... who are you?'

Jo held up her UNIT pass. 'I'm Jo Grant.'

'Jo,' he said simply, 'how long have I been here?'

'Day or so. Your dad found you.'

Noah looked troubled. 'I was out there. On the marsh. The Wing Commander and me went up to the aerodrome and –'

He cut himself off and clamped his eyes shut. Jo grasped his hand.

'It's OK. You told us all about it. You don't have to think about it any more,' she murmured gently.

Noah shook his head and opened his eyes. 'No! I do. I want to remember.'

He took a deep, ragged breath. 'There's some kind of creature out there. Living in the marshes. Like a... a snake. Or a worm. It's huge.'

Jo nodded. 'It attacked you?'

Noah turned to look at her. 'It was going to kill me. I

thought I'd had it. But it seemed to… to hesitate. I ran. God, I ran so fast.'

He put a hand to his chest as though feeling the pain of exertion all over again. 'I don't know how I got out of there.'

Jo ruffled his blond hair. 'Well, thank goodness you did. We were all very worried.'

Noah sighed. 'Who's the geezer with the white hair?'

'That's the Doctor,' stated Jo.

'Your boss?'

Jo laughed. 'Not exactly.'

She thought of how she'd felt so recently, of how she'd grown under the Doctor's tutelage. How it seemed he'd come to respect her.

'We're more like… well… colleagues,' she said at last.

The Doctor was standing with one foot on the wheel-hub of a UNIT jeep, frowning in exasperation, the receiver of a field telephone pressed to his face. The Brigadier sat next to him, leafing through a sheaf of papers and dissuading children, who assumed the vehicle to be part of the summer fête, from clambering inside it.

Jo ambled across the green, smiling broadly at the happy scene. Several floats drove slowly by, crammed with waving villagers, all dressed in a variety of colourful, home-made costumes. Two sets of Laurel and Hardys were having a heated argument by the old water pump and something had made Little Bo Peep cry.

'Perhaps she's lost her sheep,' thought Jo to herself.

She approached the jeep with trepidation. The Doctor didn't look to be in the best of tempers.

'Of course I appreciate that,' he barked into the phone.

'I know you're new to the department but I would have thought after all this time… In the files, yes. All right. Yes… I'll wait.'

He tucked the receiver under his chin.

'Man's an imbecile,' he announced to no one in particular.

'Who?' asked the Brigadier. 'The Minister?'

'Yes, the Minister. Some doe-eyed boy hardly out of short trousers, by the sound of it.'

The Brigadier smiled. 'He's a rising star, so my government sources tell me.'

The Doctor harrumphed. 'Well, I have some experience of stars. They can burn out very fast if they're not careful.'

He turned and spotted Jo. 'Hello Jo. Any candyfloss on the go?'

Jo shook her head. 'Not that I can see. But the three-legged race was quite a gas.'

The Doctor nodded absently. 'I knew a man on Taganis Six who would have won that by a mile,' he said with all seriousness.

There was a crackle on the receiver. 'Hello?' he barked.

'Are we going up to the aerodrome again?' asked Jo.

The Doctor put his hand over the receiver. 'If I can get rid of this idiot, yes. But I want you to stay with Mrs Toovey. Keep an eye on things here.'

'I've just been talking to Noah again,' said Jo confidently. 'I think I could pinpoint exactly where on the marsh he saw that thing. We should get on to it right away.'

The Doctor returned to the phone. 'Hold on.'

He flicked his gaze towards Jo. 'We will. But you'll be far more use to me here. Now off you go. There's a good girl.'

Jo felt her face flush.

'OK, colleague,' she said under her breath and stumped away sullenly towards the green.

Max Bishop and Constable Trickett were sitting on a raised platform on opposite sides of an empty chair as the Reverend Darnell approached. He glanced at them, his pale eyelashes batting in the hard sunlight, and was pleased to see how happy they were looking.

'Where's Helen, John?' he asked, trotting up the wooden steps. Trickett didn't answer at first.

'And I didn't see Nichola in the band. Aren't they well?'

Trickett's head turned but Darnell couldn't see his eyes through the policeman's thick sunglasses.

'No,' said Trickett softly. 'They've come down with something.'

Darnell tutted and turned to face the green. 'Shame.' The green was covered completely now, a sea of colours and faces.

'Going very well,' he cried. 'Thanks to you, Max.'

Max Bishop inclined his head slightly. The sun was obviously too bright for him too, judging by the thick black glasses he was wearing.

Darnell patted the pockets of his linen suit, looking for the clip-on green frames he usually attached to his spectacles.

Disappointed, he turned back to Trickett. 'Is he ready?'

Trickett nodded and got to his feet. As if on cue, a man strode out from behind the black curtains of the Legion International display, looking splendid in his police inspector's uniform.

Darnell watched as a little girl ran past and cannoned

straight into the inspector. The newcomer's face flushed with fury and he raised a gloved hand as though to strike her. Then his face softened, he glanced around and patted the girl's head affectionately.

The inspector took the steps up to the podium two at a time, extending his hand. Darnell grasped it and was surprised by the strength of his grip.

'Good afternoon, Vicar!' the newcomer enthused. 'I'm Inspector Le Maitre. How nice of you to invite me.'

The Vicar nodded. 'Well, when Constable Trickett told me we had a Scotland Yard man in the area I thought you'd be perfect to officially open our little celebration.'

Darnell failed to mention that the person he'd originally asked, an actress most famous these days for advertising 'Sparkly Suds' washing-up liquid, had cancelled at the last moment.

The guest of honour nodded. 'Only too happy, my dear fellow. It does me good to get back in touch with people. One must never lose sight of community relations, even when one is a chief inspector!'

Darnell laughed. What a charming man.

He drew the inspector to one side. 'Are you up here on a case?' he asked in a conspiratorial whisper. The Vicar was a big fan of crime novels and never let an opportunity for grisly gossip slip.

The inspector smiled. 'Let's just say I'm helping some people with their inquiries.'

Darnell frowned and then burst into a high-pitched laugh.

'Oh! Oh, very good.'

The Doctor sat down in the passenger seat of the UNIT

jeep and pulled a pad of paper from his cloak. Rapidly, he sketched the wind tunnel he had visited the previous night and the strange, chimney-like extension into which the unfortunate Legion International trooper had been sucked. He held up the L-shaped diagram for the Brigadier to see.

'Make anything of that, Brigadier?' he asked.

Lethbridge-Stewart, who was midway through a radio conversation, shook his head.

'What is it?'

'Bliss's wind tunnel,' murmured the Doctor. 'But why the vertical section?'

He continued to stare at the drawing, tapping a pencil against his chin.

The Brigadier concluded his radio call and replaced the R/T set under his seat. 'I'm afraid I've had to send Yates and Benton back to base pending further developments.'

The Doctor frowned. 'The men from the ministry again?'

The Brigadier nodded. 'We're to keep a low profile.'

'Oh I don't know,' smiled the Doctor. 'You could have got your troops to join in with the fête. Rerun a few battles or something. I'm sure the people of Culverton would be fascinated by a simulation of –'

He stopped suddenly.

'What is it?' queried the Brigadier.

The Doctor pointed ahead with his pencil. 'Just a thought. Let's get back to the aerodrome. I've one or two theories I'd like to try out.'

The Master turned to a microphone which had been set up on the platform and tapped it.

He gazed out over the packed green and watched as the Doctor and the Brigadier, oblivious to his presence, drove off towards the aerodrome.

'Ladies and gentlemen,' he announced in a clear, authoritative voice which echoed through the village. Almost at once, the crowd settled down and listened.

'Ladies and gentlemen. I'm very honoured to have been asked to open the Culverton village fête. I'm sure it will be splendid. And you're all obviously enjoying yourselves very much. I'm only sorry that the lady from the washing-up advertisements couldn't be here…'

Darnell looked up in shock.

'… but I promise that, in spite of this, we'll all have good clean fun!' concluded the Master.

There was a ripple of laughter and applause.

The Master's amplified tones settled like a blanket over the whole of Culverton. 'I declare this fête well and truly open!'

He turned from the microphone and then swung back. 'Oh and, by the way, I wouldn't miss the Legion International display. I've seen it and it's… captivating.'

He gave the crowd a cheery wave and walked slowly down the steps on to the green.

Chapter Twenty-Three
Fête Worse Than Death

The track to the aerodrome had been pummelled into deep ruts by the ceaseless convoys of lorries. The Brigadier's jeep rattled over them, dust flying from the tread of its tyres.

'So, no joy with Cochrane?' shouted Lethbridge-Stewart above the roar of the engine.

The Doctor shook his head. On his knee was the notepad on which he'd made the drawing of the strange vertical wind tunnel. It fluttered as they sped along.

'There's obstinacy and then there's wilfulness,' he said, sketching in further details with a pencil. 'Our Mr Cochrane seems very keen to keep this place under wraps.'

The Brigadier frowned. 'But he's the Defence Secretary!' he cried, genuinely shocked. 'Are you suggesting…'

'I'm not suggesting anything,' muttered the Doctor. 'But if Legion International are not from this planet – as I suspect – they may well have some pretty sophisticated methods of brainwashing.'

The Brigadier shook his head and tried to keep his mind on the road ahead. 'Good Lord.'

The jeep trundled along until it came within sight of the aerodrome perimeter.

'So where are they from?' asked the Brigadier.

'I haven't the faintest idea,' confessed the Doctor. 'But I think that wind tunnel is some kind of simulator. They've been experimenting with a process which will bring them to Earth.'

'They're definitely alien then?'

The Doctor nodded. 'I'm sure of it. And you must admit, it gives a whole new meaning to the term "friends in high places".'

He grinned broadly. The Brigadier seemed unamused.

The Doctor's attention was suddenly riveted. 'Hello.'

Lethbridge-Stewart looked through the dusty windscreen. The entire perimeter was ringed by Legion troopers, arms folded, each and every one in identical black uniforms and sunglasses.

The Brigadier pulled on the brake and the jeep shuddered to a halt. He swung himself out at once and stood with hands on hips, gazing at the human barrier.

The Doctor joined him. 'Something tells me they don't want us to come in,' he said quietly.

The cabin of the simulated Legion aeroplane was packed. Despite the heat outside, a carefully controlled air-conditioner kept it pleasantly cool. There were precisely fifty-eight passengers seated in the spacious chairs, talking in excited whispers and gazing in wonderment at the projected view visible through the small windows.

The Reverend Darnell, with the diminutive Miss Plowman at his side, gazed absently at the three-dimensional image of Zurich airport.

Bliss's honeyed voice drifted through the cabin.

'Now approaching Zurich...'

The passengers gave little gasps of pleasure as the

whole cabin appeared to tilt, shifting on invisible pistons, a simulated wing appearing to rise in their eye-line as the aircraft banked to the left.

'Or is it really Kenya?'

A wave of awed sighs washed over the cabin as the view outside altered again, this time showing a blazing sunset over the African plains. Giraffe tugged at the leaves of tall trees. A herd of elephants careered through a dusty landscape then splashed into a lake, far below.

'It's amazing!' cried Miss Plowman, her beady eyes bright with excitement.

'Miraculous,' muttered Darnell, chewing on his fingernail.

Suddenly, a small sign blinked into life. There was a soft chime and Bliss's voice returned.

'Ladies and gentlemen, we are approaching an area of turbulence. Please fasten your safety belts.'

There was rush of chatter, then a whoop of frightened delight as the cabin suddenly lurched downwards. Outside, the view appeared to be of a thunderstorm. Rain and lightning lashed at the cabin windows.

'I didn't think it would be a roller coaster too!' trilled Miss Plowman.

Darnell smiled weakly and clutched the arms of his seat as the aircraft plunged again. His stomach flipped over.

'Please do not be alarmed,' soothed Bliss's voice.

There were more excited giggles from the passengers. A little boy screeched with delight as lightning appeared to strike the wing and the cabin rocked backwards with a bang.

'Emergency!' called Bliss, her voice only fractionally

more energised. 'Emergency. Cabin depressurisation.'

A high-pitched whine filled the air. Outside, the view appeared to show the plane rapidly descending.

'Terribly… terribly realistic,' croaked Darnell above the din.

'Isn't it?'

Miss Plowman no longer seemed to be enjoying herself. 'Not a very good advert for an airline.'

Darnell shook his head.

The air in the cabin seemed to be genuinely altered. Darnell felt his ears pop. Really, this was going too far. Someone screamed.

'Oxygen masks about to be released,' said Bliss's voice. 'Do not be alarmed.'

There was a loud, splintering crack and fifty-eight oxygen masks swung down from the overhead compartments.

Some of the passengers, completely caught up in the simulation, reached for them. Others, like Darnell, looked about uncertainly.

He glanced back at the oxygen mask and frowned. There was something odd about it. The pipe which presumably led to the tanks was transparent but tinged a strange brown colour. A gelatinous slime seemed to ooze from it and the oxygen mask itself was more like the carapace of a crab, legs packed in a tight bunch, black eyes burning with malice.

The oxygen mask moved.

Darnell let out a little shriek of terror.

As the cabin appeared to plunge in a downward spiral, rolling in disorientating circles, the lights blacked out and fifty-eight slithering, living oxygen masks rocketed into the faces of fifty-eight Culverton villagers.

What little screaming there was, was drowned out by the roar of the simulated engines.

By the time the ride was over and another batch of passengers prepared to take their seats, fifty-eight satisfied customers filed out into the baking heat of the summer afternoon. It was obviously one hell of a ride. Every one of them was smiling…

The Doctor rubbed the back of his neck. Not one of the Legion troopers had moved, nor even shown any sign that they had noticed the jeep's arrival. They remained as immovable as shop window dummies the Doctor thought, then checked himself, remembering that shop window dummies didn't always stay still…

'What now, Doctor?' said the Brigadier.

The Doctor shook his head. 'I want to get another look at that wind tunnel. What we need…'

He glanced back at the jeep and then over at the ring of troopers. '…What we need is a diversion.'

Moving back towards the car, he made a quick examination of the windscreen. It was divided into two sections; a solid rectangular bottom half and a top half that was split in two. Each of these sections could be opened and angled upwards in its frame.

The Doctor opened the nearest one and tilted it until it caught the sunlight.

'Pick one,' he said.

'Beg your pardon?'

The Doctor indicated the troopers. 'Pick one of our jolly friends here. I'm going to try something.'

The Brigadier shrugged and pointed to the trooper

nearest to the firmly closed gate.

'All right,' said the Doctor. 'We'll call him Charlie.' He held up a hand and waved. 'Hello, Charlie!' The trooper didn't react.

The Doctor angled the pane of glass in its frame until it was struck by sunlight, turning it into a square of dazzling yellow. He moved the glass further until it was shining directly into the Legion man's sunglasses-covered eyes.

The trooper fell to his knees, clutching his face. Despite the sunglasses, he seemed unable to bear the direct assault.

'You see!' cried the Doctor. 'They can't stand bright light. Something else I discovered last night.'

As one, the troopers took a step forward and unshouldered their machine guns.

'How does that help us?' queried the Brigadier.

The troopers raised their weapons.

'Not a lot, it seems,' said the Doctor.

And now the cyan-blue of the room turns deeper, like the last, faint shafts of sunlight penetrating a fathomless ocean. The small creatures in their racks sleep silently, their delicate-looking, leathery chests rising and falling in soft motion.

The twelve elders still stand in the centre of the room, each contained within an elaborate network of wires and braces. Occasionally, one will slightly open its great, dark eye, as though turning over in its sleep. The Apothecaries note this as they busy themselves around the elders.

The nine-sided dais on which the elders stand gives a low hum and rises from the smooth floor. The elders are suddenly several feet higher than those who are caring for them. A forest of cicuitry has been exposed. At each corner of the shape is an empty socket.

As one, the Apothecaries cock their heads to one side, knowing that the countdown has begun. One moves swiftly to the wall and presses a claw into a recessed panel. A drawer glides out. Inside, surrounded by some silky substance, lie nine jade-coloured objects. The Apothecary takes the first and skitters back towards the dais.

Lightning illuminates the room and the whole structure shakes.

The Apothecary does not hesitate. There is no time for solemn ceremony now. It slides the first key into the socket. The key clicks into place with a satisfying thunk.

The creature moves back across the room to retrieve the remaining keys.

The smooth floor beneath its claws trembles...

CHAPTER TWENTY-FOUR

THE MARSH

The cloudless summer sky turned burnt crimson as the sun set and night came on.

The air had chilled rapidly and Jo wished she had set out in rather warmer clothes. She cupped her hands to her mouth and blew into them, then rubbed at her ring-covered fingers.

She was approaching the far side of the aerodrome and kept the long, long perimeter fence to her left as she made her way over the crumbling road. Looking ahead into the encroaching darkness she began to discern the beginnings of the marshland. Mist was creeping over the ground like a spectre reaching out from the grave.

The aerodrome was once again completely silent. In fact, there was little sound at all out there in the vast outdoors except for the occasional eerie wail of the corncrakes.

Rounding the corner at last, she saw what Noah had seen before her; the back entrance, guarded this time by a semicircle of stock-still, black-uniformed troopers, their eyes no longer hidden behind sunglasses but fixed ahead nonetheless.

Jo dropped to her knees in order to make a smaller potential target, but the guards seemed totally unaware of her presence. She turned sharply as a soft crack sounded from somewhere behind.

Jo stiffened. The sound came again, closer now, and was unquestionably footfalls on the wet ground. She shuffled backwards on her haunches and crouched low, as close to the fence as she dared, half-imagining it to be electrified or, at the very least, alarmed.

Blinking in the darkness, she finally made out a figure, bent low like herself, advancing swiftly forward on baseball boots.

'Noah!' she hissed.

The boy swung round, startled, then grinned and crept up to her, settling down on the marshy ground.

'Hi,' he murmured.

'What're you doing here? You should be in bed.'

Noah shrugged. 'I'm fine now, honestly. Besides…'

Jo gave him a quizzical look. 'Besides?'

'I can't find my dad. Or Uncle Max. I got up this afternoon and there was no one about. In fact, the whole village is pretty deserted.'

Jo frowned. 'Why have you come back here? Did you remember something else?'

Noah shook his head. 'It's still pretty vague. But I know there's something in these marshes. Something that the aerodrome people want kept quiet. And I know they've got the Wing Commander inside there.' He jerked his head towards the dark and distant shapes of the aerodrome buildings. 'Somewhere.'

Jo shot a look at the guard and then turned back towards Noah. 'What else did you and the Wing Commander see? I mean, before you were… attacked? Can you remember?'

Noah frowned. A little fear crept back into his mobile

features. There was a faraway look in his eyes. Then his gaze shifted and he stared ahead at the perimeter gates.

'Yes. I remember. Because they're at it again. Look!'

The gates were gliding open. Behind them, its engine turning over with a gentle purr, was a lorry. Gradually, a whole fleet emerged out of the darkness, queueing up behind each other. Legion troops clambered down and began unloading their familiar contents.

'That's what we saw,' whispered Noah.

Jo shuddered. 'They look like coffins.'

Noah nodded. 'We tried to open one but it was impossible.'

Jo raised herself up on her knees. 'Where are they taking them?'

'Dunno. This was as far as I got. They chased me out on to the marsh and…' He trailed off.

Jo squeezed his hand affectionately. 'It's OK. We don't have to go on.'

Noah shook his head. 'No. We do.'

He pointed ahead. The guards at the perimeter gate had stepped aside to allow a phalanx of troops to pass, shouldering their strange burden. They moved off further into the darkness until they were swallowed up by the mist.

'Come on,' said Noah, getting to his feet. Jo held back. 'What's out there?'

Noah didn't reply directly. 'We have to see what the hell they're doing with those things.' He helped Jo to her feet.

They kept well back, watching as perhaps a dozen more of the black cylinders were unloaded and carried off into the night. Noah moved in a wide orbit, always

205

keeping out of sight by ducking down among outcrops of spiky reeds.

The procession finally halted in an area of excessively boggy ground. The cylinders were lowered from the guards' shoulders and then, to Jo's astonishment, were slid slowly into the marsh. Gas bubbled to the surface, frothing over their sleek outlines. After several firm pushes, every last one of them disappeared into the ground.

Jo and Noah exchanged glances.

The Legion troops stood up, ramrod straight, and began to file back towards the aerodrome. In a few moments they were gone, leaving Jo and Noah alone on the lonely wetland.

Immediately, Noah splashed into the marsh, his legs quickly sinking up to his knees. He thrust his arms into the bog and began to grope in the cold water. Jo couldn't help smiling.

'Aren't the trout ticklish today?' she whispered.

Noah smiled back. 'Give me a hand. I think I've got one.'

Jo waded in and gasped a little as the chilly water soaked her trousers. She felt around under water, grimacing at the thought of what might be lurking down there. Leeches, perhaps, or something worse…

Eventually, her hand connected with the smooth surface of one of the containers and she plunged her arm in almost up to the shoulder, pushing the sleek black form upwards.

Noah sloshed around to its opposite side and heaved with all his strength until it began to emerge once again into the air. Filthy water seemed to evaporate immediately from its surface.

'Pretty... heavy,' gasped Jo. 'Whatever it is.'

Noah nodded and gave a final thrust which propelled the black cylinder out on to the firmer ground that surrounded them. It thudded into the soil with a wet slap.

Jo and Noah dragged themselves from the marsh then stood for a moment, hands on hips, getting their breath back.

After a quick, furtive look round, Noah dropped to his knees and began, as before, to pass his hands over the surface of the cylinder.

'We're like Burke and Hare,' said Jo and immediately regretted it. The comparison wasn't pleasant.

Noah felt in his trouser pocket and produced a Swiss army knife. He held it up in front of his eyes and selected what he thought would be the most useful application. Then he unclipped a torch from his belt and tossed it to Jo.

'Here,' he whispered. 'Keep it pointed at me.'

Jo clicked the torch on and swept the beam over Noah and on to the black cylinder.

Noah made a few tentative jabs at the surface of the container but the knife simply slid off. He beckoned Jo closer and then peered at the object with the benefit of extra light.

'Anything?' asked Jo.

Noah nodded. 'I think so. There's a little blemish here. Almost like it hasn't been...' He thrust the blade at the spot, '... sealed properly.'

There was a low groaning sound, as though someone far away had been disturbed in their sleep. Jo crouched down next to Noah, suddenly very glad of his company.

Very slowly, the black cylinder began to come apart.

There was a series of low, electronic hums and the object split into panels, each folding back like the shutter on a camera.

Shaking a little, Jo raised the torch and let the beam flood over the contents of the cylinder.

Inside, the sleek black lines contoured around her, lay Mrs Toovey, her eyes wide open and her mouth twisted into a terrible mockery of a smile. And nestling on her throat, its tendrils running up and into the old woman's mouth, was a creature the size of a small dog, its semitransparent shell glistening wet. As Jo watched, its black eyes swivelled round and regarded her with cold menace.

Jo screamed.

Discretion, the Doctor was fond of quoting, was the better part of valour. Sometimes, anyway. With this in mind, he and the Brigadier had decided against taking on the whole of Legion International single-handed and returned to Culverton to await Captain Yates and his troops, whom Lethbridge-Stewart had ordered to return.

The Doctor drove the UNIT jeep right up to the door of Whistler's cottage and jumped out. The Brigadier followed then, glancing over his shoulder, tapped him on the shoulder with his stick.

'What is it?' said the Doctor, turning on the doorstep.

The Brigadier frowned. 'Pretty quiet, don't you think?'

The Doctor shrugged. 'Villages often are. Come on.' He knocked the toe of his shoe against the door and it creaked slowly open. He exchanged looks with the Brigadier and they both went inside, looking around rapidly for any sign of life.

The Brigadier crossed to the bottom of the stairs. 'Miss Grant?' he called.

The Doctor checked the kitchen and then picked up the phone, rapidly dialling the number of the post office. He let it ring for a full minute before replacing the receiver.

'Anything?' queried Lethbridge-Stewart.

The Doctor shook his head and made for the door again.

'She'll have gone to the marshes.'

The Brigadier frowned. 'How can you be sure?'

The Doctor let out an exasperated sigh. 'Because I told her not to.'

CHAPTER TWENTY-FIVE
LAIR OF THE WORM

For once, a vehicle other than the thundering black lorries was approaching the gates of the aerodrome.

It was a coach, ultra-modern in design, its sleek lines liveried in black and yellow, its windows tinted to prevent anyone looking inside.

It purred to a halt as the gates were swung open by Legion troopers, then motored forward to park just by the old hangar. The Master stood outside the building, now dressed in his black, high-collared tunic and tight black gloves. His face was expressionless as he watched the coach arrive.

Its door hissed open and a trooper stepped out on to the broken tarmac. The Master clicked his fingers and the man stepped to one side. At once, a stream of people began to descend from the coach.

They were men and women of mostly middle age, respectable-looking; some of the men even wore Savile Row suits and bowler hats. They all seemed completely unaware of their surroundings, a fixed grin plastered over their features. A florid-faced man with a huge walrus moustache, dressed in the uniform of a general, was among them.

Jocelyn Strangeways, Chief of Staff, filed past the Master into the hangar, stepping over the threshold of the small door through which Whistler had attempted his escape, and disappeared into the darkness.

A sharp, gunpowder stink in the air.

Jo's head snapped round. Adrenalin pumped into her system.

Bullets shrieked into the marsh at her feet, thudding into the water like pebbles.

Noah was on his feet at once, grabbing her hand. 'Come on!'

Jo jumped over the black container in which Mrs Toovey lay, closing her eyes to avoid the horrible image. Then she risked a glance over her shoulder.

Fanning out in a wide semicircle from the back gates of the aerodrome were perhaps a dozen Legion troopers, armed to the teeth.

Noah pulled up sharp, his breath coming in great heaving gulps.

'We can't stop!' cried Jo. 'They'll reach us.'

Noah looked wildly around. 'If we carry on this way, we'll end up in the marsh.'

He looked suddenly very young and afraid.

'We've no choice,' said Jo firmly.

She tugged on his hand and together they raced forward, the ground beneath them becoming less and less firm.

Jo cried out as her ankles sank deep down into the cold, marshy water, spiky reeds poking into her legs through her trousers.

Bullets again tore into the ground, slapping at the marshland. Jo and Noah ducked and wove their way ahead, trying to keep low, stumbling every few feet and sinking deeper into the bog.

The cry of a curlew screeched through the still of the muggy night.

Jo was suddenly aware that their pursuers had halted. She dragged Noah to the ground and together they gazed back the way they had come. The Legion troopers were standing stock-still, like a crescent of black marble statues on some elegant driveway.

'I don't like the look of this,' murmured Jo.

Noah's breathing had grown ragged. His eyes flicked to the side.

In the marsh, about ten feet away, the water was beginning to bubble as though the temperature had risen to boiling point. Steam hissed through the reeds and soaking grass. Slimy bubbles belched to the surface and burst, releasing clouds of noxious vapour.

Noah dragged Jo back. Something slithered close by.

Jo's hand flew involuntarily to her mouth. 'Look!' she gasped.

It was as if the whole marsh had suddenly come to life. For about fifty square feet, the doughy ground was trembling and churning, with occasional flashes of some pale, fleshy-textured thing curling and snaking through it.

All at once, with a shattering, throaty roar, a gigantic creature rocketed from the marsh, teetering over Jo and Noah's cowering forms like some hideous Chinese dragon. Its massive tail was segmented like that of a crayfish and its black, blazing eyes were crab-like, but the bulk of its obscene body resembled a monstrous worm, doused in translucent slime, shuddering and clicking as it reared into the air.

*

Bliss was standing with her back to the Master, one hand on the gently humming computer banks at the far end of her office. The room was, as usual, in darkness, but the Master seemed unperturbed.

Bliss glanced round and gestured. 'You do not mind… this?'

The Master smiled, tugging at his black gloves. 'Not at all. I find it most soothing.'

'It is the natural way of things on my world.'

The Master nodded. 'I understand.'

Bliss turned around. 'Do you? Do you really?' She advanced on the Master, her chalky face looming through the darkness like the moon through cloud. 'My planet is dying!'

The Master's face was absolutely impassive. 'I understood it to be dead.'

Bliss turned sharply away, her breathing hoarse and furious. 'The Gaderene have but one chance to claim this little world. That is why you agreed to help us.'

The Master removed his gloves and regarded his fingernails. 'And have I let you down in any way?'

Bliss wiped flecks of spit from her wide mouth. 'It isn't that. The swine have been gathered but the embryos within them will not suit our purpose. The breakthrough must be soon!'

Nodding slowly, the Master got to his feet. 'We have returned a few of the villagers. Suspicion will be alleviated. Temporarily at least.'

Bliss shook her head. 'I tell you it must be soon!'

The Master sighed. 'Then bring me the Wing Commander. I have one or two tricks up my sleeve which may help us.'

*

The monster's bellowing roar thundered deafeningly over the marshes.

Noah fell on to his backside, sinking deep into the marsh, his arms outstretched in terror.

'No!' he wailed, shaking his head quickly from side to side. 'No!'

Jo snaked an arm around his waist and pulled him free from the sucking marsh.

'It's all right,' she soothed, glancing quickly upwards.

The creature was rearing over them, its eyes, like black pearls, glittering with malice. Slimy saliva gushed from its gaping maw, landing with a flat rippling sound on the disturbed waters.

Its eyes swivelled in Jo and Noah's direction.

They stiffened, trying to keep their breathing silent. Jo felt Noah's grip tighten around her hand.

The creature's lumpen face, as ill-defined as a piece of wet clay, shivered and altered as though it had detected something. Among the mass of wet flesh, some kind of sensory organ appeared to be developing before their eyes. It resolved into three black holes, like haphazard shots from a gun, arranged in a rough triangle above the creature's mouth.

The black holes distended disgustingly, membranous flesh visible through them.

'It's got our scent,' hissed Noah, pulling Jo back.

Jo felt her stomach turn as the creature moved forward, its massive body undulating through the marshland, scale by scale. A flash of something in its impenetrable black eyes made her go cold all over. With a screeching roar, it careered towards them.

Noah was about to cry out when a strange, comforting sound cut across the monster's cry. It was the blaring of a car horn.

Jo turned. Visible through the dark, its headlights shining like the beacons of twin lighthouses, Bessie was tearing across the treacherous ground towards them.

The Doctor was at the wheel, his face set in a frown of concentration as he manoeuvred the little car at a frantic rate over a section of firm ground. The Brigadier sat beside him and, as they approached the worm, he rose to his feet, steadied himself against the windscreen and aimed his service pistol.

A volley of shots rang out, striking the creature in its carapaced tail. The bullets sang off, ricocheting into the wetland. The Brigadier threw a grim look at the Doctor who chose that moment to spin the wheel, almost sending him flying.

The Doctor lifted himself up in the driving seat as Bessie raced on.

'Jo! Get down!' he called.

The creature was on the move again, enraged at the Brigadier's attack, shuffling through the boggy ground with surprising speed.

Lethbridge-Stewart aimed again, peering through the darkness and trying to hit the creature in the eyes. As before, the bullets had no effect.

'Be careful, man!' rasped the Doctor. 'You'll hit Jo and Noah.'

He powered Bessie forward, screeching to a halt just yards from the couple. Plumes of soil were thrown up in the little car's wake.

'Come on! Get in!' ordered the Doctor.

Jo and Noah scrabbled to their feet. The Brigadier grabbed Noah by the scruff of the neck and pulled him over the side of the car and into the back seat.

As Jo took the Doctor's proffered hand the creature bore down on her, screeching in fury.

She let out a piercing scream. The Doctor shifted forward, his elbow accidentally brushing the headlight control. Instantly, the two lamps on the front of Bessie's mud-splattered yellow engine powered up several notches, blazing through the night and fixing the worm in their sights.

The creature screeched and fell back.

The Doctor hauled Jo into the back seat and shot a quick look at the hideous thing before him.

'Light,' he muttered. 'Of course! They're the same!'

'What?' bellowed the Brigadier.

'They're the same creatures,' replied the Doctor with a grin. He reached down and flicked another two switches on the dashboard. Immediately, Bessie's fog lamps and indicators clicked on, and the little car blazed like a beacon.

The creature bellowed and retreated, its black eyes swivelling on their stalks and sinking back into the wet flesh of its formless face.

The Doctor nodded to himself.

'Thank… thank you, Doctor,' gasped Jo.

The Doctor looked into the back seat, frowning concernedly. 'Are you all right?' Noah nodded.

'All right,' said the Doctor, throwing Bessie into reverse. 'Let's get out of here.' The car shot backwards.

At once, the back wheels sank into the marsh.

An awful silence fell, broken only by Bessie's engine

ticking over. The funnels of light from the front headlights burrowed through the hazy night, pointing away from the monster and towards the aerodrome.

Behind them, Jo heard an ominous wet sound as the creature began to stir.

The Brigadier clambered up on his seat again, rapidly reloading his pistol. 'Come on, Doctor!' he whispered hoarsely.

The Doctor changed gear and Bessie stuttered. Still the back wheels churned through the marsh, spewing mud and grass into the air but not moving forward.

The Doctor threw a look over his shoulder to where he knew the beast to be. 'We'll have to push,' he said at last.

'We?' said Jo.

The Doctor shrugged. 'Well… you. Quickly!'

Jo, Noah and the Brigadier clambered from the safety of the car, the latter letting off a volley of shots into the darkness. The worm's shattering roar blasted over them all.

Noah pressed his hands to Bessie's boot and pushed.

'Put your backs into it!' yelled the Doctor.

The wheels span uselessly. The worm slithered forward, its eyes clicking and swivelling in the darkness.

The Brigadier pressed the gun into Jo's hand. She looked at him and he simply nodded, throwing his weight behind Noah's. Bessie moved forward an inch.

Jo dropped to one knee and tried to collect herself. Her agent's training seemed a long way off now.

She could see the worm looming through the dark, illuminated only by the car's feeble rear indicators. Its terrible face glowed red. She took aim and fired.

The Brigadier managed to lock his shoulder into

Bessie's metalwork and pushed with all his strength. The Doctor tugged at the gear lever, coaxing his beloved car forward.

'Come on,' he muttered through clenched teeth. 'Come on, Bessie!'

Noah wiped the sweat from his face and nodded at the Brigadier. 'After three,' he cried.

Lethbridge-Stewart prepared himself. With an ear-splitting roar, the creature powered through the marsh towards them, its scales slipping over one another, a great shudder rippling through its snake-like body.

Jo fired. One, two, three, four.

The Doctor slammed his foot on to the accelerator. The car gave a great lurch and bumped forward on to solid ground.

Jo threw herself back into the car, followed at once by Noah and the Brigadier, their legs poking upwards.

The Doctor span the wheel again and Bessie swung in a 180° arc.

For a moment, the creature was fully illuminated in the glare of the car's lights. It screeched again, as though the light were acid on its flesh, then fell back, water flooding over its hideous body. The Doctor patted Bessie's dashboard affectionately. Then he put his foot down and the car roared away towards the aerodrome.

He glanced at the Brigadier. 'Do you think your friend Mr Cochrane might listen to us now?'

CHAPTER TWENTY-SIX
RESURRECTION

Whistler sat down in a big, comfortable chair, the circumstances very different to his last visit to Bliss's office. He was grinning broadly and looking around him with childlike glee.

The Master pulled up a chair and sat directly opposite the old man, smiling pleasantly. Bliss was standing by the window, gazing out into the darkness. Her pale face was clammy with sweat, her great dark eyes wet and intense.

'What is it?' asked the Master.

Bliss shook her head. 'Something out there. I can... sense it.'

The Master cocked his head, interested. 'You mean your little guard dog?'

Bliss said nothing and took her seat behind the crescent-shaped desk. She raised a fat hand and indicated that the Master should proceed.

Nettled at her high-handed manner, he took his time. He pulled his gloves tight and leant forward towards Whistler's chair.

'Now,' he said calmly. 'Do you know who you are?'

Whistler's eyes swivelled from side to side. 'I think so,' he said. 'Perhaps you should tell me.'

The Master nodded. 'You are Wing Commander Alec Whistler of the Royal Air Force.'

Whistler shook his head. 'No. I don't think that can be right.'

The Master shifted forward in his seat. 'You are Wing Commander Alec Whistler and you flew Spitfires out of this aerodrome during the Second World War. Isn't that right?'

Whistler's grin broadened. 'If you say so.'

The Master's expression became grave, threatening. 'I do say so. I am the Master.'

He looked at Whistler, fixing his intense gaze on the old man's eyes. 'I am the Master. You will obey me!'

Whistler stared at him. 'I will?'

'Now,' continued the Master in his purring tones. 'You have something which I'd like to see.'

Whistler let out a peal of giggles. 'Is it a game?'

The Master rolled his eyes. 'No, it's not a game. It's very serious. Very serious indeed. You have something which belongs to my friend here.'

Whistler's face fell. 'Oh. Well I must give it back then, mustn't I?'

'Yes,' insisted the Master. 'You must. It is a small thing, like a crystal.'

'A crystal?' Whistler appeared to be fascinated. Then his attention seemed suddenly to wander, like a small boy distracted by a colourful shape elsewhere. He watched the spinning spools of Bliss's computer and grinned happily to himself. The Master sighed.

Bliss got to her feet. 'You will forgive me if I seem unimpressed by your hypnotic talents.'

The Master glared at her. 'The embryo within him is obviously preventing his personality from showing through.'

Bliss nodded. 'Naturally. It's always like that.'

'Then you shouldn't have impregnated him,' said the Master sternly.

'I didn't plan it!' spat Bliss. 'He attacked one of my men. The embryo within him was released. It found a new home. Rapidly.'

The Master nodded towards Whistler. 'We could try getting it out of him. But it's dangerous. He might not survive.'

Running her hand over her face as though feeling her skin for the first time, Bliss changed tack.

'We have most of the village now. Why don't we just tear it apart for the key?'

The Master shook his head. 'You were right. We should be cautious. It may be damaged. Or overlooked by those zombies of yours. No…'

He stared thoughtfully at Whistler who was happily watching the spinning computer tapes. 'I have a better idea.'

Jo shuddered as she recounted her experiences on the marsh.

'It was horrible. Poor Mrs Toovey…'

The Doctor laid a sympathetic hand on her shoulder. They were sitting on the bench on the village green. Next to them, the Brigadier was trying to get in touch with Captain Yates on the R/T set.

'You say there was some kind of creature?' asked the Doctor.

Jo nodded. 'It was on her neck. Just sitting there. Its eyes…' She put her face in her hands.

'It's all right, Jo,' soothed the Doctor. He glanced

around at the village green. It was still covered in stalls from that afternoon's fête, but they were completely abandoned. The eerie face of an illuminated clown grinned back at the Doctor. He looked away.

'By the way,' he said, turning back to Jo. 'I've forgiven you for going up there against my express wishes.'

Jo looked up and gave a tearful grin.

The Brigadier came over. 'Right,' he barked. 'That's that. Yates and Benton are on their way .'

The Doctor nodded. 'You managed to circumvent the exclusion order?'

'Not exactly,' murmured Lethbridge-Stewart. 'The Secretary of Defence has disappeared.'

Jo and the Doctor exchanged looks.

'In his absence, Mr Cochrane's deputy – an eminently sensible chap – listened to my story and… er… authorised us to steam in with all guns blazing.' The Brigadier seemed very pleased with himself.

The Doctor got to his feet. 'Well, I suggest we adjourn to the Wing Commander's cottage and await your reinforcements, Brigadier. We don't exactly represent a fighting force on our own, do we?'

'No.' The Brigadier looked around the deserted village. Rubbish littered the ground along with more sinister detritus: spectacles, handbags, as though their owners had no further use for them.

'Place is like a graveyard,' he concluded.

The Doctor looked up as a figure bounded across the road towards them. 'Hello, here's Noah.'

Noah strode up to the bench, shaking his head. 'Still no sign of my dad or Uncle Max.'

'Or anyone,' said Jo grimly.

She shot an appealing look at the Doctor. 'What do you think's going on?'

The Doctor frowned. 'Well, from what you've described, some kind of alien parasite. Living off the people of Culverton.'

Noah groaned disgustedly. 'And the… the aerodrome staff are helping them?'

The Doctor shook his head. 'I rather think they're one and the same.'

Captain Yates and Sergeant Benton sat in the cabin of the leading UNIT vehicle as the convoy powered along the narrow East Anglian lanes towards Culverton. Neither spoke, their mouths set in grim, determined lines as always on the eve of conflict. Both felt a quiet satisfaction that the political inertia had been dispelled and a clear call for action finally given.

Yates checked the magazine of his rifle and set it down on the seat next to him. Benton slipped his hand around the gear lever and the lorry thrummed forward with added speed.

A lone figure, like a matchstick man, stood in the box-hedge that lined the lane and watched them pass.

Captain McGarrigle's smile was unchanging. He cocked his head to one side.

The Master was in the middle of explaining an idea. 'We could gather our little herd early.'

Bliss's face clouded. 'What are you suggesting?'

The Master shrugged. 'There's little to be lost and very much to be gained. If we harvest now, the embryo within Whistler will emerge. Naturally.'

225

Bliss was appalled. 'And the embryos within all the others! They won't live long.'

'They were never meant to. Or had you forgotten? They are here merely to keep their hosts warm for the… others. Their function is simply to obey me.'

Bliss glared at him.

'I mean… us,' said the Master, spreading his hands wide.

Bliss sat down heavily behind her desk, her nose twitching. Again, something shifted behind her face, like a candle shadow flickering inside a Hallowe'en pumpkin.

The Master hid his distaste. 'Well?'

Bliss nodded slowly. 'Each life is precious to the Gaderene. We are not so numerous that we can be cavalier with the embryos. No. We must locate the ninth key, but by other methods.'

Displeased, the Master threw himself down into a chair.

Bliss suddenly stiffened and cocked her head to one side as though listening.

The Master was about to sigh when she spoke, urgently and with great rapidity, almost as though another voice were running through her. 'Troops. UNIT troops. They're heading this way.'

The Master frowned. 'They'll try and attack the aerodrome.' He slammed his gloved fist into his hand. 'Can you not use your friendly Cerberus out there?'

Bliss frowned. 'I do not understand the reference.'

The Master smiled. 'No. Of course not. It's an old Earth myth. A monstrous creature that guarded the gates to Hades.'

Bliss almost looked upset. She shook her head, sending

226

flecks of spit cascading to the floor. 'It is not so easy as it was. He… the creature, I mean, is becoming difficult to control.'

The Master looked at her with interest. 'Then raise the villagers. Order them to attack the Brigadier's tinpot army.'

Bliss considered this, then nodded rapidly.

On the desk before her stood the executive toy known as a Newton's Cradle. She took the anglepoise lamp from the desk and set it down carefully on the floor. Then she lifted back the first steel ball on the cradle and set it swinging.

As it hit its neighbour, a series of gears swung into operation with a soft grinding sound. The whole surface of the desk flipped over, revealing a complex bank of chattering screens and read-outs.

Bliss's face glowed green in the light from the screens. She flicked three switches with careful deliberation. A low, bone-shaking hum began to emanate from the desk.

'It is done,' she murmured flatly.

The Master smiled. 'Excellent. Now, let's see what we can do about our friend the Wing Commander.'

An eerie phosphorescence hovered over the now-quiet marshes like the skirts of a ghostly woman. The moon had emerged from a flotilla of thin clouds and hung low in the black sky like a sickle edged with mother-of-pearl.

Somewhere, a curlew was disturbed. Branches clattered as it took to the air. Then a low, throbbing sound became discernible, rippling out from the aerodrome like a muted heartbeat.

A fat, oily bubble rose to the surface of the marsh

water, remained for a long moment and then burst. It was followed at once by another, then another. Soon the marsh was fizzing and bubbling furiously, as though carnivorous fish were in a feeding frenzy beneath its surface.

Then, with a horrible sucking sound, one of the black cylinders shot from the water. It slammed against the bank, coming to rest by the one containing Mrs Toovey.

Another two sprang from the water, like ship's ballast escaping a wreck. Soon the marsh was awash with them; dozens and dozens of the ebony coffins, floating on the stinking water or coming to rest in the soft shallows.

Somewhere, the low, rattling hum from Bliss's desk increased in pitch.

There was a strange, sticky sound coming from Mrs Toovey's coffin. One of the old woman's gnarled hands appeared over the edge, gripping the slick surface and hauling her upright. The vile thing clinging to her upper body reacted as she stumbled to her feet, coiling itself tighter around her throat and face. Its fierce little eyes blazed.

One after another, the coffin lids shot back, folding in on themselves and revealing their contents. Men, women and even children shuffled wetly from their caskets, orientating themselves in the black night; each and every one with a foul parasite clinging to their flesh.

John, Helen and little Nichola Trickett stepped from their confinement, their faces ghastly pale, and began wading through the shallows. The embryo within John was firmly established, warm and comfortable within his face. His wife and child still bore their infection for all to see, the creatures gradually burrowing into their mouths like fungus.

The army of villagers advanced, fetid water sluicing over them as they made their way forward, staggering like an invading army; harvested early by Bliss's clarion call.

Slowly but surely, they made their way towards the village…

CHAPTER TWENTY-SEVEN

THE NINTH KEY

The Doctor sat in an armchair, thoughtfully chewing a knuckle. The Brigadier came through into the living room.

'Yates is here,' he said.

The Doctor nodded. Outside, the familiar sound of trundling trucks and jeeps formed a constant background noise.

Jo and Noah came in, holding two plates of hastily prepared corned beef sandwiches. The Doctor took one and absently stuffed into it his mouth.

'What's up, Doc?' asked Jo smiling.

The Doctor smiled in return. 'Oh, I'm just trying to think this thing through, Jo.'

He leant forward in his chair, interlacing his fingers. 'Alien parasites. That worm creature behind the aerodrome...'

Noah shrugged. 'What's to work out, Doctor? The Legion people are obviously behind it all.'

'Yes,' nodded the Doctor. 'But why wait this long? Surely they could have taken over the village if they'd wanted to. And what about the Wing Commander?'

The Brigadier frowned. 'What about him?'

The Doctor gestured towards Noah. 'Well, he was captured according to our friend here. And then they sent someone to search the house. He seems very important to them.'

'Because of something he knows?' queried Noah.

'Or something he has,' said the Doctor.

Jo sat up, almost choking on her sandwich. 'It couldn't be his Spitfire, could it?'

The Doctor looked suitably astonished. 'His what?'

Noah smiled. 'Oh yeah. The old fella's got a working Spitfire from the war. It's in the garden. He usually flies it for the fête.'

The Doctor and Brigadier both seemed startled, then the former got to his feet, smoothing down the creases in his narrow black trousers. 'I'd like to see it.'

The front door opened and Yates came inside. He saluted. 'Ready when you are, sir.'

'Really, Doctor,' muttered the Brigadier, returning Yates's salute. 'This is hardly the time for pottering in antiquated aeroplanes. I think a frontal assault on the aerodrome will do us more good.'

'Yes, well, as usual, you're opting for the most obvious solution first, Lethbridge-Stewart.'

The Doctor slipped an arm around Jo's waist. 'Come on, Jo. Show me this aeroplane.'

The Brigadier sighed in exasperation. 'Very well, Doctor. While you're playing toy soldiers, I'll see about sorting out this situation. Captain Yates…'

'Sir?'

'We'll use this room as our HQ. I want to see Benton right away.'

Yates saluted smartly. 'Right away, sir.' He turned smartly on his heel.

Noah was already leading the Doctor towards the

French windows at the back of the room. 'We can go through here,' he said, unlocking the white-framed door. 'I used to come here all the time when I was a kid.'

The Doctor gave a rueful smile but restrained himself from commenting that Noah was still little more than that. All three stepped across the threshold on to the lawn. Noah pointed ahead to a cluster of lime trees, adjacent to a barred gate which led directly on to the road.

Beneath the trees, was a bulky mass of canvas, bone-white in the moonlight.

The Doctor strode towards it.

'It's the one he flew from the aerodrome, according to Mrs Toovey,' said Jo.

The Doctor examined the tarpaulin, rapidly unfastened a couple ropes and flung back a corner.

The fuselage of a sleek, dark-coloured plane glittered in the moonlight. The Doctor let out a low whistle then let his hand move gently over its surface, coming to rest on the tinted windows of the cockpit.

'What a magnificent machine,' he whispered. He turned to Noah. 'Do you think you could lay your hands on that torch?'

The boy nodded and dashed back to the house.

'Give me a hand, would you, Jo?' asked the Doctor, pulling back more of the canvas.

Jo joined him and soon the entire plane was revealed, the red, white and blue circles on its wings like the markings on a butterfly.

Noah returned with the torch.

'Thanks,' the Doctor muttered, taking it, and clambered on to the Spitfire. Within a few moments he had unlatched the bubble-hood of the cockpit and swung it back. He shone the torch inside and illuminated a confused view of the interior; switches, dials, levers, old photographs tucked into the corner plus a pervasive smell of well-worn leather.

'What are you looking for, Doctor?' Jo climbed on to the wing next to him.

The Doctor shook his head. 'I don't know. It just seemed to me that…'

His voice trailed off as he spotted a small, grey box, jammed under the controls of the Spitfire. Leaning down, he snaked his arm over the seat, tossed aside the heavy old safety belt and plucked the box from its hiding place.

'What is it?' asked Jo.

The Doctor shrugged. 'Looks like a tobacco tin.' He tapped the heavily dented object. 'Appears to be made of lead.'

'Lead?'

'Yes.' The Doctor helped Jo back to the ground and then jumped down himself. He handed the torch to Noah who trained the beam on his hands. Carefully, the Doctor lifted the lid of the lead box.

Inside lay a variety of odds and ends. A winged RAF badge, a Swastika pin – no doubt taken from the body of some unlucky German – a dog-eared photograph of a very pretty girl and a small, crystalline object, shaped roughly like a key.

'Hello.' The Doctor lifted the object out and held it in the palm of his hand. It seem to glow, a beautiful jade colour.

'What is it?' asked Noah. 'Funny looking thing.'

The Doctor's eyes were shining. 'It's more than "funny

looking", my boy,' he beamed. 'It's a matter transference encoder.' He waved his free hand theatrically. 'From another world!'

Private Billy Dodds wiped a drip of moisture from the end of his snub nose and sighed. He glanced quickly from side to side to make sure none of his superiors were watching, then sat down heavily on a low wall and reached into his uniform for a packet of cigarettes.

With practised skill he drew one out, struck a match off the rough old brickwork beneath him and was soon drawing the smoke gratefully into his lungs. After a few contented moments, he gave another sigh. Hardly a man's life, he thought ruefully.

Dodds was new to this UNIT lark. He'd been in the regulars for over two years, working on radar experiments up north when his CO had put his name forward for a transfer. Dodds had been pleased – as far as he was concerned anywhere was better than the dull confines of Catterick garrison – but this new outfit had been strange from the outset.

His cousin, who was something very minor at the MOD had told him it was all very hush-hush but Dodds hadn't had time to find out much more before being hauled in for this job. Some kind of security thing to do with an aerodrome. His superiors were called Benton and Yates and they were both said to take orders from a Brigadier, whom Dodds had yet to meet. Some of the more experienced lads also spoke of a scientist called the Doctor who helped out sometimes. When Dodds had asked the men what exactly he helped out with, they had just grinned, winked and told him he'd soon find out. So, none the wiser, Dodds and a couple of dozen others had been bundled into lorries and driven up to East Anglia, secretly excited at all the mystery.

The village was pretty and deathly quiet but then it was the middle of the night. Dodds felt a little foolish, patrolling a quaint English street armed with a rifle as though he were on the streets of Belfast.

He tried humming a pop song but soon gave up. He put out his fag and thought about lighting another, hoping that his relief was on the way.

Footsteps broke the silence.

Dodds peered through the darkness. Someone was coming round the corner, about three hundred yards away.

Dodds straightened up and was about to unshoulder his rifle when he realised the figure was a civilian. A middle-aged man by the look of it and shuffling along in the most extraordinary way, almost like a sleepwalker, hands slightly outstretched. Drunk, more than likely, thought Dodds.

Another man emerged directly behind the first, then two more. Then a woman and a child. They seemed to be grinning. Dodds frowned. What was this? A family outing?

He walked forward a few steps, trying to make out details in the gloom. One of the figures appeared to be wearing a white vicar's collar but his rumpled linen suit was filthy and stained with water. Also, there was something very wrong with his face…

Dodds swallowed anxiously and raised his rifle. The vicar-figure, shambling forward, water pooling at his feet, seemed to have some kind of creature pressed into the flesh of his face. It had a segmented body like a worm and a mass of spindly legs which pierced the man's skin. It was almost as though the thing were controlling the vicar, squatting in his head like a pilot in a cockpit.

Dodds felt himself go very cold.

'Sir!' he croaked.

More figures emerged, swelling the group.

'Sir!' shrieked Dodds.

Two soldiers appeared from behind him and stopped in their tracks.

'What are they?' hissed Dodds. His comrades shook their heads.

'Get the Sarge,' barked one. The other soldier raced off towards Whistler's cottage.

The strange group of villagers shuffled inexorably forward. Dodds' hands began to shake uncontrollably. He shot a glance over his shoulder towards the cottage, then back at the vicar or, rather, at the vile, multi-tendrilled thing which was hanging from his mouth.

Then Private Billy Dodds lifted his rifle, took aim at the vicar and opened fire.

The Reverend Darnell fell to his knees and keeled over, blood pouring from his left leg.

The crackle of gunfire brought Benton, Yates and the Brigadier spilling out of Whistler's cottage and on to the street.

'What the hell –?' barked Yates. He took in the situation at a glance and knocked Dodds' rifle down.

'Wait, Private, wait!'

The Brigadier peered at the advancing villagers. 'Doctor!' he bellowed. 'Doctor!'

The Doctor came haring from the cottage, tucking

the jade key into the pocket of his smoking jacket. Jo and Noah brought up the rear.

All three froze as they took in the sight of the zombie-like inhabitants of Culverton.

Jo suddenly gripped the Doctor's arm. He and Noah peered ahead. Stumbling behind the Vicar, water sluicing through their sodden clothes, were Ted and Max Bishop.

Chapter Twenty-Eight
IMPROVISATION

The Master's hands hovered over the flaring panels that had emerged from Bliss's desk.

He glanced over at Whistler, who sat facing the computer, then flicked three switches in rapid succession.

Bliss stood immobile in the shadows and, despite himself, the Master found the woman's stillness slightly unnerving.

'The computations must be exact,' said Bliss quietly.

The Master's face was impassive. 'Of course.'

He tapped part of the steel console. 'This is where the signal would come from?'

Bliss detached herself from the darkness, nodding. 'When the time is right, the embryos will be given the instruction to leave their hosts.'

The Master nodded to himself. 'Then all I need to do is remodulate the signal to make it more localised.' He pointed a black-gloved finger at Whistler. 'So that only the embryo within him is summoned.'

Dexterously, he punched a series of commands into the complex machinery. A soft chiming sound began to emanate from the desk. He adjusted a button and the pitch of the sound dropped. A further, delicate adjustment and the sound became scarcely audible.

The Master's intense gaze swept over the console screens.

Bliss stared at Whistler's vacuously grinning face and shook her head.

'It isn't working.'

The Master held up his hand. 'Patience, patience.'

He stabbed at a button and a series of numbers appeared on the glowing panel.

There was a sudden, ugly, burping gulp and something shifted inside Whistler's face.

'There!' hissed the Master. 'There!'

Spindly legs, like pale, hollow straws, were appearing at the corners of the old man's grinning mouth as the embryo within him was summoned. The tendrils waved about in agitation, pressing into his cheeks and nose.

Bliss stared anxiously at the thing as it crawled from the Wing Commander's face. She waited a full minute until the bulk of its slimy body was exposed and then carefully, tenderly, pulled it from his mouth. Its fleshy body flowed over her hands like wet dough. The Master grimaced.

With a wet slap, Bliss placed the thing on the carpet where it writhed in confusion, its legs scrabbling at the air.

The Master tutted. 'Brave little soldier.'

Bliss glared at him, then touched her forehead and chest three times, finally placing the flat of her palm over her heart. 'This Gaderene has served us well. He may die with honour.'

The creature on the floor had begun to crawl pathetically back towards Whistler.

Bliss lifted her foot and, with deadly accuracy, brought

down her heel on the embryo's head. Its transparent skin popped and blistered as its life was extinguished.

Bliss let out a low groan, as though appalled at what she'd had to do.

She looked down at the shattered remains of the embryo at her feet and then swung round to point at Whistler. 'Now,' she barked. 'Get the information out of him!'

The Master came round from behind the desk and leant over Whistler, his hands clasping the arms of the chair.

'Mr Whistler?'

Whistler groaned. Saliva and a small amount of blood tumbled from his lips.

'Mr Whistler,' continued the Master. 'Wing Commander. How're you feeling?'

Whistler managed to open his bloodshot eyes.

The Master's expression became stern. 'You know who I am. I am the Master. Now, tell me. The final part. The ninth key. Where is it? Where is it?'

The Doctor stared at the horrible sight of the infected villagers staggering towards him like gas-blinded soldiers.

'Great Scott,' whispered the Brigadier. 'What do we do, Doctor?'

He raised his revolver. Most of the UNIT troops were now assembled around the cottage, bristling with weapons.

'You can't shoot at them!' cried Noah.

The Doctor shook his head. 'No. You can't. They're merely the vessels for these creatures. Without them, the people of this village might be entirely human again.'

Benton gestured helplessly.

'But we have to do something, Doctor. They'll be all over us in a few minutes.'

The Doctor frowned. 'I wonder... This could be some kind of distraction.'

Noah winced as he saw the vile creature occupying his father suddenly move within his mouth and widen his lips into a taut, manic grin.

The villagers' pace suddenly increased. They rushed forward en masse, arms outstretched.

The Brigadier turned to Yates. 'Captain Yates! Fire at their feet. See if they react.'

Yates nodded. 'Right away, sir.'

He turned to address the line of troops and barked an order. At once, a volley of shots rang out, splintering the road at the villagers' feet. Chips of tarmac bounced upwards cutting into flesh but the possessed people lumbered on.

The UNIT troops rapidly reloaded.

'Well, Doctor?' cried the Brigadier.

The Doctor looked round rapidly, taking in the parked lorries and the garden of Whistler's cottage.

'I've got an idea. We can't risk hurting any of those people but I think they're here to try and prevent you from attacking the aerodrome.'

'So what can we do?' asked Jo.

'Attack the aerodrome!' said the Doctor. 'By the time they get there, we could be inside. Leave half your men here, Brigadier. The rest of them go up in force.'

The Brigadier nodded. 'Divide and conquer, eh Doctor? Splendid.'

He swung round towards Benton. 'Sergeant, you stay here. Captain Yates and I will lead the assault on the aerodrome.'

Benton saluted. 'Yes, sir.'

The Brigadier cast a worried look at the approaching villagers. 'I want you to do whatever you can to restrain those… people. Without resort to firearms. Is that understood?'

Benton answered in the affirmative.

The Doctor nodded confidently to himself. 'Right. That might buy us some time.'

He took Jo by the elbow. 'Jo, I need your help.'

Jo allowed herself to be steered back towards the cottage. The Doctor grabbed Noah and forced the boy to look away from the strange and horrible sight of his father and uncle.

'You too, Noah. I think I may know a way to disable these creatures. At least temporarily.'

Noah looked pleadingly at the Doctor. 'Will… will they be OK?'

The Doctor looked far from sure but gave him a winning smile. 'I hope so, Noah. We can only do our best.'

He ushered the boy through into Whistler's cottage.

'Just what have you got planned in that devious mind of yours, Doctor?' asked Jo brightly as they stood on the threshold.

'Tell me, Jo,' said the Doctor. 'Do you have green fingers?'

Jo gave a puzzled frown.

Sergeant Benton approached his troops and gave them the order to shoulder their rifles.

The possessed inhabitants of Culverton were gathering again and stumbling forward.

Benton swallowed nervously and ordered his men to link arms. Above all, they must not let the villagers through.

Chapter Twenty-Nine
ATTACK!

Bliss placed the last of eight jade-coloured objects on a small table in front of Whistler. Each was almost identical to the key which the Doctor had found in the Spitfire but with subtle differences in the shaft; tiny microcircuitry made up a complex pattern that sparkled and shimmered as though alive.

Bliss arranged the keys in a rough semicircle.

Whistler tried not to look at them, working his mouth open and closed, feeling the strain of the ejected creature on his old jaw. He felt a violent urge to be sick.

'Look at them, Whistler,' urged the Master. 'Look at these objects. You've seen one like them before haven't you?'

Whistler shook his head and clamped his eyes shut.

'What's going on?' he mumbled, raising a shaking hand to his temple. 'Who are you people?'

The Master stared at him. 'That's not important now. There's nothing at all that's important except that you show me where the last of these objects is hidden. The ninth key.'

Whistler steadied his breathing. He was severely disorientated and could remember very little of his recent experiences, but he knew an interrogation when he saw one and he wasn't about to let these people have what they wanted.

'I've never seen anything like those things in my life,' he said carefully.

Bliss barrelled towards him, moving swiftly despite her bulk. 'Lies!'

She raised a hand to hit him but the Master grasped her wrist.

'Do you have to be so drearily unsubtle?' he hissed. 'Please, allow me to do this my way.'

Bliss snatched her hand away. The Master turned back to Whistler. 'Focus on the keys, Wing Commander. Let me see into your mind.'

Whistler gritted his teeth and tried to turn away. The Master grabbed his chin and wrenched his head round. Despite himself, Whistler looked directly into the stranger's eyes. When he tried to look away, all he saw were the whirling spools of tape on Bliss's computer. They seemed to be as one with the Master's eyes; merging, blurring, spinning…

The Master's voice was persuasive, Whistler had to concede. Fella must've had some training. Probably a Russian. Though he didn't look it. His appearance and the tone of his voice were more like a Turk. Or a Spaniard. The voice was… the voice was…

'Look at the keys, Wing Commander. There are eight of them. Where is the ninth? Let me see.'

The Master's voice was warm and soothing. It was almost as though Whistler could see it. Its colour. Brown. A warm brown. Whistler felt his befuddled mind clearing a little. He saw a huge canopy of blue sky and a beautiful, dusty landscape. Vineyards and olive trees dotting the soil like cloves pressed into a Christmas orange. His plane was soaring overhead, giving a victory roll. Beneath, the crowds were cheering and cheering. It was all over. The war was finally over. Whistler smiled beneath his large goggles. His face was black with smoke and oil but he was happy. Happier than he'd ever been. He'd got through it. Feeling inside his leather jacket, his fingers found the small, crystalline object he'd come upon that day in the grounds of Culverton aerodrome. The day after she'd been taken from him by the bloody bomb.

He cradled the thing in his palm now. It was warm to the touch…

The Master snapped his fingers in front of Whistler's eyes and the old man started.

'What? Where was…?' he stammered.

'Well?' asked Bliss.

The Master smiled. 'I know exactly where it is. Shall we go?'

Bliss's chalky face split into an impossibly wide grin. 'The configuration will be complete. The invasion can begin!'

Whistler sank back into his chair, feeling utterly worthless.

The Doctor threw off his smoking jacket and, quickly and efficiently emptied the unwashed dishes from Whistler's sink. He rolled up his sleeves and then looked up as Jo and Noah stumbled in from the garden, each carrying a bag of fertiliser. Jo let hers flop to the tiled kitchen floor and groaned.

'Mind telling us why we're doing this, Doctor?'

The Doctor shook his head. 'No time just now. Noah,

go back out to the garden. There must be a potting shed of some kind. Bring back all the tools you can lay your hands on.'

Noah looked puzzled but shrugged and dashed out.

The Doctor turned both taps on and water thudded into the old, square porcelain sink.

Without looking at Jo, he began to speak. 'We have to stop the villagers' advance in order to help the Brigadier, yes?'

'Yes,' said Jo.

'But we can't risk harming any of them. Yes?'

Jo sighed. 'Yes.'

'And what we want most of all is for those people to be free of the aliens' influence.'

'Obviously.'

'Well,' cried the Doctor happily. 'If I'm right, this may be a way of killing two birds with one stone.'

Noah kicked open the gated kitchen door and came back inside, staggering under the weight of an old grey canvas bag. He dropped it to the floor with a loud clunk. A quantity of hammers, files and nails spilled over the tiles.

'Splendid,' said the Doctor. He nodded towards the front room. 'See how they're getting on, would you?'

Noah raced from the kitchen. The Doctor rapidly sorted through the tools on the floor. 'Right, Jo. You're a practical sort of girl, aren't you?'

Jo shrugged. 'I like to think so.'

The Doctor pointed towards Mrs Toovey's cooker. 'Can you get that going? I need it heated to about two hundred degrees.'

'OK.' Jo moved towards the cooker.

The Doctor pulled a chair from under the kitchen table. Its legs scraped over the tiles. Feeling inside the pockets of his abandoned smoking jacket, he retrieved his sonic screwdriver and a few other objects that Jo had never seen before. One of them appeared to be some sort of compact glass retort. He ransacked the tool bag, hurling a metal ruler and a hammer over his shoulder.

'What're you looking for, Doctor?' asked Jo, bending over the cooker.

The Doctor didn't look up. 'If we're out of luck, I'll have to use a file to create my own – ah!'

He held up a jam jar filled with some black substance and beamed triumphantly. 'I knew the Wing Commander wouldn't let me down. He's a tinkerer like me.'

Jo tried to make out what was inside the jar. 'I don't…'

'Iron filings!' cried the Doctor. Then, without pause, he got up, dragged one of the bags of fertiliser across the floor, hefted it on to the table and split the packaging apart with a well-aimed blow with a Stanley knife. Dark, peaty matter spilled out on to the table.

Noah ran back in from the front room.

'How's it going out there?' asked the Doctor.

Noah's expression was grave. 'Not good.'

Benton let fly with a devastating punch, knocking a burly man in a cable-knit sweater to the ground. The man, grinning madly, simply rolled over and came at him again, his spade-like hands outstretched. He made to grab the sergeant around the throat but Benton ducked and dodged, slamming the butt of his rifle into the man's side.

Around them, the scene was very much the same. The dozen or so troops left after the Brigadier and Yates had left for the attack on the aerodrome were struggling to keep back the villagers. Most had now fully absorbed the disgusting embryos and wore the same fixed grins. Some, less advanced in the conversion process, had strange, lumpen disfigurements as though they were suffering from the mumps. What they all had in common was their determination to break through the UNIT platoon.

Private Billy Dodds fell backwards at the combined assault of Ted and Max Bishop. He yelled in terror as their hands clawed at his face, then managed to kick his booted foot into Ted's groin.

Silently, Ted rolled off him and fell to the ground, his smiling face smacking off the bullet-pocked tarmac. Dodds dragged himself to his feet and retreated behind the makeshift barricade the UNIT men had constructed.

Panting with exhaustion he sank to the ground and noticed Sergeant Benton next to him, hastily reloading his rifle. Benton cracked the magazine into place and then got up on one knee. Aiming carefully, he shot at the road in front of the villagers' advance.

'You lad!' he yelled at Dodds. 'Go into the cottage and tell the Doctor we can't hold them any more!'

'But, Sarge –'

'Do it!' cried Benton, aiming again with one eye closed.

He gave Dodds covering fire as the inexperienced private scuttled across the road and into Whistler's cottage.

Dodds ran through the front room and into the kitchen where a strange sight met his eyes. Burst bags of what looked like fertiliser were scattered all over the floor and red rubber hoses snaked from the cooker into a sink full of water. There was a pervasive, sweet smell and for one crazy moment Dodds thought someone might be making jam.

A tall, white-haired man in shirtsleeves was at the sink. A girl and a young boy stood nearby looking extremely worried. All three had wet handkerchiefs or tea towels over the bottom half of their faces.

The tall man was filling milk bottles, but Dodds peered at the dozen or so on the side of the sink and they appeared to be empty. Each had been sealed with what looked wax; a pan of melted candles on the stove bore witness to this.

'Would one of you be the Doctor?' asked Dodds lamely.

The girl pointed to the white-haired man, who was too immersed in his work to reply.

'It's all right,' came her muffled voice. 'We don't know what he's doing, either.'

Dodds walked up to the Doctor and saluted. The Doctor looked up, noticing the private's presence for the first time.

'Begging your pardon, sir,' said Dodds. 'But Sergeant Benton says he can't hold them any more.'

The Doctor nodded. 'Right. It's time we got everyone inside the cottage.'

He thrust two of the milk bottles into the private's hands. Dodds looked down at them and frowned. 'What do I do with these, sir?'

The Doctor doled out the remaining bottles to Jo and Noah, then grabbed three for himself. 'Come on,' he ordered.

Marching off through the cottage with the others close

251

behind, he opened the front door with the toe of his boot and dashed outside.

He took in the chaotic scene in an instant.

'All right, Sergeant,' he shouted. 'Call off your men.'

Benton appeared from behind the barricade and yelled the order to retreat.

'Get everyone inside,' shouted the Doctor.

The UNIT troops gratefully retreated, racing past him and into the cottage. Benton paused on the threshold as the last two of his troops piled inside.

'Fisher! Dodds! Get upstairs. I want your rifles trained on the attackers.'

He looked worriedly at the Doctor. 'We may have no choice, Doctor.'

The Doctor nodded. 'We'll see.'

He raised the first of the milk bottles into the air as Jo and Noah appeared in the doorway. 'Are you ready?' he cried.

'For what?' asked Jo.

The Doctor looked affronted. 'Chuck 'em, of course!'

He hurled his bottle in a wide arc and it smashed in front of Ted Bishop. It was immediately followed by two more.

Almost at once the heavy, sickly-sweet smell grew stronger.

Ted Bishop staggered slightly and then something extraordinary happened. He began to laugh. A strange, high giggle rolled out from his distended face, building to an almost hysterical pitch. Then, just as suddenly, his dark eyes rolled over white and he fell to the ground, unconscious.

The Doctor's eyes, the only part of his face visible

beneath his wet handkerchief mask, sparkled with triumph.

'Doctor –' began Jo.

'Don't just stand there!' cried the Doctor. 'Throw!'

He grabbed the bottles from Jo's hands and threw them into the crowd of villagers. One after another they stumbled and fell, convulsed by hysterical, frightening laughter.

Noah hurled his bottles at his uncle's feet. The glass shattered into shards and Max Bishop fell to the roadside, arms flailing. In seconds, he had blacked out.

'Doctor...' gasped Jo. 'What... what's going on?'

The Doctor watched the chaos with satisfaction. 'Nitrous oxide, Jo,' he said above the chorus of insane giggling coming from close by. 'I isolated the nitrates in the fertiliser and heated it with the iron filings. Now we know it works, we need to produce as much as we can.'

He grinned as Jo suddenly fell down flat on her backside, giggling. 'Nitrous...' she gasped.

'Oxide,' said the Doctor. 'Of course, there are lots of impurities in it, the way I knocked it up. Causes some side effects. You probably know it better as laughing gas.'

He helped her to her feet and pushed her back inside.

'You two had better stay in there. We don't want you affected too.'

The Doctor shut the door firmly behind him as he re-entered the cottage. He raced up the stairs towards Benton.

'All right, Sergeant. That should keep them unconscious for a while. We've done all we can here. I think it's time we helped the Brigadier out.'

None of them noticed that Noah Bishop had slipped

outside and was running towards the unconscious body of his father.

Whistler pulled against the ropes that bound him to the chair. He cursed and tugged again, the harsh fabric cutting into his wrists. He had let himself down. Badly. That Master fella had bamboozled him into revealing his secret. Though quite what they wanted with his good-luck charm, he couldn't begin to tell. The point was he had failed as an officer and a gentleman. And now it was up to him to make amends. The first thing to do was get the hell out of the aerodrome.

The ropes were refusing to budge. Whistler struggled to his feet and lifted the chair bodily. Just across the room, the crescent shape of Bliss's desk still glowed with light.

He shuffled closer to the desk, his gaze flicking over it for any sign of something useful. In turning itself over, the crescent of the desk had exposed what appeared to be quite a sharp metal surface. The old man made straight for it, grunting with effort as he carried the bulky chair behind him.

He banged against the desk and swore as he cracked his wrist against it. Then he manoeuvred himself so that the ropes which bound him were flush with the sharp edge of the half-moon and began to rub them swiftly against it.

With agonising slowness, the fibres of the rope began to unravel.

Whistler bit his lower lip. Sweat dripped from his forehead at the combined effort of keeping the chair off the ground and leaning against the desk. Just as he felt one hand coming free, the door opened and Captain

McGarrigle stood there, his big, dark eyes glowering at him.

The old man realised at once that another of the vile creatures had found a home within the Captain.

With the speed of a panther, McGarrigle strode across the room towards Whistler.

In a searing flash of memory, Whistler saw the Captain attacking him outside by the perimeter fence.

As the younger man leapt at him, he pulled one hand free and swung the chair round, catching him a brutal blow on the side of his head.

The Captain crashed to the floor but rolled over at once, bringing his fist up and punching the old man in the stomach.

Whistler cried out and fell backwards against the desk, his spine connecting painfully with the hard metal.

In a second, the Captain's broad hands were on his face and Whistler knew at once what was happening. Fingers flashed to cover his nostrils and a warm palm was suddenly clamped over his mouth. McGarrigle was trying to suffocate him.

Whistler was no longer a young man. He had no hope of defending himself against an adversary like the Captain, six feet of sinewy muscle possessed by an alien intelligence. But as he struggled under his opponent's deadly grip, rapidly losing consciousness, he knew that he owed it to the traditions by which he had lived his life not to go down without a fight. He still had his wits. And his wits told him that the Captain always carried a pistol in his belt…

The alien's hands were clamped firmly across Whistler's face, strong and implacable. The old man struggled violently, almost convulsing himself beneath the Captain's grip, and his hands thrashed at McGarrigle's belly, raining ineffectual blows on the wall of hard muscle. But then he found the gun, felt its cold presence and struggled to release it from the belt.

The strength was draining from his limbs. The room, already dark, was swirling into a deeper, everlasting blackness and there was a roaring in his ears. Then something else came back to him. The interrogation. Bliss's interrogation. The lamp. She had reacted to it as though scalded. There was a black lead by the side of the desk. He knew there was. With one hand still struggling to release the gun, Whistler made a final effort and slapped his other hand hard against the side of the desk. He found the cable at once. His fingers slid down its length and came upon a bulky rectangle fixed into it. He clicked on the anglepoise lamp.

The Captain reeled back, hissing like a reptile, his hand flying from Whistler's face to cover his eyes.

Whistler gulped air into his bursting lungs and shook his head to clear the explosion of red dots that was bursting before his eyes. He knew he only had seconds.

His opponent was already recovering. His hands flew to Whistler's throat. The old man tugged at McGarrigle's belt. A press stud opened and the gun clattered to the floor. Whistler grabbed it, took aim and pumped six bullets into the Captain's chest.

The alien was slammed back against the desk, his head hit the metal with a sickening crack and he slid down, blood smearing the elegant blond wood behind him. The lamp fell to his chest, throwing its harsh light on his face. Whistler saw the Captain's huge dark eyes dilate and then something hideous stirring beneath the skin of his face.

Getting shakily to his feet, Whistler didn't need to see any more. He pulled the gun belt from the corpse, reloaded the pistol and raced from the office.

CHAPTER THIRTY
SIEGE

The ring of black-uniformed Legion troopers outside the aerodrome's perimeter fence had been boosted by some new arrivals.

The Brigadier watched as Mrs Toovey and Jobey Packer emerged from behind the soldiers, taking their place in the human barricade, both smiling. Soon after, they were joined by Graham Allinson and Anthony Ayre.

'They're using pensioners and boys now,' said the Brigadier bitterly. 'It's like they know we won't attack.'

Yates nodded. 'What I wouldn't give to be facing a gang of straightforward monsters right now.'

The Brigadier gazed steadily at the enemy. 'But that's what they are, Yates. Inside them, anyway. Hostile invaders.'

He straightened up and moved swiftly towards the truck full of UNIT troops.

'Right, attention all of you,' he barked. 'The enemy has us at a disadvantage. They assume we won't attack because what we're facing here are innocent human victims. I say again, they assume we won't attack.'

Yates was surprised. 'Sir?'

'Desperate times call for desperate measures, Captain,' said the Brigadier. He pulled himself up into the cabin of the nearest truck.

*

The Doctor held up the crystalline key and turned it around and around in the light.

'What exactly does that thing do, Doctor?' asked Jo.

'I thought I'd explained.'

Jo grunted. 'Hardly.'

The sound of gunfire and smashing bottles filtered in as the Doctor adopted the tone of a teacher explaining a very hard sum to a very dense child.

'It's a matter transference encoder. Probably one of many. They need it to travel to Earth from wherever they're based.'

Jo frowned. 'If they've got some already, why would they be after this one?'

The Doctor weighed the key in his hand. 'Very good question.'

'So we're presuming they don't have space ships or anything? Like the Daleks?'

The Doctor nodded. 'It seems likely. They must have to travel an unimaginable distance. Perhaps even…'

His voice trailed off and he stared into space.

'Doctor?'

'I was just thinking. Remember what Mrs Toovey said about the lightning. Summer lightning. That could have been these creatures arriving.'

He tapped the jade key against his chin thoughtfully.

'Arriving in… embryonic form. They could pass safely through space without all the requisite encoders being in place… but they would need them all. Eventually.'

'What for?' said Jo.

The Doctor's expression was grave. 'For the adults to come through.'

Jo looked down and then quickly around. 'Where - where's Noah?'

In the hangar, Bliss was anxiously watching the line of VIPs she had gathered. They were lying flat on sleek black surgical tables, blanketed and grinning.

She checked on Cochrane, Secretary of Defence, feeling his pulse and frowning.

'The breakthrough must be soon,' she muttered to herself.

Bliss rubbed a hand over her face. A shape beneath the skin shifted.

'These human shells are weak.' She turned her fat face up towards the ceiling. Her great dark eyes blinked slowly as though she were gazing through space.

Then she laid a hand on Cochrane's forehead. He was tossing and turning restlessly, as though agitated.

'Not long now, my friends,' whispered Bliss, looking down at the row of people. 'And then you will have new homes. Warm homes.'

Sergeant Benton stood by the window of the boxroom on the upper floor of Whistler's cottage. He hoped against hope that his men's ongoing battle with the Culverton villagers had given the Brigadier a chance to attack the aerodrome, but there had been no word from his superior for almost half an hour.

Peering through the window, he saw the disorientated villagers beginning to stir.

The Doctor had warned him that the nitrous oxide gas would provide only temporary anaesthesia, but they seemed to be making a remarkably speedy recovery.

Benton was about to order Private Dodds downstairs to tell the Doctor when he noticed something strange.

Ted Bishop had recovered and was standing stock-still only yards from Whistler's cottage. His brother was next to him in a similar pose.

Benton swallowed anxiously. He pointed his rifle directly at Ted Bishop's face.

'What're they doing?' asked Dodds, lowering his gun a fraction.

Benton shook his head. 'I've really no idea. Maybe the Doctor can –'

He stopped dead as a figure emerged from the shadows outside.

'Oh no,' said Benton quietly.

The Master positioned himself between the Bishop brothers and put his hands behind his back.

'Doctor!' he called. 'Doctor, if you're in there, I'd like a word.'

Benton trained his rifle on the Master. 'Now you know not to try anything silly,' he shouted from the window.

The Master looked up and smiled.

The door of the cottage opened and the Doctor came out, shrugging on his smoking jacket. He caught sight of the suave, bearded figure just ahead and grunted.

'Well, well. Look what the cat dragged in.'

The Master smiled affably. 'How nice to see you again, Doctor. Do you know, I think I've actually missed you.'

The Doctor's face was serious. 'I wish I could say the same.'

Jo came out behind the Doctor and quietly closed the cottage door behind her.

'You're working for these creatures, I take it?' said the Doctor.

The Master inclined his head a fraction.

'Dear me.' The Doctor rubbed his chin. 'Always the bridesmaid, never the blushing bride. How does it feel always to be someone else's lackey?'

The Master bristled. 'As the Brigadier's pet monkey, I should think you're better placed to answer that, my dear Doctor.'

The Doctor glared at him. 'What do you want?'

'The encoder, of course.'

The Doctor avoided his gaze. 'I don't know what you're talking about.'

'Don't play games with me. I don't have time.'

The Doctor looked around. 'For once you seem to have forgotten to surround yourself with thugs. Your threats don't seem entirely persuasive.'

The Master dropped his hands. Benton's finger tightened on the trigger.

'Despite your amusing efforts, Doctor, these people are still quite capable of killing. They will do my bidding. If I order them to attack, they will do so. Do you really want your soldier friends to cut them to pieces?'

The Doctor considered this. 'Well, exchange is no robbery. I may give you the encoder... if you'll give me information.'

The Master inclined his head to one side. 'Go on.'

The Doctor pulled the crystalline key from his coat pocket and tossed it into the air, catching it deftly a moment later. 'These creatures. Who are they?'

The Master kept his eyes on the key, twitching slightly as the Doctor toyed with it. 'They are the Gaderene,' he

stated. 'They came to Earth some thirty years ago and…
marked it.'

The Doctor frowned. 'Marked it?'

'Like a cat marking its territory,' said Jo quietly.

The Master nodded. 'A crude analogy, Miss Grant, but
essentially correct. Two of them arrived in embryonic
form. They had this planet down as a useful fall-back
should anything unforeseen occur.'

'And what happened?' asked the Doctor.

'Something unforeseen occurred. Their world is dying.
I managed to get them back in touch with their nearest
and dearest. They need a new home.'

The Doctor set his face into a stern frown. 'But this
planet is occupied already. They can't just be allowed
to… move in.'

'Oddly enough, Doctor, that's not the way they see it.
They do not intend to ask the human race politely to leave.
They intend to… ah… what is the modern parlance?'

'Squat?' said Jo.

'Squat,' replied the Master. 'Yes. And now, if you'll
hand over the encoder, I shall help them get on with it.'

The Doctor regarded him steadily. 'You know I can't
allow that.'

The Master sighed. 'Good old Doctor. Always so
tiresomely fair.'

He clicked his fingers and two of the recovered villagers
appeared, dragging Noah between them.

Jo cried out in horror.

The Master picked up an abandoned UNIT pistol and
pointed it at Noah who was now crouching at his father's
feet. 'Don't move!' he commanded, glaring at Benton on
the upper floor. 'Get up, boy. Move here, next to me.'

Reluctantly Noah did so. The Master tugged at his arm and pressed the cold barrel of the pistol to Noah's cheek. 'Now, Doctor, the encoder. Or this boy dies.'

The Doctor thought at once of General Gogon. He wasn't about to go through all that again. He glanced towards the horizon, as though expecting a distant pyrotechnical display to distract the Master. Nothing happened. He stepped forward.

'Doctor!' called Jo.

The Doctor glanced back at her. 'I've little choice.'

He threw the key to the Master who caught it in one black-gloved hand. 'Thank you, Doctor.'

The Master pushed the barrel of the pistol further into Noah's cheek.

The boy whimpered. Suddenly he seemed very young indeed.

'You know, I seem to remember we had a little falling out, you and I. Back at the Academy,' mused the Master, as though he were at a summer garden party. 'That was about not keeping my word. I told you then and I'm telling you now, you must be more realistic, Doctor. You're too trusting.'

The smile on his face melted away. He pocketed the jade encoder and backed away, motioning with the gun for Noah to follow.

'Now!,' he yelled. 'Kill them! Kill them all!'

The villagers rushed forward, mouths wide open, a horrible, gurgling roar escaping from their possessed bodies.

In the confusion, the Master took to his heels, dragging Noah behind him.

CHAPTER THIRTY-ONE
SCRAMBLE

Bliss stepped over the body of Captain McGarrigle and, in silence, picked up the eight encoders from the desk. The time for the transference was rapidly approaching. The embryos within her swine would have to be released in order to make way for the adult Gaderene. The timing was critical but Bliss felt nerveless as she turned on her heel, left the office and walked swiftly towards the runway. This was the moment she had waited for.

'Fall back! Fall back!' screamed Sergeant Benton as the villagers smashed and hammered at the cottage door.

He raced down the stairs to find the Doctor and Jo heading for the kitchen.

'I've got no choice but to fire on them, Doctor!'

The Doctor nodded. 'I suggest we head for the aerodrome, Sergeant. We've done all we can. Any word from the Brigadier?'

Benton shook his head.

'All right,' said the Doctor. 'I suggest you and your men fan out from the back of the cottage and head up there on foot. You'll be less conspicuous and, anyway, I think they'll be more interested in me.'

'Why?' asked Jo.

'Because,' said the Doctor, 'I intend to go up there in a

rather more ostentatious form of transport.'

Jo's jaw dropped. 'Not the Spitfire?'

'Naturally.'

'But you can't! I mean…' stammered Jo.

The Doctor shrugged. 'Why not? I admit I'm a bit out of practice but we have to get Noah away from the Master and stop the Gaderene. We need every weapon at our disposal. Besides, it'll be good to go back up in one of those old crates. I haven't flown a Spitfire since 2154!'

So saying, he strode through the kitchen, pausing only to pick up the remaining bottles of nitrous oxide, and made his way into the garden.

Benton shook his head and began to shout orders up the stairs to his men. Jo raced after the Doctor.

He spoke to her over his shoulder as they approached the tarpaulin-covered aircraft. 'If I'm right, Jo, then the Gaderene's grip on Earth is precarious to say the least.'

'What do you mean?'

'Well they only have the embryonic forms inside the villagers. They're no good for anything much except brute force. No, if they're to exert real control, they need the adults to come through.'

'And for that they need the Wing Commander's encoder?'

The Doctor nodded.

'But what about Bliss?' queried Jo. 'She seems completely in control of things.'

The Doctor shrugged. 'From what the Master says she must have been one of the original two who landed here. Some luckless soul became host to her but it's taken all these years for the creature to mature. It's more than just occupying a body. It's become her.'

Jo looked back towards the cottage. 'So the Master helped them set up a… a bridge between their world… their dying world and Earth?'

'That's right, Jo. There must be something special about this area. Perhaps because it was the original landing point.'

'And they had to send embryos because they're young… mindless?' said Jo.

The Doctor nodded and began to pull at the tarpaulin. 'The link wasn't properly established, so only embryos could stand the trip unscathed.'

Jo blanched. 'But now the Master has the final key. They'll be able to mount a full invasion.'

'Unless we can stop them,' said the Doctor gravely.

He pulled at the hood of the cockpit and dragged it over, then jumped up on to the wing and swung his legs inside.

'Hey, Doctor!' cried Jo. 'You're not leaving me here!'

'No choice, Jo. These things were only built for one.'

He loaded the milk bottles into the cramped space at his feet. 'You stick with Benton. You'll be fine. I'll see you up there.'

He pulled out his pencil torch and pointed the beam at the instrument panel. After a moment, his hands raced over the dials and switches and the aircraft's old engine thrummed into life.

Benton and his men appeared at the back door of the cottage.

'Just the chap!' called the Doctor over the Spitfire's roar. 'Jo, I need help starting the propeller.'

Jo gave a rapid thumbs-up sign and signalled for Benton to join her. He raced across the lawn and yelled orders for Dodds and Fisher to open the gate at the far end of the garden which led on to the road.

The Doctor paused before closing the hood over him.

'Chocks away!' he yelled and then motioned to Benton to start the fighter's propeller.

After two or three spins, the propeller sputtered into noisy life. The blades raced round in a whirl, flashing white in the moonlight.

Almost at once, the plane began to shunt forward over the grass. The Doctor smiled and waved as he powered the Spitfire past Jo and Benton, manoeuvring carefully so that the wings just missed the posts of the now-open gate.

As he moved on to the road and prepared for take-off, the possessed villagers finally broke through into the house and began to stream into the garden.

Benton let loose a volley of shots over their heads and grabbed Jo by the elbow.

'Come on, miss. Time we weren't here!'

They raced through the gate and on to the road, followed by the rest of Benton's troops just as the Spitfire powered down the empty road. With a whining roar it soared into the sky, banking to the left almost at once.

'Good luck, Doctor,' said Jo quietly.

'Don't worry, miss,' said Benton as they ran over the road and into the fields beyond. Once the Brig and the Doctor get through, we'll take the aerodrome in no time.'

Jo nodded, casting an anxious glance over her shoulder at the pursuing villagers. 'That may be true, Sergeant,' she gasped, breathlessly. 'But you're forgetting something.'

'What's that?'

'The creature in the marsh,' said Jo.

*

Charles Cochrane MP woke with a very sore throat. He leant forward on the black table he found himself upon and retched. There was blood in his saliva and the sight of it made him properly sick. He stared at the pool of vomit on the hard concrete floor and then lay back, his head swimming. He had no idea where he was and all kinds of theories, from kidnapping to some Fleet Street scandal, raced through his mind. He reached down and felt himself all over to make sure he was all in one piece, fully clothed and not – heaven forfend – wearing women's underwear. Assured on all three counts, he breathed a sigh of relief and risked a glance to his left.

He appeared to be in some kind of aircraft hangar. It was old and very dusty but there were about two dozen more tables arranged along the wall. On each lay a person. Some were asleep. Others seemed to be recovering like himself. Most had some kind of disgusting animal lying on their chests or close by. Cochrane shuddered and then looked down. A semitransparent creature with a segmented tail and round, pitch-black eyes like a shrimp's was tucked up by his side.

He screamed and knocked it to the floor. It landed with a wet slap. Quite dead.

Hauling himself up on to his elbows, Cochrane peered along the line of his fellow inmates. He recognised most of them. There was at least one other Cabinet member. And surely that was the Strangeways, the Chief of Staff?

He was about to open his mouth when the door swung open and a large, heavily built woman marched inside.

'Madam,' cried Cochrane indignantly. 'Would you kindly explain what on earth is going on?'

Bliss's face, still fixed in its perpetual smile, was

nevertheless chilling. She didn't answer. Instead, she took a large black canister from her pocket and twisted a silver knob on its end. There was a sibilant hiss and gas began to flood the room.

Cochrane felt his head swimming again. He tried to get up from the table but his legs seemed to turn to water beneath him. His last recollection before he slipped into unconsciousness was the door opening again and a bearded man striding inside, dragging a boy behind him and holding some kind of crystal aloft. The man was grinning triumphantly.

CHAPTER THIRTY-TWO
DESPERATE MEASURES

The Brigadier and Yates sat in the cabin of the leading UNIT truck. The remaining two were directly behind, having driven some five hundred yards or so back down the Culverton road, away from the aerodrome.

'Right,' said the Brigadier. 'Get this transport turned round. We'll give it a couple if minutes and then we'll storm the place.'

Yates looked worried. 'And if we hit the civilians, sir?'

The Brigadier's mouth set into a thin line. 'Then we hit the civilians, Captain. The Doctor's explained just how dangerous these creatures are. We have to do whatever it takes to get in there and stop them.'

Yates nodded. 'Yes, sir.'

He reached down and put the truck into reverse. Within moments it was facing back towards the aerodrome.

The Brigadier nodded his approval. 'Now they've seen us retreat in force. The last thing they'll expect is one of our trucks to come back. We have to drive through them, if necessary.'

Yates gave a solemn nod and reached for the gear lever. To his surprise, the Brigadier leant over and stopped him.

'Move over, Captain,' he said quietly.

'Sir?'

Lethbridge-Stewart didn't look him in the eye. 'I wouldn't ask you to do anything I wouldn't do myself. Move over.'

Yates shuffled over, allowing him to take up his position in front of the steering wheel.

Clenching his teeth until the muscles on his jaw stood out, the Brigadier pressed his foot down on the accelerator and the truck roared forward. The other two, packed with troops, followed.

'Operation Trojan Horse, eh Captain Yates?' said the Brigadier.

Yates nodded. 'Yes, sir. Operation Trojan Horse.'

He looked down at his knees.

And now all nine keys are in place.

There is so little time. The ground beneath the steel palace groans and rocks. For the first time, a crack has developed in the thick plate glass of the observation window.

The Apothecaries look round in fear, the warm blue atmosphere is altered by the thin hiss of the filthy air from outside. The wind screams and scrabbles at the breach, like a living thing, jealously trying to gain entry.

Efforts are made to seal the gap but to no avail. They cannot be diverted from the great purpose. A translucent column of blue light has begun to shoot upwards from the dais, bathing the twelve elders in its glorious effulgence.

The Apothecaries stand back now. Their work is almost done. Soon, when the elders have passed through, it will be the turn of the embryos. And then the Gaderene race will have been saved. They will have survived.

And the Apothecaries will remain, as they volunteered to remain, to watch the dying hours of their home world…

The column of blue light pulses regularly. Waiting…
Waiting…

The old airstrip, plunged into darkness, stretched out like a bolt of black silk.

The Master jerked his thumb over his shoulder towards the hangar. 'They're secure?'

Bliss nodded impatiently at the question. 'Of course. The gas will keep them unconscious until their new occupants arrive.'

A stiff breeze had blown up, flapping Bliss's lank hair into her large eyes. Noah cowered at the Master's feet, the barrel of the pistol dangerously close to his temple.

A circular area about a hundred feet across had been marked out in the parched ground next to the airstrip, like some kind of black-magic pentagram. At equidistant points, narrow depressions were sunk into it. Bliss let her gaze flick over them and then turned to the Master.

'It is time.'

The Master nodded. Bliss moved away and one by one began to insert the crystalline keys into hollow metallic sockets inset into the ground.

The wind suddenly increased in strength and, as each key was put in place, it began to hum with power.

'Will… will my dad be all right?' asked Noah in a small voice. The Master and Bliss ignored him completely.

Noah watched, awestruck, as what appeared to be blue fire crackled between the keys, forming a glowing halo just above the ground. Bliss inserted the eighth key and there was an ear-splitting roar of power. The blue halo grew more solid, spiralling upwards into the sky in a regular, pulsing pattern. But it was still oddly insubstantial, flickering like a film beam or distantly observed summer lightning.

The Master too, seemed impressed by the sight, the light washing over his saturnine features.

Bliss walked up to him and held out her fat hand.

'The ninth key,' she ordered.

The Master smiled. 'You haven't forgotten our little bargain?'

Noah scowled. 'What have they promised you? Control of the world?'

'Hardly, young man,' purred the Master. 'That is why the Gaderene are here, after all.'

Bliss looked down at Noah. 'He wishes merely to see the destruction of your kind.'

Noah was appalled. 'That's sick.'

The Master shrugged. 'As I told the Doctor once, it's a big, bad Universe out there.'

Bliss jerked her hand in his face. 'The key! Come on, we're wasting time.'

The Master glanced over at the hangar. 'First bring out the swine. They'll need to be infested at once.'

Bliss considered this. 'Very well.'

'And do hurry,' said the Master. Bliss shot him a deadly look.

'Take the boy. You'll need help,' he concluded.

Bliss didn't move for a moment and Noah thought she might strike the Master but then the woman grabbed Noah and dragged him back towards the hangar.

The Master smiled as he watched the alien's retreating back. He held the ninth key aloft and watched as it sparkled in the dazzling column of blue light.

*

The Doctor's hands gripped the controls of the Spitfire as he banked the plane to the right and then forward again as he headed for the aerodrome.

He glanced down at the controls which he knew would operate the fighter's machine guns. His thumb hovered over the red button but he took his hand away. That wasn't his style at all. No, he would try and put the plane down somewhere close by and get the nitrous-oxide bombs to the Brigadier.

Glancing out of the bubble-hood of the cockpit, he could see some kind of activity below.

Suddenly, the night sky appeared to explode into a blazing blue. The Doctor threw a hand in front of his eyes and squinted through his fingers. A vast column of light was extending from the ground into the sky. It burned with a fantastic magnesium brightness, like fire trapped in amber.

The Doctor thrust the joystick of the plane down and the Spitfire roared towards the earth.

The ground rushed up to almost meet it. In the light from the blue column, the Doctor could suddenly make out the perimeter fence. As before, Legion troops surrounded the place, but they had been joined by others, clearly villagers, whose ordinary clothes stood out against the black of the soldiers' uniforms.

Three trucks were hurtling along the road towards them.

'Oh no,' whispered the Doctor.

CHAPTER THIRTY-THREE
INVASION

Jo and Benton were tearing across the fields towards the aerodrome, the other troops and the possessed villagers close behind them.

They stumbled through waist-high crops damp with dew, then suddenly flattened themselves as the pillar of blue light sprang into life before them.

'Look! Look!' cried Jo. 'The Gaderene. They're coming!'

Moments later, she and Benton crouched low again as the Spitfire roared overhead.

'Good,' said Jo. 'The Doctor's almost there. Come on, Sergeant. He'll need all the help he can get.'

She grabbed Benton's hand and pulled the burly soldier from the ground.

The Doctor knew his timing had to be perfect. If he was right about what the Brigadier was planning, there wouldn't be time for another pass.

The Spitfire roared through the air towards the Culverton road.

Beneath, the UNIT trucks were powering towards the perimeter fence and its human shield. The Doctor could make out Mrs Toovey in the front rank.

He reached down between his knees and plucked out two of the gas-filled milk bottles.

Keeping the plane steady with one hand, he managed to unclip the hood of the cockpit and, with a tremendous heave, threw it sideways.

He gasped at the change in air pressure and squinted as the wind screamed in his face, flattening his cheeks and mane of white hair.

He moved the joystick to the right, and the plane suddenly turned sharply, allowing him a clear view of the road. Desperately, he flung the bottles one after another out of the cockpit.

They plummeted to the road about fifty feet below and shattered just in front of the assembled crowd.

The Doctor reached for the last of the bottles and hurled those out too, watching in satisfaction as they broke open on impact. Almost at once, the Legion troopers and the remaining villagers began to keel over.

The Doctor managed to haul the bubble-hood of the Spitfire back into place and then flew back around to see the results of his handiwork.

To his delight, the people had fallen back in a broad fan, like the petals of a dying flower, leaving the entrance to the aerodrome virtually clear.

Bliss paused as she pulled the first of the surgical tables from its position by the wall.

Noah watched as her head shifted to one side, almost as though it were too heavy for her neck. She closed her great, black eyes and a strangely troubled expression flitted over her face.

Her eyes screwed up tight. One last time.

The worm must prevent the troops from reaching the airstrip. One last time…

She reached deep into her subconscious. Found an image, a memory of them together on the Gaderene planet before all this. She replayed in her mind the moment when they had been sent into space, the brief childhood they had known together as sister and brother.

Bliss shuddered as the memories washed over her. She had made the dimensional jump unscathed.

He had not been so lucky. For years he had slept on in the marshland while she made her way in the human world, desperate to find a way back to the planet of the Gaderene. And then the Master had found her, told her that her people were on the verge of extinction, that she could become their saviour. He had provided the equipment to track down the missing key; the encoder which had gone astray after their craft had crash-landed on the aerodrome during wartime. Now their plans were almost complete.

Monstrously overgrown and mutated, her brother had become useful only as a guard dog. Except for that tiny part of him which kept calling out to her for release.

Release…

She would give it to him at last.

Bliss focused all her thoughts on the creature she had once loved and bade him rise from the marsh…

In the truck, Yates suddenly pointed ahead. 'Look, sir!'

The Brigadier glanced up from the wheel just as the Doctor's Spitfire roared overhead. He saw the unconscious villagers and smiled with relief.

'Right,' he cried. 'No time to waste.'

He rammed his boot down on the accelerator and the truck ploughed forward, missing the human shield and smashing into the perimeter fence which collapsed in a chaos of steel and mesh.

The two other trucks powered through the hole, their tyres flattening the mesh as they drove towards the airstrip.

The leading truck screeched to a halt and the Brigadier and Yates jumped out. They could already make out the blazing column of light, flaring over the rooftops like a firework display.

'Seems like as good a place as any,' muttered the Brigadier. 'Come on.'

'Right, sir.' Yates moved swiftly to the parked trucks and ordered all the men out.

Just as they were dismounting, the air was filled by a deafening, throaty roar.

The ground shook beneath the Brigadier and several soldiers toppled over, their arms and legs splaying wide as they struggled to remain upright.

Then, with a massive splintering of glass, an adjacent building crumbled into fragments as the gigantic marsh-worm hove into view. Brittle, antennae-like protrusions bristled around its head, its black eyes bore down on the troops below.

The Brigadier's face fell. Then he recovered himself, pulled out his pistol and took up position with his men.

'Commence firing!' he yelled.

Jo and Benton had crossed the marsh and reached the back of the aerodrome. The non-appearance of the creature puzzled Jo until they both heard the crackle of nearby gunfire.

'I think the Brig's got company,' said Benton quietly.

The fence had been flattened as the creature passed over it and they clambered over it comparatively easily. The remaining UNIT troops were close behind them. Legion men and villagers were milling around, seemingly disorientated.

Benton tapped Jo on the arm.

Jo shielded her eyes against the glare of the light column. She could just make out three figures at its base, close to the hangar. Bliss and Noah were moving a series of what looked like hospital operating tables out on to the airstrip. The Master was close by, gazing up at the light.

'Come on,' said Jo urgently.

Swiftly, she and Benton ran the remaining distance.

CHAPTER THIRTY-FOUR
LAST OF THE GADERENE

The Doctor put the Spitfire down behind the hangar. A section of road, cracked and broken, connected some of the aerodrome's outbuildings with the control tower. Black Legion lorries had been neatly parked at one end but there was enough room for the old plane to touch down, her heavy rubber tyres screeching over the tarmac.

As soon as the fighter came to a halt, the Doctor threw back the hood and clambered out. He raised an arm to shield his eyes from the incredible glare of the blue light and ran as fast as he could towards it.

For a few moments, there was silence around the Spitfire. Then a figure emerged from behind the metal stairs which led to the control tower.

Wing Commander Whistler, hobbling and exhausted, stumbled towards the plane, smiling ecstatically, and patted the fuselage as though it were an old friend.

The Doctor approached the base of the column of light in silence. He spotted Jo approaching too, and Benton peeling away from her and heading for the Brigadier. Behind them, the UNIT troops were still being pursued by the possessed villagers.

Jo raced to the Doctor's side and took his hand. She looked over at Noah and gave him an encouraging smile.

The boy looked miserable and scared.

'A magnificent spectacle, don't you think, Doctor?' said the Master, without turning round.

The Doctor looked into the light, his eyes hidden in the lines on his face. The column's unstable pattern showed that the ninth key had yet to be inserted.

'The dimensional bridge isn't completed,' he cried. 'There's still time. You don't have to go through with this madness.'

The Master turned round, his features bathed in blue light. 'Don't I, Doctor? I've made a deal with the Gaderene. I can't deny them. Isn't that what we all fight to defend? Hearth and home?'

The Doctor shook his head. 'But not like this. Earth does not belong to them. There must be another way. If they make the leap, every living thing on this planet will be at their mercy.'

'Exactly!' The Master's eyes were blazing. 'They will drain this little world dry. And I shall have my revenge.'

He glanced over at Bliss who was still smiling her wide, wide smile. 'You have defeated me more times than I care to admit, Doctor. But now, at last, the hour is mine!'

Without another word, he tossed the ninth key over to Bliss. The alien caught it in her spade-like hand and hugged it, briefly, to her chest.

'No!' cried the Doctor, stepping forward.

The Master's hand reached into his tunic and brought out a long, black cylindrical object. He resembled a gunslinger, a UNIT pistol in one hand, trained on Noah, and his deadly tissue-compressor in the other, pointed squarely at the Doctor's chest. 'Stay where you are, Doctor. It would be a pity if you missed the... fireworks.'

Bliss strode forward and calmly inserted the final key into the ground. The pitch of the humming roar changed again, rising, rising, rising. Jo shielded her ears.

The Doctor looked back. The creature was still keeping the UNIT troops at bay. There was nothing he could do.

And now the journey nears its end.

The twelve elders stream through space in their component particles, bridging the dimensional gulf between their world and Earth. They feel no pain, no fear, no exhilaration, sleeping still and cocooned in the power of the nine jade keys which hold their existence secure.

Flashing through the inky blackness of space, they spearhead the Gaderene invasion force; three hundred thousand embryos glittering in their molecular wake…

The Brigadier ducked as a section of the aerodrome building crashed to the ground. The worm reared above him, its mandibles thrashing wildly, and wriggled forward, crunching the old tarmac beneath its scaly body.

Several soldiers lay dead around the base, crushed by its monstrous bulk or casually tossed aside by its maw.

A lone soldier raced towards the action. Close behind him came the remainder of the troops, the villagers on their heels.

'Benton!' cried the Brigadier. 'Glad to have you back.'

Benton saluted breathlessly.

'Bring in the bazookas!' ordered the Brigadier.

Benton tore off to the rear of the UNIT trucks. The newly arrived troops immediately took up their positions.

'Now, Yates,' said the Brigadier, turning to his deputy. 'If we can just get the creature into that passageway…'

Yates nodded. 'I know what to do, sir.'

Keeping low, he scurried along the side of the hangar, revolver in hand, until he was perilously close to the monster's underbelly.

Ahead of him, a broad passageway connected the hangar buildings to the main body of the old control tower. Yates waited until the worm was at the top of the passage and then gave three sharp blasts on a whistle. At once, the troops to his immediate left began a vicious assault, blasting into the creature's flank until blood pumped from its gelatinous flesh.

Roaring in pain and rage, the worm slithered backwards down the passage.

The Brigadier smiled, raised his hand and then dropped it to his side.

At once, every one of the UNIT vehicles switched on their headlights. The worm was suddenly lit by a fierce illumination, pinioned back against the hangar buildings as though pierced by arrows. It howled in agony, its evil black eyes retreating back into its fleshy face.

The Brigadier raised his R/T set. 'Now, Benton,' he barked.

There was a short pause. Then, with a multiple crack, the bazookas let rip, sending shell after shell into the monster's head.

Clenching his fist in triumph, the Brigadier looked over to see the possessed villagers shambling towards him.

Bliss's face had taken on an ecstatic look. She stepped back from the fiery blue light, which now seemed as solid and palpable as a glass column. Dark shapes had begun to swirl within it. Jo peered closer but couldn't make out anything definite.

'Doctor,' hissed Noah in an urgent whisper. 'What're we going to do?'

The Doctor shook his head. 'I don't know. If the Brigadier can get through we can still destroy the matter encoders…'

Everyone stiffened at the sound of the multiple bazooka barrage close by. Bliss looked away from the light, but she seemed untroubled.

She felt the creature's agony as the human soldiers shattered its flesh. The pain coursed through her own veins, jagged, dreadful. But the tiny voice in the back of her mind called not for help but for release. *Release…*

In a very few moments, she would allow the worm to die. Its part in the great plan would finally cease. But not yet, not just yet. The encoders must be protected. The time for the breakthrough had come.

'Look at her face!' Jo's voice cut across the deafening sound of the column of light.

Bliss did indeed seem to have altered. It was almost as though her bulky frame was merely hanging loosely over another, more angular, body; like a butterfly about to cast off its chrysalis. The mouth was impossibly wide, more like a wound, and there was something visible behind it, chitinous, slimy. Only the huge, dark eyes seemed the same, and they blazed like burning pitch.

'Everything I have striven for is about to come to pass,' she hissed, something like wonderment in her voice. 'The last of the Gaderene are on their way. We have found our new home.'

The Doctor struggled to make himself heard over the noise of the light-column.

'There must be another way.'

Bliss shook her head. Fragments of skin came away.

'When the elders arrive, they will take charge of the invasion. We will gather all those humans we have converted. All of them, from across the globe. Enough to provide shelter for my people!'

She turned to the Master, a kind of sneer twisting her distorted features. 'And now all that is no longer useful can be disposed of. Even a Time Lord.'

The Master's face fell. 'What are you talking about?'

'I have been tolerant of you for too long,' spat Bliss. 'You have been a faithful servant, but you remain *only* a servant!'

The Doctor smiled slyly. 'Trouble at t'mill?'

The Master ignored him. 'You would be nothing without me! I made contact. I have saved your people!'

Bliss's voice seemed to drop in pitch. A solitary, straw-like mandible began to creep its way around the wet corner of her mouth. 'And you have taken every opportunity to humiliate me. Well, no longer… *Master*,' she sneered.

The Master raised his pistol to cover Bliss. 'Might I remind you that if only one of the encoders were removed, then your invasion force would be obliterated.'

Bliss shook her head. Great gobbets of saliva flew from her mouth. 'That is no longer a concern. To enter the column now would mean certain death for anyone. It is finished!'

The Master swung round and covered the Doctor. 'It seems they have me at a disadvantage, Doctor,' he said blithely. 'Therefore, you will enter the column and remove one of the encoders.'

'No!' cried Jo. 'He can't. He'll be killed.'

The Master moved back so that everyone, including Bliss, was in his line of fire. 'The Doctor won't mind, Miss Grant. What do you say, Doctor? Your life or the fate of the whole world?'

The Doctor looked the Master up and down, his face impassive.

Then he took a step forward.

Jo grabbed at his smoking jacket. 'No, Doctor!'

He turned and grasped her hand. 'I've no choice, Jo.'

Noah was shaking his head violently. 'No!'

Bliss's eyes bobbed in her loose flesh like grapes in a winepress. 'You are too late! *They are coming!*'

Jo looked up at the column of light. The dark shapes she had seen earlier were finally coalescing. Strange, hideous, twisting forms, like spiders washed down a huge, translucent drain.

The Master pointed the pistol directly at the Doctor. 'If you would be so kind, Doctor.'

Bliss darted forward, her hands stretched out like talons, a gurgling roar belching from within her.

Suddenly, a strange droning sound cut across the roar of the blue column. The Doctor looked up. A shape zoomed overhead, like a great bird. He frowned, puzzled, and then smiled broadly.

'Good grief!'

The shape came by again, its engines taking on a familiar drone. 'It's the Spitfire!' cried Jo.

The old plane flew dangerously low and a downdraught of air forced everyone to scatter. The Master rolled over and shot a wild bolt of energy high into the air.

The Doctor kicked out and knocked both weapons from the Master's hands. He grabbed Noah's hand. 'Come on!'

He, Jo and Noah began to pelt away across the tarmac.

'Doctor!' gasped Jo. 'Where are... we can't leave now...!'

'Must get to the Brigadier,' called the Doctor over his shoulder. 'If we can get in touch with the Spitfire...'

Jo dragged on his arm and pulled him up sharp. 'No need.'

'What?' he barked.

Jo pulled her own R/T set from her bag.

The Doctor threw up his hands. 'Well, why didn't you say so?' He grabbed the radio and immediately clicked to the correct frequency. The set crackled.

'Trap one? Trap one, are you receiving me? Over.'

All three listened anxiously. Overhead the Spitfire was circling.

'Trap one here, Doctor. Over.'

Jo sighed in relief.

'Brigadier, you've got to get in touch with that plane. It's armed. Over.'

The R/T set crackled. 'Roger, Doctor. Over.'

The Doctor nodded to himself. 'Tell him to concentrate his fire on the circle of light. Over.'

'Will do. Over and out.'

The Doctor tossed the radio back to Jo. 'Right. Let's see if that gets us anywhere.'

The worm roared again and staggered backwards into the hangar, smashing the old glass roof and sending hundreds of deadly shards streaming to the ground.

'It's weakening, sir!' called Benton above the din.

The Brigadier nodded. Half a dozen troops were wrestling with the villagers in hand-to-hand combat. He turned to Yates who was once again crouched at his side. 'Any luck?'

Yates shrugged. 'I'm not sure, sir. There's no way of telling… ah!'

The R/T set gave a positive-sounding squeal and Yates thrust it into the Brigadier's hand.

'Hello, Spitfire. Hello Spitfire. Are you receiving me? Over.'

The radio crackled.

The Brigadier clicked again. 'This is Brigadier Lethbridge-Stewart. Is that you up there, Alec?'

The Spitfire roared over the aerodrome.

Inside the cockpit, Alec Whistler suddenly felt forty years younger. He peered through the glass at the terrifying but beautiful column of blue fire which lit up the heavens. He could see it stretching away through the clouds, seemingly into infinity, like a vast tornado frozen to the spot. Then he saw the monstrous, wounded worm thrashing about in the ruins of the hangar buildings. He thrust the joystick down and prepared to make another pass, then raised the radio receiver to his masked face.

'Alistair! What a lovely surprise. Can I be of assistance? You look like you've got your hands full. Over.'

The ancient device hissed and the Brigadier's delighted voice came through.

'Don't worry about us, Alec. I've got some very specific instructions. Now listen very carefully. Over.'

*

293

The Master was pointing his sleek, black pistol, hastily retrieved after the Doctor's attack, at Bliss. She seemed in the grip of a convulsion, her flabby white skin rippling and puckering.

'Even if you kill me now, the Gaderene will destroy you, Time Lord.' Her face juddered and a whole section fell away, revealing a gaping, mandible-stuffed maw.

The Master considered what she had said. He glanced over at the row of gurneys and then up at the terrible creatures taking shape within the column if light.

'Your weapon cannot affect the encoders,' chittered Bliss. 'You know that.'

'And what if I simply destroy your... swine?' said the Master simply. 'Then where will your precious race take shelter? You won't get far trying to take over the world if you're stranded on the runway of an East Anglian aerodrome.'

He smiled and swung the weapon round to cover the recumbent form of Charles Cochrane. The Secretary of Defence slept soundly, unaware that death was poised to claim him.

With a screeching howl, Bliss threw herself bodily at the Master, knocking him to the ground. His weapon rolled out of sight without firing a single blast.

The alien's bulk was immense and the Master struggled to get his breath as it straddled him. He put both fists together and smashed them into its chest. Bliss howled and slumped slightly, clothes and flesh falling away to reveal more and more of the vile creature beneath. A segmented tail burst from what had been one of Bliss's legs and wrapped itself around the Master's throat.

Gasping, he rolled on to his side and slapped his

gloved hand on the grass, desperately trying to locate his weapon. Bliss's tail tightened, scale sliding over scale. The Master retched and hammered his fists against the unyielding flesh. The alien reared over him, the last vestiges of Bliss falling in disgusting clumps from its massive, locust-like head. Now the great dark eyes were fully revealed, gazing down with terrible malice at the prone Time Lord.

A rapid staccato of gunfire bit into the parched soil. Grass and dry mud flew into the air as the Spitfire rained down bullets, aiming for the column of light.

Again and again they came, stabbing at the earth. Then bullets hit scaly flesh and dark fluid pumped into the soil.

Wisps of smoke filled the air. The Bliss creature opened its mouth and howled in agony.

The Doctor stood some distance away from the column of light with hands on hips. He shook his head. 'It's no good, Jo,' he said at last. 'Whistler's not even touching the encoders. I have to go in myself.'

Jo shook her head violently. 'But you heard what Bliss said! Anyone who goes in there will be killed. It's suicide!'

The Doctor detached himself from her grip and squeezed her hand affectionately. 'Nevertheless,' he said quietly.

He raised a hand and touched her cheek. Then he turned on his heel and walked swiftly towards the column.

Jo's whole frame sagged. Noah crawled forward and put his arms around her. She closed her eyes. At last, she took the R/T set from her bag and made contact with the Brigadier.

'You can call off the Spitfire,' she said flatly. 'The Doctor's going in alone.'

'What?' came the Brigadier's reply. 'Say again.'

Jo let the radio fall to the ground.

The Doctor stood as close as he dared to the boiling, twisting column of light. The twelve elders were almost formed now, standing as though behind a shimmering curtain, just waiting for the moment to break through. They fluttered and jerked like an old film, shadowy impressions of the creatures' full forms. They moved in and out of focus, testing the waterfall of light with their claws.

The Doctor looked for a moment into their pitiless black eyes and then over at their intended homes, the people lying prone on the black couches only feet away.

The nearest encoder was visible, thrust into the ground about five yards away from him. He could try and reach through the curtain of light, of course, and only risk destroying part of his body, but he had to be sure. He had to uproot the encoder and send the Gaderene streaming back into space and inevitable destruction. It gave him no pleasure to contemplate this. They were merely striving to survive. But he could not allow them to destroy humanity.

The Doctor took a deep breath, gathered himself and stepped forward.

With a bellowing scream, the Bliss creature was on him, sending them both flying backwards. He gasped, winded, and tasted earth in his mouth. He tried to turn over but the massive, wounded beast was holding him flat, mandibles chittering, fathomless eyes dilating with evil intent.

The Doctor managed to chop at its neck and the alien croaked throatily, spewing its saliva on to his chest. Managing to raise one leg, he kicked blindly at it and sent it rolling head over tail.

Jumping to his feet, the Doctor made straight for the column.

The Bliss creature's tail coiled around his ankles like a snake and dragged him to the ground. He fell heavily, his face connecting with the iron-hard soil. With lightning speed, the tail was around his throat, crushing the life out of him.

The Doctor gasped for air, eyes bulging.

He tried to get his fingers between the scales on the monster's skin, to find any vulnerable spot. But there was nothing. He felt the alien's spiny claws bite into his clothes as it grasped him in a deadly bear hug.

He tried to crawl forward. He had to make it into the column. He had to remove the encoder and destroy the Gaderene. Had to. If it was the last thing he did…

A dark figure suddenly swam into view. The Doctor tried to focus on it, but consciousness was leaving him as the alien throttled him to death. He was vaguely aware that the figure was raising its arm…

Then there came a sharp, electric crackle and suddenly the Doctor could breathe again.

He sank to the ground, dragging breath after ragged breath, and finally managed to look over his shoulder.

The Bliss creature was shrinking before his eyes, scales impacting upon one another, the lethal tail winding itself up like a spring, the mandibles crushing themselves, the black, black eyes popping like over-ripe fruit. The creature's roar diminished into a pitiful squeal as it grew smaller and smaller and smaller and finally lay still.

The Doctor rubbed his eyes, scarcely able to believe what had happened.

The Master stood before him, his black weapon in his hand. 'I could hardly deny myself the pleasure of killing you myself, Doctor.'

He grinned and raised the weapon.

Whistler banked the Spitfire to the left, peering through the cockpit hood at the scene below. A white-haired man was lying prone on the grass, a figure in black pointing some kind of gun at him.

The man in black was obviously one of Bliss's mob. His jaw setting grimly, Whistler powered the plane forward, his finger hovering over the machine-gun control.

The Doctor heard the bullets hit the ground before he saw them. Two smashed into the parched soil, scoring a direct hit on the ring of encoders. With a loud crack, one of the keys came loose, like a rotten tooth.

More of the deadly bullets smashed to earth and suddenly, with an agonised cry, the Master pitched forward on one knee. He toppled backwards and the weapon rolled from his gloved hand.

The column of light flickered uncertainly. The Doctor could see the adult Gaderene shuffling perplexedly, their claws tearing at the blue light.

In an instant, he was at the Master's side. Blood was pouring from the Time Lord's hand.

'Don't try to move,' said the Doctor gently.

The Master shook his head. 'It's no good. It's finished.'

The Doctor threw a quick glance at the Gaderene. They seemed impatient to be free, writhing and pushing through the column of light. The loose key rocked in its socket.

'I should have listened to you,' said the Master softly.

The Doctor nodded. 'You could never have controlled them.'

The Master managed a small shake of his head. 'No. I mean... I mean I should have listened to you years ago...' He succeeded in smiling, then coughed. 'I liked this body,' he said at last. 'It had style.'

The Doctor stared down at him, then over at the column. The Gaderene had still to be stopped. His work wasn't over.

The Master suddenly sprang to his feet.

Taken by surprise, the Doctor fell sideways. He clutched at the Master's tunic but his old enemy pushed him back.

'Dear Doctor,' he laughed. 'I was always better at play-acting than you!'

He stepped into the blue incandescence.

The Doctor watched helplessly but it seemed that without the ninth key in its proper order, the dazzling column was safe to enter, just as it had been when Bliss inserted the key some time before.

The Master pushed through the half-formed Gaderene creatures towards the loose key. In moments he would reinsert it, step out and the invasion would be complete. The Doctor had no choice but to enter the blazing light. He moved swiftly forward, his cloak streaming behind him.

*

Whistler listened to the Brigadier's voice on his radio. He was deep in conversation with a young girl named Jo. She was very upset. It seemed this Doctor fella was about to throw his life away by trying to remove Whistler's good-luck charm. There was no other way to stop this invasion. The Wing Commander still had no idea why the jade-coloured thing was so important to Bliss and her cronies but important it obviously was.

As he flew, Whistler managed to open the little lead tin that sat next to him. The dog-eared, white-bordered picture of his one-time love looked up at him, her smile still as vivid to him as on the last day he saw her. He touched the picture with his left hand and then set his jaw determinedly. He had one last mission. One last chance for revenge.

The Master fell to his knees, put his uninjured hand around the ninth key and struggled to ram it back into its proper place.

He was genuinely shocked when the Doctor grabbed his shoulder, span him round and punched him to the ground. Kicking out savagely, the Master caught the Doctor on his shins and brought him slamming down on to the earth. For a long moment, the two men grappled, the flickering blue incandescence boiling around them. The half-formed adult Gaderene and the thousands of embryos swirled over their bodies like wraiths.

The Master reached out a gloved hand towards the ninth key. It was only inches from his fingertips.

The Doctor rammed his hand under the Master's arm and held onto it in an iron grip. Grunting, the Master slammed his elbow into the Doctor's side and the Doctor fell back, gasping in pain.

'You're too late Doctor!' screamed the Master triumphantly as his hand closed around the key.

Just as he was thrusting the key back into place a tremendous roar, louder even than the deafening cacophony of the light-column burst upon them and both he and the Doctor looked up. A great dark shape was powering down from the sky. Dive-bombing.

'No! *No!*' snarled the Master as the Spitfire entered the blue light and spiralled round and round towards them. The ninth key slipped back into its socket without a sound.

The Doctor stepped out of the column as though hopping off a bus. In seconds, the intensity of the light increased again. He could see the Master as though through a sheet of ice.

Their eyes met for a long, long moment. Two Time Lords. So similar in so many ways. Yet separated by a gulf as wide as the Universe itself. Two Time Lords. One safe. One doomed.

The Master held up his hand but the gesture was unclear.

Then, with a tortured whine, the Spitfire crashed into the centre of the column.

The Doctor threw himself to one side, rolling over and over until he deemed it safe to look back.

The column of light lit up with a new and fiery radiance as the aeroplane exploded into flames within it. There was a colossal boom and then a horrible, tortured, wretched scream blasted through the night. It echoed across the aerodrome and out over the wide, flat fields.

Within the column, the Gaderene shimmered and began to diminish, stretched into fibrous shapes as they were sucked backwards into the heavens. Light seethed over them, splitting them into tiny pixels of flesh, blood and bone, as the nine keys disintegrated in the firestorm and the aliens were dragged back along their dimensional pathway.

The Doctor peered ahead, struggling to make out the Master, but there was no sign of him.

He got to his feet and ran back towards the column. There was a final juddering scream, then it was all gone. The column of light. The roar of its energy.

Suddenly there was nothing but a devastating silence.

The Doctor sank back on his haunches.

Release… It felt her passing and it mourned. Every fibre of its hideously mutated flesh cried out in agony. But now it could let go. The struggle was over…

Sergeant Benton had his rifle trained on the worm, ready for one last desperate assault, when the creature suddenly and inexplicably crashed to the ground, quite dead. Benton looked up, not quite daring to believe his eyes.

Its flesh was steaming, like overcooked meat. The Brigadier came over and gave the worm's carcass an experimental kick. It didn't move.

Around them, dazed villagers were slowly coming round, expelled Gaderene embryos hanging from their mouths like ectoplasm.

The Brigadier looked over towards the airstrip where he had seen the Spitfire crash. There was absolutely no sign of it.

*

And now the searing column of light streams back along the path it followed, rippling like a ribbon, crazed, unfettered, out of control. Blazing through the poisonous atmosphere of the planet, it thunders into the steel palace, vapourising the entire structure, along with the Apothecaries who have laboured so long and so hard.

But the destruction of the palace is lost in the global catastrophe as the planet ends its days. Tectonic plates crumple into one another, great volcanic masses vomit fiery lava into the black, black sky.

The ground rolls and splits and engulfs itself.

And the last of the Gaderene are no more…

CHAPTER THIRTY-FIVE
PEACE-TIME

Max Bishop was more surprised than he could adequately express to find himself lying in a wet field with his brother by his side.

He looked up at the sky, which was just showing the first streaks of dawn, and blinked repeatedly. There was a very nasty taste in his mouth.

Glancing down, he could just make out a small, almost formless thing, lying in the corn to his right. It was rather like a crab, or some kind of worm, but its flesh was blackened, twisted and dead. There was another one lying by Ted who was slowly coming round.

Max sat up and shook his head. His clothes were filthy and wet. His favourite bow tie was torn and hanging over one shoulder. But he was all right.

He glanced across at his brother and tried to smile. It hurt to do so. Max settled instead for a touch on his brother's hand.

'Hello Ted,' he said quietly.

Mrs Toovey was already moving between the confused villagers who had woken to find themselves in a ring outside the aerodrome. She fussed over them, wishing fervently that there was a tea urn close by.

She recognised many of her friends. Miss Arbus, Mrs

Garrick, even Commander Tyrell who looked most confused of all. He gazed through the fence at his beloved aerodrome and then down at the disgusting crab-like creature that was curled up on his chest.

Mrs Toovey frowned as she saw something unpleasant nearby. A skinny boy – Graham, she thought he was called – was standing over another boy she didn't recognise. Graham was kicking the boy repeatedly in the ribs.

Mrs Toovey raced up to Graham and pulled him away.

'Really!' she admonished. 'I don't think that's very nice at all, is it?'

Anthony Ayre looked up from his prone position on the ground and then over to Graham Allinson. The bully remembered what had happened at the bottom of the garden and he felt suddenly cold and sick.

Graham smiled a natural but nicely smug smile. Somehow he didn't think he'd be having much trouble from Anthony again.

It was Noah who saw the parachute first.

As his father ran up to embrace him, Noah glanced over Ted's shoulder and saw the old-fashioned silk canopy as it floated gently to the ground. Wing Commander Whistler landed expertly and was gathering the 'chute behind him as the Brigadier ran up.

'Alec, old man. Well done!' he enthused, pumping Whistler's hand.

Whistler waved away his praise and together they walked towards the airstrip. The old man paused by the great carcass of the Gaderene worm, its scales glittering in the dawn light.

The UNIT troops gave Whistler a hero's welcome and Jo gave him a peck on the cheek.

'Nice to meet you at last,' she said.

Whistler smiled. 'Charmed, Miss... er...?'

'This is Miss Josephine Grant,' said the Brigadier.

Whistler looked around. 'Where's this Doctor chap, then?'

Jo glanced across the airstrip.

The Doctor was standing where the column of light had been. There was nothing there now but a wide circle of scorched grass. His hands were thrust deep into his pockets as he gazed ahead.

Jo took Whistler over to meet him and the Doctor shook the old man's hand. But he didn't smile and soon detached himself from the little group. Jo followed and fell into step with him.

'Are you all right?'

The Doctor gave a small, sad smile. 'Yes. Yes, of course, Jo. We've won. The Earth is safe. The Gaderene have been defeated.'

Jo nodded. 'And wiped out.'

The Doctor nodded. 'I wish there'd been another way. In the end, they just wanted a home.'

Jo sighed. 'And the Master? What happened out there on the airstrip?'

The Doctor looked into the middle distance. 'He's gone.'

'For ever?'

The Doctor didn't answer. He walked ahead, his head sunk low on his chest.

Jo walked slowly back towards the Brigadier.

*

Whistler was looking down at the scorched earth. He could just make out the remains of his lucky charm, projecting from the blackened soil just as it had all those years before.

He thought briefly of the girl again but pushed the memory aside. Time to move on.

He sniffed. 'I say. Who was that chap I saw? He was down here when I made one of my passes. Dark-looking chap. With a beard. Assumed he was one of Bliss's lot.'

'Not exactly,' said the Brigadier.

Whistler shrugged. 'Oh. Friend of the Doctor's?'

Jo and the Brigadier exchanged glances.

Jo watched as the Doctor walked slowly back towards his car, a tall figure against the rising sun, his cloak flapping in the fresh wind.

'Just someone he went to school with,' she said.

Next in the Doctor Who 50th Anniversary Collection:

FESTIVAL OF DEATH

JONATHAN MORRIS

ISBN 978 1 849 90523 7

The Doctor Who 50th Anniversary Collection
Eleven classic adventures
Eleven brilliant writers
One incredible Doctor

The Beautiful Death is the ultimate theme-park ride: a sightseeing tour of the afterlife. But something has gone wrong and, when the Fourth Doctor arrives in the aftermath of the disaster, he is congratulated for saving the population from destruction – something he hasn't actually done yet. He has no choice but to travel back in time and discover how he became a hero.

And then he finds out. He did it by sacrificing his life.

An adventure featuring the Fourth Doctor, as played by Tom Baker, and his companions Romana and K-9.

DOCTOR WHO
The Encyclopedia

Gary Russell

Available for iPad
An unforgettable tour of space and time!

The ultimate series companion and episode guide,
covering seven thrilling years of *Doctor Who*. Download
everything that has happened, un-happened and
happened again in the worlds of the Ninth, Tenth and
Eleventh Doctors.

◊

Explore and search over three thousand entries
by episode, character, place or object and see the
connections that link them together

◊

Open interactive 'portals' for the Doctor, Amy, Rory,
River and other major characters

◊

Build an A-Z of your favourites, explore galleries of imag-
ery, and preview and buy must-have episodes